Dedalus Original Fi

FONTOON

John Schoneboom is a New Yorker who now lives in Newcastle Upon Tyne.

He has studied international affairs, played the funky bass guitar, sold ice cream from a van, sneaked into numerous venues, and foiled a purse snatching.

His play *Dreams of Jimmy Bannon* won the Artist Fellowship Award from the Massachusetts Cultural Council.

Fontoon is his first novel.

John Schoneboom

Fontoon

Dedalus

Supported using public funding by
ARTS COUNCIL ENGLAND

Published in the UK by Dedalus Limited,
24-26, St Judith's Lane, Sawtry, Cambs, PE28 5XE
email: info@dedalusbooks.com
www.dedalusbooks.com

ISBN printed book 978 1 909232 89 1
ISBN ebook 978 1 910213 02 5

Dedalus is distributed in the USA & Canada by SCB Distributors,
15608 South New Century Drive, Gardena, CA 90248
email: info@scbdistributors.com   web: www.scbdistributors.com

Dedalus is distributed in Australia by Peribo Pty Ltd.
58, Beaumont Road, Mount Kuring-gai, N.S.W. 2080
email: info@peribo.com.au

First published by Dedalus in 2014
Fontoon copyright © John Schoneboom 2014

The right of John Schoneboom to be identified as the author of this work has been asserted by him in accordance with the Copyright, Designs and Patents Act, 1988.

Printed in Finland by Bookwell
Typeset by Marie Lane

This book is sold subject to the condition that it shall not, by way of trade or otherwise, be lent, resold, hired out or otherwise circulated without the publisher's prior consent in any form of binding or cover other than that in which it is published and without a similar condition including this condition being imposed on the subsequent purchaser.

A C.I.P. listing for this book is available on request.

To sinkholes, supernovas, and spontaneous combustions

To the Tom Zmoos Wrecking Company and the Fred Meuser Futon Factory

To Abby and Oscar and Maisie

Chapter God

General Rule 34. Any balls potted or leaving the table as a result of non-Player interference including Acts of God, shall remain out of play (pocketed). Any remaining balls that were so moved are to be respotted as close as possible to their original positions.

General Rules of Pocket Billiards
Billiards Congress of America

Chapter Hang

I am not, nor will I ever be, a morning person, mused Admiral Fontoon, subliminally noting that it was perhaps the only thing of which he felt truly certain. He winced and made a sucking sound through his clenched teeth as he gingerly touched the bump that had risen on his head.

He was hanging upside down, swaying gently now after swinging wildly for some time. His arms hung limply in mute surrender. One leg extended to the side and bent like a branch that did not know where to grow, drifting half-heartedly, searching to no avail for a plausible position in which to await death or redemption. The one straight and rigid limb was his other leg, which had a tightened noose around the ankle. From there the rope looped through a pulley attached to the ceiling, and routed thence to a spinning spool at the foot of his bed, anchored firmly to the floor with steel bolts. It was the furious spinning of the spool that had yanked the rope so suddenly, resulting in the tightening of the ankle noose and the unceremonious hoisting of Admiral Fontoon. The entire apparatus had been triggered electronically by Fontoon's alarm clock; more specifically, it had been triggered by the seventh sounding of the snooze alarm, a result, in turn, of Fontoon's obstinacy, and of his lethargy.

Son of a bitch, thought Fontoon, dangling. He was supposed to have gotten out of bed before all this. That was the whole idea: a clock to inspire fear, ergo motion. Fontoon spoke several profanities aloud to his uncaring apartment, and punched the air viciously, which caused him to spin.

He felt the lurch of nausea and struggled to control it. He did not think he could bear either the sound or the sight of his vomit hurtling out of his mouth and splashing onto various of his possessions some nine feet below, and he especially did not relish the thought of cleaning it all up. *Agh, or the taste of it,* he thought, which only made it harder to control.

Admiral Fontoon looked around the room while the spinning gradually subsided, trying to get a fix on something for as long as he could in order to combat the dizziness. He admired his good oak table, against which his head had slammed as his body was ripped helplessly into the air. As always he remembered the good price he had gotten on it, even though that had been many years ago. Directly below him was an imitation Oriental rug that had caused bitterness at how quickly it had begun to look dingy. Must everything be cheap? Must everything be tawdry?

Partly on the rug was a huge and disorderly pile of newspapers, three months' worth, which he had been meaning to take down to the recycling centre as required by law. How inconvenient it all was. That pile of papers made him feel a sense of futility, and disgust as well, disgust with the disorderliness that made his whole life seem contemptible.

A good part of his kitchen was exposed to his view, and although he could not see the sink itself, it reminded him that he had not washed his dishes from the night before. He tucked his chin to his chest and looked at his captured foot. It was beginning to go numb. His sense of futility spread a little more, starting from just below his sternum and claiming territory in all directions outward, filling his chest, spreading towards his nether region. He looked out of his window at the kaleidoscope of changing colours and twisting shapes. He knew it was a mistake to have looked.

It was always foolish to engage any aspect of the city while in a state of infirmity or irresolution.

Once he felt the first tiny taste creep through, it was all over. He immediately disgorged the contents of his stomach, here we go, this again, the terrible sudden yielding, the wrong-wayness, the taste, the warmth, the picturing yourself as others would see you, the whole awful pitiless spectacle. He believed that his ears got the worst of it, all in all. In the anticlimactic silence that followed, Fontoon swayed gently from his rope, wiping his mouth with the back of his hand, and determined to get himself down.

He tried to reach up to grab his foot, thinking that he might free it manually. *But then what?* It was a moot point; he could not reach it; his stomach muscles weren't strong enough. He looked at his flabby belly, which hung now unnaturally in the direction of his head, quivering just ever so. Sucking in his stomach, he peered at it until he could almost see the vague indentations that would have been where muscle definition would go. Thus satisfied that his physical condition was not so terrible, certainly not beyond reclamation, Fontoon felt a moment of contentment before a surge of real concern at his plight annihilated his serenity.

He had felt inconvenienced, to be sure, but had subconsciously assumed that there would of course be a way for him to get down. Now he was beginning to question that assumption. How *would* he get down? What if he couldn't? It was a horrible and absurd possibility, but surely history was nothing if not a relentless continuum of the horrible and the absurd. People died in all manner of ridiculous ways. What if this was his destiny? No way to get down.

How would it happen? What exactly would get him? A slow

death from starvation, followed by decay until his skeletal foot finally slipped through the noose and sent his bones clattering into an untidy pile on top of dried vomit? Or would the pressure from the blood pouring into his head get him first, causing his brain to haemorrhage, or his neck arteries to burst? Perhaps a heart attack, for some reason, or a stroke. The stress might cause some sort of clot to form, or a kidney to fail. There was nobody who might save him. His few friends were far too self-involved to worry that something might be wrong, even if he hung there drying for months. He couldn't complain. He had been a poor friend too. How often did he take the initiative to call? The chickens had come home to roost. How terrible it was to be lonely. How terrible to acknowledge the merciless justice of it all. How strangely satisfying to oscillate idly and indulge in self-pity.

He might just do one quite personal thing to pass the time. Yes. Yes well why not? It would certainly be a novel way of going about it, if he could manage it. It would be a good experiment, if nothing else. His mind could return to his predicament afterwards.

It was possible that his mother would call, but of course he would be unable to get to the phone. It would go to his answering machine and she would think nothing of it for a long time. She might never think anything of it. He might not survive until her second call. Or she might become obsessive and vicious, full of blame. He might receive dozens of rapid-fire, increasingly insufferable calls from her, unable to do anything but listen and rage impotently. And her calls would be in the slightest German accent, as almost everything she said had been in a slight – slight but distinct, and to a German ear, wrong German – accent since the day decades ago it first appeared from out of some clear dark suburban psychosexual wormhole. It had only been questioned once, early on.

"Fot accent?" she had replied.

It had never been mentioned again.

There was no way to tell which way it would go, and it really didn't matter. She would never believe he was really dead, although it would certainly rank high among her accusations if she turned on him. Even when she was eventually faced with her dismal, piteous, pile-of-bones son, she would only tell the story as the tale of a lamentable imbecile. *And jesus god,* he thought, *she'd be right.* From all vantage points, his tragedy would be ignominious.

His neighbours, he knew, would laugh. Yes old Ed and Marla would have themselves one of their big old country-style laughs all right. At least Arthur and Minnie downstairs would have a kind word; they were originally from overseas and north of the Tyne, and they always said nice things over a cup of tea. Everyone called them Uncle Arthur and Aunt Minnie.

Desperate. Desperate now. Something must be done and done while there's still strength left, but what? The first job, certainly, was to quell the rising panic that along with the unpleasant smell from below threatened to nauseate him once again. He dedicated his powers of concentration to this task until he heard the first creaking sound from the ceiling. He looked up and saw that the plaster around the screws that held the pulley was bulging and cracking. *Oh god.* He looked down at the rancid puddle of vomit far below him. *No!*

Admiral Fontoon shut his eyes as the creaking grew more urgent and the first bits of plaster powder began gently to rain.

And then, with a disappointingly weak crumbling sound, in a hail of plaster and rope, he plummeted earthward.

Chapter Rewind

"Gentlemen, let's call this meeting to order. Jenkins, what have you got for me?"

"Right JB. We've confirmed that he definitely bought the alarm clock, which means that right about" – Jenkins paused here to look at his watch – "now, he's probably wondering what the hell hit him."

The whole room broke out into self-satisfied chuckling.

"Excellent work, that's tops. Are we monitoring him at all times? Edgars?"

"We're getting reports almost hourly now, sir."

"Good, good. Let's see if we can confirm that the clock has been activated."

JB pressed a button on the intercom in front of him at the head of the long, mahogany executive meeting table. Out in the reception area, his secretary Shirley was ready in case the big man needed her like he needed her now.

"Shirley hon, can we get a read on Fontoon's current situation please?"

"I'll get Sheila on the phone pronto, Mr. Bentley."

When Shirley had a task to do for Mr. Bentley, she always did it right away rather than find other things to do first or think up reasons not to do it. It was one of the reasons Bentley valued her as an employee. She also showed up on time very dependably, although she generally took a bit more than the mandated thirty minutes for lunch. Bentley noticed, but looked the other way. Bentley knew as well as anyone that it was almost impossible to get lunch and eat it within thirty minutes. The thirty-minute rule was something of a convenient administrative fiction that nobody apart from Alison in human resources took terribly seriously. Bentley was the sort of boss who knew when to be strict and when to cut a little slack. Shirley's forty-minute lunches were something to be tolerated with detached amusement and filed in the back of the mind for possible use as a weapon should Shirley ever complain about time or cross an unspoken line in some other way.

Bentley was above all else a professional and he knew where to draw the line between employee and sex partner. Shirley and her hips and her special skirts were off limits. Bentley took the philosophical view. Sometimes when you'd really like to do a thing but you know it's complicated and wrong, you're able to refrain from doing it by overcoming it mentally.

Shirley picked up the telephone within one second of finishing her intercom conversation with Mr. Bentley and dialled her friend Sheila. Shirley had only made friends with Sheila because Mr. Bentley had asked her to do so.

"Hi Sheila, Shirl. So!"

Sheila and Shirley had a giggly-gossipy-girly conversation, which Shirley cut off after only a few minutes, having gleaned the information requested by Mr. Bentley.

"Listen, I have to go, I'm at work. Good to talk to you, babe."

Shirley hit the button on her intercom so she could report back to Mr. Bentley.

"Yes, Shirley, what have you found out?"

"Mr. Fontoon has definitely triggered the alarm clock, sir. Sheila can see him very clearly."

"And he hasn't found some way to escape yet?"

"Not at all, sir. He's stuck up there but good."
"Good, good. Any other information?"
"Well..."
"What is it, Shirley?"
"Apparently he's been, you know, at it again." Shirley blushed. "Right there in the trap. Upside down."
"Did you hear that, boys? Fontoon's been at it again! Upside down this time!"

The room broke up into hearty laughter and clapping. Finding out about somebody else masturbating was always an hilarious event.

"That's all for now, Shirley, thank you. Top work, top drawer. All right then, what's the employment report? Adams?"

"Thank you, sir. His position is quite stable at Wossafocken Point, and he doesn't spend much time in focused critique of his situation. He thinks big, real big. I think we can safely assume that he'll be parked in his useless dead-end job for some time to come."

"Top drawer. Love life? Watkins?"

"Feeble, sir. He is one hundred percent alone and has no realistic prospects. There's a girl at the grocery store he has a bit of a crush on. A very young, very pretty girl who has plenty of men available to her of any sort she might want. She smiled at him because she is *une créature souriante*. She looks right at you and smiles, and if that sort of thing impresses you, you're done for. No, there's nothing to report here. It's the café counter girl story all over again."

"Excellent, excellent. Gentlemen, I commend you. Everything seems to be in very good order indeed. Work is so easy when you've got a good team around you. It's just tricks and horizons left now I think. Let's have tricks first. Weasby?"

"Just small things really. The lab has developed a way of

making his toenails grow faster by focusing infrared magnetic waves on them. He cuts them, you see, and then forgets about them. He thinks he has so much time before attending to them again, but they are growing faster now. Soon, he must cut them again."

"And that annoys him."

"Oh, very much sir. Close to rage at times. We're having an effect."

"All right, Weasby, that's fine, that's fine. Horizons? Hornbottom? Any major humiliations upcoming?"

"Thank you, sir. We've been setting up a fairly elaborate fatelet for him that's sure to end in financial and emotional disaster if he bites. It's his grad-school fantasy, wanting to do international relations or poetry – we've been encouraging it, sent him a couple of brochures about programmes at local universities. This is a low probability event, but if he does bite, we're looking at a two-year journey to nowhere, and a ton of money and emotional capital drained. I hardly need explain to this group how long those loans are going to be in the picture."

"About as long as the shame, I'd say."

"Not quite! Not quite!"

Laughter all around.

"I like it! Well done! Well, let's move..."

"Sir..."

"Yes, Hornbottom?"

"There is one more thing, sir. We've detected something potentially troubling on the horizon as well."

"Very good, what is it?"

"We're not sure. We do know he's being watched, and not by us. But we've been unable to find out anything else so far."

"Hmm. Can we think of anybody who might want to help him?"

"Not a pigeon, sir. But at this point we're not ruling out anything."

"Well, that's fine, that's fine. I'm sure it's nothing you boys can't handle. Continue to monitor the situation and let us know as soon as you learn anything, that's all. Gentlemen, that's enough for now. This meeting of the Fontoon Wrecking Company is adjourned."

Chapter Buttocks

Admiral Fontoon felt like a complete idiot and he knew his feeling was right. His rude awakening had left him in a state of profound inanition. He had drawn a mental line at one o'clock in the afternoon, a time after which he felt getting out of bed was demoralising. Well, what if he did sleep all day? Why shouldn't he? Nobody would blame him because nobody would know because nobody would care. He wasn't expected at Wossafocken Point for hours.

Fontoon sat numbly now at his kitchen table and pressed Cheez Bombs, which actually burst in tiny explosions upon contact with saliva, into his mouth. He had showered and made desultory cleaning motions, not so much tidying as pushing everything into a centralised quasi-Olmec pre-Columbian mound before which to collapse in ceremonial despair. He had sustained no injuries worthy of medical attention, but his left knee and forearm had both received impressive bruises, and he could legitimately limp. His head was still tender from its encounter with the oak table. A vomitous aroma lingered.

You must face yourself strictly, with severe eyes. That's what the handsome Japanese man ahead of Fontoon had said to the sprouty nose-hair corner grocer as Fontoon waited to pay for his spaghetti and sauce one day. Fontoon didn't know the context but he always remembered those words, which seemed true, and ruthless. It was almost as if, once you knew a fierce axiom like that one, you didn't even have to face yourself strictly with severe eyes any more. You could simply state the axiom and create an effect serious enough for most purposes.

Fontoon also remembered the words of pocket billiards champion Willie Mosconi, who had started his classic work on the game, right at the beginning of chapter one (Fundamentals), with the timeless phrase: *There's only one way to play pocket billiards – the right way.* How true those words were as well, and how equally unforgiving and generally applicable to life itself. Fundamentals indeed. It was about getting serious. It was about cutting the fat, the distractions, the excuses. Fontoon didn't need to face himself particularly strictly nor with especially severe eyes; even from a timid sideways glance he knew he wasn't playing the pocket billiards game of life the right way. With a sigh he looked out of the window at the always-unfamiliar view of the city outside, the very sight that had made him cross the line into nausea.

He stood up and approached the window, that he might gaze through it while striking a reflective pose with his hands clasped thoughtfully behind his buttocks. As he stood there, Fontoon secretly enjoyed the effect created by his own posture, standing so thoughtfully and quietly before a window like that. He felt somehow romantic. He bet himself that history's best philosophers no doubt stood in similar attitudes while pondering the meaning of life. He felt in the perfect mood to have an insight of his own. He sniffed the air around him with grave dissatisfaction, and frowned.

"Alone I stand," he said solemnly in the emptiness of his apartment, secretly enjoying the dramatic sound of it despite his real sense of ruin, and straining to hear its faint reverberations in the room.

Fontoon watched as the building across the street went through its continual permutations. It was of no fixed colour, but changed constantly according to combinations of its internal chemistry, the mood of the viewer, and the way the light would hit it. The patterns into which these colours fell also continuously changed, as did the shape of the building itself. It remained more or less a top-tapering rectangular box, but would oscillate like a huge building-shaped elastic tube full of thick liquid, as if there were an enormous building-sized woman belly dancing very slowly inside it.

The streets and sidewalks rolled along in waves, usually subtly, but sometimes with such force that it was hard to keep one's footing. Beyond one's immediate vicinity, the city blended into a bubbling backdrop of melted crayons, with colourful balls emerging, spreading, breaking into smaller balls, joining to form larger ones, or sinking away entirely. Overhead, multi-hued clouds formed and dissipated like time-lapse films, and mirages appeared and faded everywhere. And down on those rolling streets, people moved, synchronising their body motions as best they could to the motion of the city itself.

Admiral Fontoon was beginning to get hypnotised. His eyelids, which had been fixed narrowly in an attitude of wisdom and perceptiveness, had relaxed and were drooping. Likewise, his jaw had gone slack, and indeed saliva was pooling beneath his tongue, and rising to such a level that spillage was imminent. Sometimes when this happened he would start awake, with some hurried imperative in his head, such as 'Action stations!' Other times, like now, he simply gazed until his saliva pool flooded over the banks of his lips, setting off a sudden shamefest of wiping and slurping. He shuffled across the room and sat back down at his kitchen table.

On the table was a swell of bills and junk mail that Fontoon had been accumulating and avoiding for several weeks, if not months. This unkempt splash of envelopes needed tending badly. Fontoon resisted the urge to do nothing. Instead, he made a very orderly stack out of the dishevelment and pushed it neatly to one corner. *Hmmm.* Some brochures for graduate courses in poetry. *Interesting.* He had long harboured poetic ambitions and fancied himself a latent talent of potentially great repute. Statistically speaking, the peak of his fame, were it coming, ought most likely to have been well over a decade ago. Fontoon extinguished this disturbing inkling the very moment he noticed it arising. Impudent thoughts of this kind only create needless anxiety. Brash, young, sexy, and self-confident were only four among innumerable possible qualities of an emerging poet. Taking the world by storm was only one way to make an entrance. Surely there were plenty of examples of less grasping people slinking onto the poetic stage quietly through side doors at uncharismatic later stages in life. Well then Admiral Fontoon could be one of those.

Fontoon greedily imagined himself now giving a public reading in a bookstore full of devoted fans, now at a fancy party on an equal footing with famous celebrities from other walks of life. It is true that he had never written a poem that he felt was a success on his own artistic terms, and indeed he had produced only three or four failures. The fact of greater importance was that he was living his life, accumulating the sorts of experiences and thoughts and attitudes that would one day serve him so well in the world of poetry.

He had nearly started hundreds of poems, mostly in random snatches of words that would occur to him during the course of the day and would have the magic ring of poetry. For example, he might combine the word 'vanishing' with the word 'distance' and consider there was a phrase with poetic possibilities, or the word 'gabble' with the word 'wahine' and reckon there was something in there somewhere. It was never convenient to write these down, but he felt reasonably confident that these promising beginnings remained trapped in a subconscious netherworld and could be retrieved once he simply sat down with a sharpened pencil, a clean sheet of paper, and an entire free afternoon ahead of him with no masturbating. All he needed to do was dip into this vast well of dissociated snippets and allow them to coalesce before his gently coaxing mind's patient eye.

Fontoon spent nearly a full additional minute basking in imprecise reverie. He thought of the word 'nabob' and the word 'kaput', and nodded his head earnestly. The immediate afternoon was nothing if not full of tightly constrained possibilities. *I should start now,* thought Fontoon, a thought that somehow triggered a profusion of other things he ought to do that afternoon as well. Where to begin?

I'll make a list, Fontoon decided. A list always clears things up. Fontoon felt that finally he was about to get things organised. Without a list, it was impossible to do anything, but once you had one, all you had to do was go through it and tick things off. *I should have done this a long time ago.* He got up to try to find a pen and a piece of paper. He could have sworn he kept some blank paper on his kitchen table, but if so, it had moved elsewhere. He looked all over his apartment, starting with the places he could have sworn he kept blank paper and then moving on to places he knew he never kept blank paper. It was infuriating. He had only just barely embarked on his organisational crusade and he was already being driven up the wall by it. Was it too much to ask that a piece of blank bastard paper could be found when it was wanted? Must everything be stupid and irritating?

"Dammit!" he suddenly yelled. He intended to punch the

soft fleshy bit of his other hand, but somehow the back of a chair got in the way. Fontoon dropped into a pained crouch and indulged in a few moments of feeling angry and stupid before rising with the decision to make his list on the back of an envelope. There were loads of envelopes right there on the kitchen table. Now he needed a pen or a pencil. Where to look? By the phone? No, nothing there except a pad of blank paper. Stuck on a bookshelf somewhere? No, no, nothing. Ah. Pencil. On the floor by the laundry pile. Success. However, he discovered he was unable to hold a pencil very happily now in his swollen red writing hand. Placing the pencil awkwardly in his left hand, he attempted some uncoordinated scribbling, only to break the fragile point. He hurled the implement across the apartment and it rolled under his refrigerator, where it remained for the rest of eternity. Fontoon put his head down on the kitchen table until realising there was something he could easily do without thinking. Thank god for egestion. It would take up some time and nobody could blame him for doing it.

He had an uneventful time of it, producing the sort that anyone could understand, went through his rather thorough cleaning ritual, and then he did something relatively unusual. He opened up the little cupboard under the sink, and took out an empty glass jar and a strainer. Using the latter, he dipped into the toilet water, held his breath, fished out his not insubstantial prize, placed it carefully into the glass jar, and screwed the cap on tight. Only then did he flush the toilet. Only then did he breathe.

He looked around the apartment furtively, even though he knew nobody else was there to see, except of course, as always, the invisible omni-connecting tendrils of the all-feeling universe. His knuckles whitened a bit as he clutched his jar and went for the special cupboard.

Fontoon

Fontoon opened the cupboard. There they were – some thirty jars of impounded bowel movements of various vintages. *I need to get rid of some of these,* he thought. *Cull the herd.* Fontoon felt dirty in a fascinating way as he placed the newest recruit among its brethren and paused to look at them all, some nearly as unsullied as the day they were made, others wholly desiccated and crumbling. It sure was interesting. How strange they looked. Look at that one, three years old. *Crusty little thing.* Fontoon shut the cupboard door and exhaled decisively. He was very ashamed of himself, and quietly thrilled.

I could do the dishes, Fontoon considered, looking at the pile still twiddling its thumbs in the sink, a pile that was obviously prepared to wait forever. A glance in the other direction yielded only the pile of puke-soaked newspapers. Piles everywhere. Smells. People were supposed to take their recycling down to the Recycling Centre. It was clearly a tedious and untenable system. They ought to make it easy for people, very easy. Do you want the recycling done or not?

Enough. He stood, and in an act that already felt heroic, he set his jaw, held his breath, and grabbed a large, lawn-sized garbage bag from under the sink in the kitchen. He began stuffing the papers into the bag. It felt good. The triumph of filling the first bag was followed by the disappointment of discovering that it was the last bag he had.

No matter. Fontoon fixed his eyes on the sink and permitted a thin smile. He removed some of the papers from his garbage bag to make room. Two minutes of clinking and crashing later, the dishes were gone. *I have more dishes,* he said to himself, giddy with the liberating feeling of 'anything goes'.

He lifted the big bag and cradled it in his arms. It was heavy, and he was already feeling faint. He narrowed his eyes and looked both ways, as if he were about to cross Secret

Agent Street. He fumbled with the front door knob until he succeeded in opening it, and staggered out into the hallway of his apartment building.

Nobody. Fontoon made his way along the corridor and over to the rubbish chute, got it open, took a look at the 'No Newspapers!' sign and one last look both ways, and then wedged the big bag into the opening. He had to push as hard as he could to force it through the hole. The bag plummeted for long silent seconds before landing with an earthenware smash at the bottom of the chute.

Hah, he thought.

He hurried gleefully back to his apartment, where he grabbed a large armful of newspapers. Before entering the hallway, he poked his head out and looked both ways. All clear. As swiftly and quietly as he could, he approached the rubbish chute again. A few papers slid off the top of the unwieldy pile and landed on the floor behind him. Again he got the chute door open and shoved the papers inside. Again he looked around. Still clear.

Just as he was retrieving the fallen papers, however, he looked up to see a pair of eyes peering intently at him through a door that was opened just a crack.

"I see what you're doing Fontoon," said the voice attached to the eyes, "and I'm calling the police."

It was Tommy 'The Fink' Pinkston from down the hall.

Tommy was eleven years old. He was called The Fink because he had blown the whistle on Culoso one school day back in third grade. Culoso was a charismatic child who could lead less self-assured others astray. Culoso had a naked lady pen, the kind where she has an ink bathing suit that drains away down to one small strategic triangle. That's how Culoso originally roped in Tommy.

The pair of them, Culoso and Tommy, kept claiming to have to go to the bathroom, and when they got permission they'd go to the bathroom all right, only not on official business. They'd just lean against the sink and look at Culoso's pen for a few thrilling minutes. Then it was arguing about who was bigger, King Kong or It from *Mad Monster Party*. Tommy was a Kong man; Culoso shot him down. Tommy objected at first, but Culoso was adamant. Tommy had no choice but to concede that compared to It, King Kong was fairly small.

The teacher, Mrs. Dubin, a beautiful woman with dark sweaters full of bosom, caught them and was angry. Culoso and Tommy had lied to her and taken her for quite a little ride. For the first half of the year Mrs. Dubin had been Miss Kirschner, but then she married Mr. Dubin. All the students preferred Miss Kirschner. She used to belong to them, but now she had come under the spell of this Dubin. Unspoken tension crimped the shoulders of everyone in the class since the wedding day. Even so, Tommy was genuinely remorseful upon seeing Mrs. Dubin's indignant face. He understood all at once that Miss Kirschner was still there below the surface, kindly and warm and accessible, only she was wounded and felt forced against her own loving nature to draw a disciplinary line in the sand.

However, he did really and truly now have to go to the bathroom, and she wouldn't let him. He gave her a pleading look and clutched his penis imploringly through his trousers, but no; she was in a punishing, Dubinesque mood.

To his credit, Tommy had refused to beg. He didn't say for the love of god, Mrs. Dubin, I'm going to wet my pants, punish me however you like, but please in the name of decency don't make me wet my pants in school. In her anger she probably hadn't considered the idea that Tommy might realistically wet his pants if he couldn't get to the bathroom. It's probably not what she really wanted. It was probably just the Dubin in her.

Tommy held out as long as he could, but the day was young and eventually he had to let go. The ensuing pants infusion changed how everyone perceived him from then on; his job prospects and future happiness suffered accordingly. Tommy turned against Culoso that day; he blamed him for everything and told on him about the naked lady pen, which was promptly confiscated. It was Culoso who named him The Fink.

Fontoon had never met Tommy's family and wondered if he lived alone. He wondered if the boy's parents were perhaps living a slapdash life of moral relativism. In fact, they were a sneaky little couple, but their worst actual crime had been placing a bag that said 'meter broken' over a functioning parking meter – actually they always did it, and always had plenty of marked bags.

"Don't call the police, Tommy," said Fontoon now in a measured tone, "because if you do I'll..."

"You'll what?" taunted Tommy. "What'll you do?"

"I'll make you regret it."

"Big man! I'm calling the police."

A scowl took Fontoon's face as he turned to confront the boy, his arms still full of newspapers. He was immediately blinded by a succession of bright flashes, as Tommy blasted him with a dozen rapid-fire rounds of snapshot.

"You little bastard!" yelled Fontoon, dropping the papers and rushing the door, which slammed in his face. He could hear the sound of a chain sliding into place. He could see only spots.

Chapter Jail

"I'll have your badge for this! You'll be spending the rest of your life giving out parking tickets!"

"Oh, I'm sure," said Officer Malone, locking Fontoon into a cage of steel bars and nodding as if he had seen everything there ever was in the world. "You'll have my badge. I'll be giving out parking tickets. I can see it all now." Malone took off his cap and scratched his manly head. Fontoon grabbed the bars of the cell door and rattled them.

"Throwing his papers away, was he?" asked Officer Farrell as he strode purposefully up to Fontoon's cell. He put his hands on his hips. He was chewing gum, and wore a frown on his handsome face. "Piece of shit."

"Throwing them away like dirt. Like you'd throw away a goddamned banana peel."

"Let me tell you something, dickhead. You don't throw your newspapers away. They're not garbage. What the fuck?"

"He'll think twice before doing that next time, won't he?"

"You better fucking think twice about it, asshole."

"They were covered in vomit!" shouted Fontoon. "I had to get rid of them!"

"And throwing away your dishes, for god's sake!" exclaimed Malone. "What is that? You don't throw away your dishes! You wash them! Wash them and put them away!"

"Punk-ass motherfucker. Just remember one thing, dirtbag. You're not just throwing away some dishes here. You're throwing away your life."

Fontoon

You're throwing away your life. The words echoed in Admiral Fontoon's mind as the policemen walked away, still clucking. It was a definite sore spot. It had taken years of tortured half-attempts at self-examination for Fontoon to approach the broad outlines of that same conclusion, and still he had never perceived it with the beautiful stark clarity that Officer Danny Farrell so instantly had.

"O that some Power would give us that little gift," a voice sang out from behind Fontoon, "to see ourselves as others see us. It would from many a blunder free us, and foolish notions as well, oh yes!"

Damn, Fontoon thought. *Roommate.* He turned around reluctantly to survey his surroundings for the first time. It was a small cell, with bars for a front door and three of the four walls. The fourth, outer wall was concrete and had bars on a tiny square window narrower than one of Fontoon's thighs. The floor was concrete, with a small hole in the middle of it that served as a toilet.

A metal bunk bed took up one wall, with some sort of square-jawed criminal sitting up top. His strangely bright blue eyes sat moist and blinking in a field of deep creases, a filamented topography of recklessly ill-conceived plans. Fontoon's mind raced through a threat assessment. They had poetry in common. They would probably get along all right.

The criminal reached a meaty hand under his mattress and pulled out a toilet brush with a sharpened bit of metal taped to the end of it. He pointed it in the general direction of Fontoon's stomach.

"I'll chiv ya!" he spat, grinning maniacally. He repeated it: "Heh heh, I'll chiv ya!"

Fontoon felt the alarm that the words were intended to produce. At the same time, he was pleased to hear an authentic prison word on his very first day in jail, one connoting both a crudely fashioned weapon and the means of employing it. It took little imagination to get a sense of what it would be like to be chivved, even if one couldn't provide a strict dictionary definition on demand. Some awful blend of stabbing and slashing and tearing, no doubt. It would hurt and it would be horrifying, and nobody would do much to make you feel better after it happened.

"I'll chiv ya, I'll chiv ya!" he cried again, and then curled up beside himself laughing. "I'll chiv ya," he gasped between laughs, "I'll chiv ya!" He laughed until he coughed and then he coughed for a long time.

"I'm just messing with you," he said at last. "Make yourself at home. Try anything funny and I will shank you where you stand. You ever been shanked?"

"No."

"Me neither. Try it and I'll skiv you."

Fontoon didn't say anything. All this skiv and chiv and shank. There could be poetry here. This was an experience. This was real life. There was an authenticity here that would be invaluable to the poetic enterprise.

"Let's escape," said the criminal with a sudden change of tone. "Sure, we could dig a tunnel. All we need is a place to hide the dirt. Imagine how much dirt there would be from digging a big long tunnel out of here. Think the guards aren't going to notice? Don't be naïve. This cell would probably be completely full of dirt, they'd have to be blind not to notice it. No, something has to be done about it. I could dig, and you could eat the dirt. I'll dig and you eat. I'm not eating dirt. Dish chucker. I don't suppose you'd risk it. You'd rather apologise for existing than try to be a man for a change."

He paused here to scrutinise Fontoon critically before

continuing.

"I bet you want the top bunk. Everyone does. Can't have it. I was here first."

"I don't care about having the top bunk."

"That's what they all say. Name's Singleton. Richard. 'Dicky James.' Listen, look what I've got here. Here's the difference between you and me. I'm armed. Steel carpenter's square, shaved to a point. Keep it right here under my mattress. And that's not all. Look. Simple shard of plexiglass, wrapped up on one end with electrical tape. Prison sign shop. You can get all kinds of stuff in there. Check this one out. Gardening gloves. I was on landscape detail for six months. You put a smaller glove on the inside, with inverted upholstery tacks stitched to the knuckles. You get the tacks from the furniture shop. I gotta introduce you to Bernie. Bernie works the shops, he can get you anything. If he likes you. Hang on, there's more. Legal point: they've got to let you have access to typewriters so you have the opportunity to prepare your own defence papers. It's a law, you understand me? Check this one out. Carriage return. U clamp attached to one side, handle wrapped up with boxing tape from the gym and a little upholstery thread. Furniture shop again. You would love Bernie. You ram this into a fellow's bread basket, it's a real conversation stopper. I love this one. Unbreakable comb. Razors wrapped on with tape. Simple but sweet. What do you say, you want to escape? We dig in shifts. You go first and I'll be lookout. Hell, I'll eat some dirt. Think I won't? Jesus if there's any worms in there I'll puke. Are you with me?"

"Whatever you say, man."

"Don't be like that. I'm not really going to chiv you. Not unless you go all skink on me. That's a prison term. Stick with me, kid. I'll get you up to speed."

"All right. Thanks."

Fontoon got into the bottom bunk and lay down to take stock of his life. Officer Farrell had been exactly right. He was throwing his life away, little by little. A new day would be handed to him every afternoon, and he would immediately cast it onto the burning trash heap of waste and futility. He was just like the man in the story of the man who had a million potatoes but could never figure out what to do with them. He had made practically no progress in virtually all areas. And he had only himself to blame.

The time I've wasted, he thought.

Fontoon curled up on his bunk bed and felt cheated. He'd be missing a shift at the lighthouse for this. No doubt that would mean trouble. There would be repercussions. Mr. Pappy had little tolerance for any nonsense out at Wossafocken Point. Fontoon would write a letter, many letters. The mayor would get one. The newspapers. Perhaps he could become a *cause célèbre*. Surely he was not the only person in the world who felt that the system had become absurd with authoritarian arbitrariness. There would be others, others who might rally around him. His letters could provide the tipping point. Everyone might rise. Maybe this ridiculous episode could be put to good use in the end. Yes, his letters would be in the form of poems, trenchant political poems. He'd be asked to speak at college graduations. He would speak metaphorically of prison life and liberation. Young women in provocative dress would gather around him and look up at him with undisguised admiration and tell him what an inspiration he'd been to them. He'd invite them back for late night sessions with wine and intellectual flirtation. One of them, possibly more, would remain at the end of the night and would tentatively touch his trousers while gazing earnestly into his eyes. In short order,

Fontoon

Fontoon was asleep. He dreamed about running away from things.

"Wakey wakey! Aww, look at him, all curled up on his bunk!" Officer Malone was running a tin cup noisily along the bars of Fontoon's cell.

"On your feet, sunshine," added Officer Farrell. "I hope you enjoyed your little beauty sleep, but I got bad news for you. You're still ugly."

Fontoon awoke with a start and instinctively reached for his snooze button before collecting his wits.

"What's going on?" asked Fontoon, propping himself up on his elbows. "When do I get to talk to a lawyer?"

"Never. What we say goes. That's the only law in here."

"Let me tell you something. I'm writing some letters, all right? And everything you say to me is going to be in them. Throwing a man in jail over tossing out some compromised newspapers? Taking his rights away? It's not going to look too good for you boys."

"And your dishes," said Officer Malone. "Just like they were garbage.

"So what? It's not a crime, is it? A man can do as he pleases with his own dishes in this country, the last time I checked, no?"

"It may not be a crime, dickwad, but it's criminal just the same," said Officer Farrell.

"It's a crime of the mind," injected Singleton from his position on the bunk bed.

"Enough out of you, Richard 'Dicky James'," barked Officer Farrell, "I'll beat you funny with this stick!"

"You wouldn't dare, copper!"

"You can lose your skiv privileges, you know!" yelled Officer Malone.

Singleton took his muttering to inaudible levels.

"Shavvy skivver," grumbled Officer Farrell.

"Listen," interrupted Fontoon. "Can you just tell me..."

"It's *morally* criminal," added Officer Malone, confirming that he understood the precise sense in which it was criminal to throw away one's dishes instead of washing them and putting them away, that he understood it even more finely than this criminal Singleton. What did criminals know about morals?

"I'll be honest with you," said Officer Farrell in a low whisper. "I don't even personally care about the newspapers. What kind of idiot throws away his dishes? What kind of vermin?"

"Let me ask you something if I may," said Officer Malone. "What do you do on a Sunday?"

"A Sunday?" asked Fontoon.

"You're not a religious man?"

"Me?" said Fontoon. "No. I mean, I have certain ideas..."

"Irreligious, you might say? Would that be fair enough?"

"Irreligious, yes, I suppose so. Is that a crime now too?"

"Not at all. No, what interests me is, in what sense?"

"I don't follow."

"Irreligious has two shades of meaning, Einstein," offered Officer Farrell impatiently. "Indifferent or hostile to religion."

"Precisely," confirmed Malone. "I'm wondering whether this one considers himself more indifferent or more hostile."

"What does this have to do with anything?" asked Fontoon.

"I think the question is raised quite naturally in view of the behaviour you've exhibited, which you'd have to admit would be a far cry from God-fearing."

Fontoon tried to manifest a patient and kindly expression, but, as others saw him, he appeared smug.

"Gentlemen," he began. "I'm a citizen. I pay taxes. I have

rights. I would like to get out of here. What are the steps, where do I pay the fine? Let us bring this ridiculous matter to its conclusion."

"Sounds a bit godless to me," said Malone, shaking his head wearily.

"You don't need to be a tax-paying citizen to have rights, dish fucker," put in Officer Farrell, with a somewhat more heated tone than the situation perhaps called for. "You are a human being, with rights inherent. What people never get is that the Framers of the Constitution did not purport to create any rights. Rather there were rights and liberties that were presumed to be self-evident and pre-existing, the function of the law being only to prevent the government from infringing upon them."

"So I get a lawyer, right?" ventured Fontoon, palms out, shoulders up, eyebrows raised.

"Fuck you," said Farrell. "Fucking wise-ass."

"Although it is a kettle of fish," added Malone, "when you consider one man's government intrusion is another man's fair play. For example taxing the rich. It's like being a cop. A cop for whom, if you get my drift. However, regardless, there is ever the divine paradox in which the enslaver is enslaved as much as the enslaved, that is, the other, original, enslaved. And that for any to be free, all must be freed."

Officer Farrell gave him a quieting look.

"So we all getting freed?" shouted Singleton. "After all, the man just said..."

"Shut the fuck up, 'Dicky James' Singleton!" said Officer Farrell.

"Only this turd right here," he continued, nodding at Fontoon. He put the key into the cell door and turned it with a satisfying clanky sound. "You're free to go. You and your rights are free to go home to your crumpled little cretin hole and be as godless and asinine as you please."

"Out you go," added Officer Malone, wanting to be fully involved in the release of the prisoner.

Fontoon stepped quickly out of the door and Farrell locked it back up. Singleton snorted contemptuously.

"So," said Fontoon. "What happens now?"

"Whattaya, want me to tell you what to do with your life?" said Farrell.

"That's it, I'm out? No charges, no fine, no lawyers. So you admit I was wrongfully imprisoned?"

"Not at all. We were within our prerogatives," said Malone.

"Well within," added Farrell.

"It's a judgement call," clarified Malone.

"A judgement call?"

"Yes," continued Malone. "A legal concept meaning that it is up to the discretion of the authoritative officer in charge and we thereby lawfully chose jail time in this particular instance in accordance with the relevant statutes. Now, you could eventually have brought legal challenges to your own incarceration thanks to what we call the rule of law, with its protections even for the likes of you. And it could have turned out that, in the judgement of those whose job it is to judge, we had over-incarcerated, so to speak, in which case justice would have been served and you'd have been released just as you're being released right now. Naturally if you continue to stand here questioning us in this aggressive fashion, and we perceive a threat here, we do have additional discretion for vigorous responses."

Fontoon chose not to pursue the discussion and indicated as much to Officer Malone by folding his arms and smiling sarcastically. The two policemen escorted Fontoon to the front lobby area of the jail, where he collected the personal artefacts that had been confiscated from him and a few free brochures.

Fontoon offered his hand to the officers for shaking, and after the slightest pause Officer Malone took it and shook it; Officer Farrell followed suit. Fontoon wheeled around and, as Malone and Farrell shook each other's hands, strode out into the growing daylight feeling tentatively hopeful and glad to be a free man with a world of possibilities before him. *I'm going to contemplate all this one day,* he thought. Surely Mr. Pappy would understand that he had been unavoidably detained.

He hailed an inflatable taxicab and went bouncing and careering into the heart of the city.

"Asshole," said Officer Farrell.

Chapter Stomach

"How was Uncle Ned's stomach cough today?"

The fact is Uncle Ned's stomach cough was disgusting, but Zoom Zoom knew his mother didn't want to hear some vivid description of it. Nobody wanted to hear anything about anybody's horrible cough or which organ seemed to be the source of it. Zoom Zoom's mother wasn't some kind of extraordinary person who wanted to hear that somebody's horrible cough sounded like a jelly stomach turning inside out, so Zoom Zoom said something encouraging and put away the last of the dishes.

"Enough with your chores, come and chat with me," said his mother. "You've done enough, working the garden, taking Ned his groceries, cooking me dinner, getting a new cushion for my wheelchair. You must be exhausted."

"Nahhh, I'm fine, really ma."

Zoom Zoom's mother smiled. She knew he wasn't fine. He had thrown his back out of alignment in a cycling accident two days earlier trying to carry too many groceries out to Uncle Ned and his repulsive cough. He wouldn't be riding that bike again any time soon, unfortunately. He couldn't even sit up straight; he was forced to slump over somewhat to the right. He'd have to take the bus to do his errands.

"Look at you, you can hardly turn your head!"

It was true. Zoom Zoom's neck was in bad shape too. He couldn't turn his head left or right. To look to the side, he'd have to turn his whole body – a fairly difficult proposition with his back in the shape it was. The most viable position for him was to sit slumping to the right and staring straight ahead. It was still painful, although it helped if he could prop his right elbow up on something.

"You should get yourself to the doctor, Zoom Zoom."

"I know, ma. I will. I just don't know when, that's all. Tomorrow I've got errands. And then Friday I'm down at the orphanage all day. Well, I'll get to it when I can, no worries.."

"You're a sweet boy, Zoom Zoom."

"Aw, ma."

"You be careful on that bus tomorrow."

"I will, ma."

Chapter Space

Admiral Fontoon's commute out to the lighthouse at Wossafocken Point was a time-consuming multi-modal bit of business that required catching a certain Purple Train in time to connect to a certain Orange Train in time to catch a certain bus out to a certain row boat, with only the tiniest margins for error. A natural dawdler, Fontoon had to muster an exhausting amount of determination simply to get to work on time. And if he was late, there was trouble.

If you've missed the crucial Purple Train, you're on to vastly inferior Plan B. Plan B is the N45 for about twelve miles to the corner with the hardware store, and then you have to sprint a block to get to the stop on time for the P28, which doesn't even drop you that close to the pier.

It takes forever, but the worst thing about the P28 isn't how late you get to work. It's the sick knowledge that you've burned life hours unproductively because you can't even read. You can't read on the corner because it's cold and windy, and you can't read once you're on the bus. You can't read when you're that late to work. You just have to sit and burn.

Time cannot be separated from space because of the velocity of objects relative to the speed of light and the strength of intense gravitational fields, which can slow the pace of unfolding, and because without space there is literally no time. There is a relationship between commuting minutes and personal space that is similarly non-Euclidean. Take the Boingy Boingy Man. The Boingy Boingy Man has Admiral

Fontoon's exact subway habits, only he shows up everywhere ten seconds earlier.

When Fontoon arrives to ascend the stairs to the elevated platform of the Purple Train, there is the Boingy Boingy Man ahead of him, a good six foot seven and only perhaps a hundred and sixty pounds, boinging his angular high-kneed way up the stairs, his enormous sticky-out ears quivering with the impact of each foot as it lands. He takes those stairs two at a time, briskly, whereas Fontoon grunts out loud with each step. Then across the platform he goes, boing boing boing in enormous bouncy steps, to Fontoon's exact favourite spot by the pay phone. Fontoon has to limit himself to the periphery of his own favoured area. Then the Boingy Boingy Man strides big strides into the Purple Train and takes up Fontoon's favourite space there by the opposite door. Fontoon shrinks into an available seat, all resentful.

Personal space narrows with the approach into the Orange Station. People begin to mass near the Purple Train doors that let out to the stairs that lead eventually down to the Orange Train, positioning themselves to burst out ahead of as many other people as possible, even as greedy crowds outside poise to push in at the same time. Fontoon tries to resist it, but he stands up a bit too soon, reluctantly moving into place behind somebody who looks fast.

Once the doors open, it's all-out mayhem. People flood out, some of them actually breaking into a run. A run! Grown people, men and grown women who should be at their most dignified age of life, running toward the stairs in some mysterious panic, their tongues practically hanging out. At the same time, people trying to enter the train push against the tide, wedging in an elbow here, a knee there. The train isn't going anywhere while people are still getting out, so why must they push in? They cannot help it. They must get in. They must get in now. They must get in first. Must they must they must.

On the stairs Fontoon finds himself behind a woman who has to get both her feet on a step before she can take the next one. It is her way, her style, her defect, her hell. One foot, two foot. One foot, two foot. She must feel alone in the station. Perhaps soft music plays dreamily in her head. Perhaps for her the madness does not exist. How else could she move like that without screaming? Fontoon restrains an impulse simply to kick her in the back, muffles the idea that old people should not leave the house, just as the woman behind Fontoon battles the urge to push him down the stairs, struggles to justify the idea that people in front of her are stupid.

Finally at the lowest level, Fontoon awaits the arrival of an Orange Train against the roar of an industrial ventilation system aurally evocative of run-amok computers and lonely death in deep space. There, as always, is the Boingy Boingy Man, impossibly, leaning against Fontoon's favourite support beam, reading a newspaper that he did not have on the Purple Train, looking like he's been there ages.

Fontoon has no book and no newspaper, and he feels the waiting keenly. He takes to pacing and indulging in furtive micro-glances at the astonishing shape of the skinny woman with the long curly hair that is always wet, she with her impossibly tight trousers and her regal bearing and her acne-scarred yet fiercely defiant face.

What must her voice sound like? Fontoon imagined it as sounding like the tiny twin fairies from Mothra movies, conjuring distant bongo drums in the background. There was one time that she did speak, because some quite elderly man approached her in a friendly fashion that Fontoon envied. The man naturally asked her some natural-sounding questions, smiled at her, seemed perfectly at his ease. *Sure it's easy if you're old,* that's what Fontoon thought as he strained to hear what her voice sounded like, hoping it wouldn't be disappointing. But somehow he couldn't quite hear her even though he was no more than ten feet away. It was fairy twins with distant bongos after all, obscured by train screeching and gigantic other-dimensional ventilators. She smiled at first, but her smile faded as the man failed to disengage graciously and leave her to her lonely scarred beauty. She seemed embarrassed; no, annoyed. She had been forced to emit her special sounds. Fontoon was glad and frightened. He bet she smelled really fresh. One day he must brush past her and have an exquisite sniff.

Fontoon wished he could speak to her just as easily as the old man, only without becoming annoying. Anything he could say would come uncomfortably out of the blue. It would also violate the unspoken No Communities code of the subway.

If only she was at his bus stop instead. Bus people speak to each other, tease each other about their unusual backpacks, comment on the Tuesday driver who tends to arrive late, chastise each other for not bringing an umbrella. There are entire social hierarchies within bus-stop communities.

Andy was the leader of Fontoon's bus-stop community. Andy was fifty-something and wore caps and always had a wry comment at the ready. He knew how to say things, emphasising important points with rhetorical flair, such as 'They're not giving us Veteran's Day off, I'm taking it off anyway. Yeah, I'm *taking* Veteran's Day off.' Whenever people were waiting for the bus and Andy wasn't there yet, most of the conversation centred on the fact that Andy wasn't there yet. Someone might speculate that if Andy didn't hurry, he might miss the bus. Somebody else might say that Andy had missed the bus last Thursday. Someone else might rejoin that they thought Andy was sometimes getting a ride and then everybody would go 'ohhhhhh.' When Andy showed up, you greeted him by saying, 'There he is.'

Andy's leadership was unquestioned. If the bus was especially late and everybody had to consider the possibility that it wouldn't come, that they might have to walk the long journey to the Q46, they looked to Andy to decide when the time was right to give up waiting and take action. If Andy would wait it out, they would wait it out as well. If Andy had had enough waiting, they had also had enough. Nobody was going to go walking off after a Q46 while Andy was still waiting for the P47.

The Q46 was a frequent subject of conversation at the bus stop, in particular its merits as a Plan B way to get home. It was Andy's preferred Plan B bus, but not the only possible choice. There was also the P28 to the N45 to consider, an option at which Andy scoffed. Fontoon secretly questioned Andy's wisdom on this matter, but wouldn't feel right about speaking his doubts aloud. That conversation would have gone like this:

"I don't know, I think the P28 to the N45 might be even better. Number one, the P28 is closer to here than the Q46, and number two, the N45 gets you to a closer subway stop."

Andy might say, "Really?"

"Yeah."

Then Andy might shrug and say, "Q46 is a better bus. Take you right to Union Turnpike."

Everyone would nod, including Fontoon.

One time during a conversation about the Q46, Andy marvelled at its efficiency.

"I took the Q46 on Thursday, got out of work a little early.

Man! Twenty minutes I'm walking up the hill to my house. *Twenty minutes.*"

"That's if you get the express," said Rosalia.

"There is no express," corrected Andy.

"Yes, the express bus, it doesn't make all the stops. If you get the regular, forget it." Everyone's attention was piqued now because they enjoyed seeing Andy respond to being contradicted.

"There is no express."

"Did it make all the stops, all the local stops?"

"No, that's the thing, it made two, maybe three stops, two three stops. Q46. Twenty minutes."

"That's the express."

"No, no, that's the limited."

"The limited?"

"Yeah, the limited. It makes fewer stops. I'm telling you, you get the limited and you are moving. You are *moving* on the limited."

"That's the express."

"No, the limited."

"What's the difference?"

"There is no express on the Q46. This is the limited."

That was the end of the discussion. Everybody always called it the limited after that. That was the power of Andy's leadership.

Fontoon boards his P47 to the pier. It's the nice driver, the one with a cheerful hello and some eye contact for every single person who gets on. The bus is nearly full. One seat is somewhat available, except that the young man in the next seat is sitting improperly, slumping strangely to one side, occupying territory to which he is not entitled. His elbow is even propped up on the adjoining seat. To accept this impudence meekly would be to yield to the inner coward. Fontoon also feels a budding feeling that, if allowed to mature, would become rage. Nothing good has ever come from allowing cowardice and rage to lie and fester together. Resolute yet afraid, Fontoon wedges into the compromised seat. The young man slowly retracts his elbow, although judging from his grimace he is not happy about doing so. He continues to lean into the other seat's space, forcing Fontoon into an awkward position, holding his elbows against himself in an unnaturally tight way.

Did this young ruffian think he could intimidate Fontoon? Did he expect Admiral Fontoon to accept this treatment meekly?

What should be done? Physically push back? Fontoon possessed excellent aesthetic instincts and instantly understood that resorting to such an act would lack beauty.

A few choice words would be a fine thing, but where were they? The best realistic thing really would be to stare at the offender and have him not look back. That way, anyone looking would see Fontoon's anger, would understand that he was not afraid. Indeed they would see that it was the young instigator who was shrinking, and that only a highly evolved sense of decorum prevented Fontoon from going apeshit.

Fontoon gave Zoom Zoom a first class stare down. Zoom Zoom didn't turn to face Fontoon because his neck was killing him, but he could see him with his peripheral vision. More than that, he could sense Fontoon, could feel the heat from his eyeballs. Fontoon kept staring, just to make sure everyone could see who was afraid and who wasn't. Zoom Zoom kept looking straight on ahead.

"This man is insane," thought Zoom Zoom.

The moment passed. Fontoon's anger turned to hydrocarbons and got stored with the rest. Zoom Zoom got his errands done and made it to Uncle Ned's later that day with more groceries. His back got much better over the next six weeks. Uncle Ned's stomach cough kept getting worse.

Chapter Light

Two hundred and fifty-nine, two hundred and sixty, two hundred and sixty-one...

Admiral Fontoon always counted the well-worn steps on his daily trudge up to his office. Initially this was just a way to pass the time during the trudge; now he was also trying to solve one of life's little mundane mysteries. One day he noticed that the number of steps seemed to vary quite a bit; from then on he began to keep meticulous track of the daily totals, ascending and descending. Thus far he had documented a range from a low of two hundred and sixty-nine to a high of two hundred and eighty-one. There was of course nothing to be done about it. The police weren't interested.

Blasted steps. They were enough to drive a man mad in any case. If Fontoon had his way they would modernise the old lighthouse and put in an elevator, but Wossafocken Point was a designated historical monument; improvements were strictly forbidden. It had an odd shape, as if it were not a tower in itself but the reflection of a tower in a badly warped mirror, with all manner of bulges, this part seeming to have shrunk, that part seeming to have bubbled. The shape shifted, slowly, like a stiff old man shifting his weight from one leg to another, now stretching his old back and shoulders out a bit as he leaned on his wooden cane, so that the bulging bits would move around, up and down the tower, and from one side to another. Fontoon was nearly at the top.

Two seventy-two, two seventy-three, two seventy-four,

two seventy-five. *God damn.*

Fontoon was well out of breath, as always, as he pushed open the heavy wooden door at the top of the steps. He had to take a little rowboat at the end of his commute over to where the lighthouse stood on a small piece of rock off the coast of the city. Wossafocken Point. It was just a short row of perhaps a hundred yards to the island. He was on time, but that would do nothing to help him with regard to the shift he had missed due to imprisonment. It was not possible to call Mr. Pappy, the head keeper, because Mr. Pappy didn't use telephones. He didn't believe in them. He believed in people showing up when they were supposed to.

First thing Fontoon had to do was go to the locker room and put on his uniform: regulations. The uniform consisted of a coat, waistcoat, trousers, and cap, all of dark indigo flannel. The coat was double-vested and had a double row of five yellow metal buttons running down the front of it. A yellow metal official badge was pinned to the cap just above the visor. There was also an optional canvas helmet for cold weather. Shoes were black and polished to shine. Mr. Pappy was very particular about all this. Everything had better be clean and neat. Mr. Pappy was generally a taciturn fellow who kept to himself, but if he turned to face you strictly with severe eyes, any physical or mental sloppiness would weigh upon you heavily.

Fontoon checked himself in the least warped mirror available, and deemed himself presentable. Numerous tasks awaited his attention. He began by cleaning and polishing the copper and brass fixtures of the lighting apparatus before moving on to the utensils used in the lantern and watch room. It was beautifully mindless, utterly absorbing work. He moved on to sweeping and dusting the tower landing, doors, windows, window recesses, and passageways from the lantern to the oil storage area.

Finally he got to the lens itself, a second-order Fresnel number that Fontoon referred to as The Bad Boy. These tasks were saved for last because they were the most thrilling. A second-order Fresnel lens is a magnificent and daunting device, and Fontoon hardly dared look at it until it was time to tend to its needs. The lens resembles a gigantic beehive, with prisms at the top and bottom to bend the light from the single lamp so that it comes out in a narrow, highly focused sheet. Four wicks, hollow to allow air to flow on both sides of the flame, increasing its brightness, were arranged in concentric circles. A powerful magnifying glass further intensified the light at the centre of the lens so that the overall result of the lamp architecture was an extraordinarily bright plane of concentrated light emanating from the top of the tall tower. It was an ingenious design, a perfect meeting of art and science, and anyone who saw it could appreciate its beauty.

Very gently and carefully Fontoon cleaned and polished the lens, filled the lamp with oil and wiped it clean and dry, dusted the housing, trimmed the wicks. Mr. Pappy was a real traditionalist, lighthouse-wise. Didn't like kerosene. He was a whale-oil man. Whale oil burned the steadiest and gave the best light.

Every once in a good long while, Mr. Pappy would somehow or other procure a freshly killed whale. Admiral Fontoon was never sure whether the old man would go out and harpoon one himself, or whether he would buy them from an audacious band of seafaring chancers, or whether indeed he would occasionally simply find one floating past. All he knew was that sometimes he would arrive at work to find a drying sperm whale on the island with a hole in its head and the oil sucked out. The whale oil did last a long time. The light it made really was pure and gorgeous. Using whale oil was wrong, but Fontoon loved it because it made him feel like he was living hundreds of years ago.

At last, with tasks complete and the evening sun melting away into a great purple-orange wash, Fontoon got to light the lamp. Each time that thing got fired up Fontoon was filled with an almost numinous lyrical feeling. Then he would stand there, looking out to sea, smelling the air, and wishing somebody could see him and appreciate exactly how poetic he could be. If his essential qualities could just be noticed by the right sort of person with the right sort of connections, Fontoon felt certain of his ability to blossom as a personage.

Fontoon had started out at Wossafocken Point as an intern but was now the assistant keeper, and was considered competent. What pride he took in the work was mitigated somewhat by the knowledge that the only two actual job requirements, as written in the official description, were a 'modicum' of intelligence and basic motility. Furthermore, it was lonely work that, whatever its merits, contributed virtually nothing to maritime safety, lighthouses having long since been rendered irrelevant by technological developments such as sonar, radar, radio, and infrared detectors.

But people still liked them, and they were everywhere protected by zoning laws, interest groups, and tradition. And if they were worth keeping, they were worth keeping properly. That's the way Mr. Pappy looked at it, and he approached the management of Wossafocken Point as if sailors' lives still depended on it. So when Admiral Fontoon turned from the window and saw Mr. Pappy standing at the entrance to the lamp room with his arms folded, he knew the old man was unhappy with him.

Fontoon

"I can explain," said Fontoon, grasping for the words that would make his recent incarceration for carelessness in matters pertaining to the earth's fragile resources seem sympathetic.

Mr. Pappy lived on site, alone, and tended to the lighthouse as a way of life. He was generally either in his living quarters or in the watch room. When Fontoon worked, they stayed out of each other's way. A short, wiry man of seventy-some-odd years, Mr. Pappy would always greet Fontoon with a curt little nod of his head, but he rarely said anything else. If he did say anything, it wasn't usually directed at Admiral Fontoon; it was usually directed at nobody. 'Hundred potatoes a pig and a pot,' he would say, gazing out of the window, or 'Ain't a man but a man with his ass on a can.' Most of the time he said nothing.

Mr. Pappy's wife had lived with him there for the better part of three decades but had passed away many years ago. Their young daughter, an only child, had died in a terrible storm early in their marriage, when powerful winds sent waves and rocks smashing through the windows of the little house and buffeted the tower. Her mother was ill in bed, and the girl had been frightened by the storm's fury. She was running to the tower to find her father when she was knocked down and carried out to sea by a huge wave. Mr. Pappy could only watch in tears from the walkway as he struggled to keep the flame burning in the lamp room. He had banged his hands hard on the cold stone wall and shouted 'No!'; he hears the word echoing around the room to this day.

Admiral Fontoon didn't know any of this history, but he could tell that the head keeper lapsed into sadness at times, and it was something that Fontoon respected. Fontoon looked at him now and wondered what might be going through the older man's head.

"Kinsmen cold and belly keel," said Mr. Pappy.

"Yes," said Fontoon. "You'll never believe it. It's a funny story, actually."

Just then the Fifth Auditor appeared from behind Mr. Pappy. The Fifth Auditor was top dog of all lighthouses, the administrator of administrators. He had no nautical experience himself but personally oversaw all hiring and firing of lighthouse staff. He had hired Fontoon because he thought he was an important navy man when he saw 'Admiral' on the job application. In fact, Admiral was just Fontoon's first name; Fontoon's father was a big fan of the navy, collected plastic navy toys, and named his only son after his favourite rank. When the Fifth Auditor realised his mistake, he was displeased and had taken a dim view of Fontoon ever since. He had not seen fit to fire him as of yet, although there were numerous applicable technical grounds for dismissal, among them 'slovenliness'. The Fifth Auditor liked to consider himself a man of immense forbearance.

"Admiral Fontoon," said the Fifth Auditor, slowly, emphasising the word 'Admiral' just slightly. He paused here to take in the view of the magnificent Fresnel lens and its intense plane of light.

"A beautiful light," he continued, nodding as if he were weighing his options. "You do keep a fine light here. There's no question of that."

"Thank you, sir," said Fontoon, but he received only a disapproving glare in response.

"I just happened to be in town, making my rounds, and of course it's always a pleasure to drop in for a visit with Mr. Pappy."

The Fifth Auditor smiled at Mr. Pappy, who reciprocated with a thinly disguised sneer, causing the Fifth Auditor's smile to wane.

"I understand there was a little problem here last night?"

"A problem, sir?"

"A certain assistant keeper failing to turn up?"

"Ah yes. I am very sorry about that, sir. Both of you. Very sorry. It was, unfortunately, completely unavoidable and beyond my control."

"And why is that?"

"I had been unfairly imprisoned."

"I see. By whom?"

"Frankly, sir, an out-of-control despotic..."

"I see," said the Fifth Auditor, cutting him off abruptly.

"It was all a big misunderstanding. Had there been a phone here to call, I might have..."

"Do you see these?" interrupted the Fifth Auditor, producing a copy of the lighthouse bylaws.

"I do."

"What are they?"

"The lighthouse bylaws."

"I don't think I need to remind you that failure to take an adequate interest in one's work is grounds for dismissal."

"No, sir. I assure you, I am..."

"Do you think failing to show up indicates an adequate level of interest?"

"Not on the face of it, no, I agree, but, as I was explaining..."

The Fifth Auditor began leafing through the bylaws theatrically.

"Hmmm," he said. "There's nothing in here about explanations or excuses that I can see. Nothing at all. Nothing whatsoever. Would you like to have a look, 'Admiral'?"

"No, sir."

"Very good. So. What is to be done? I'm afraid there are grounds for dismissal here, there is regrettably no ambiguity on that score here in the bylaws. It is my unfortunate job here to..."

Just then one of the large windows of the lamp room smashed inwards with a flock of wayward birds. Shards of glass and feathers sprayed everywhere, and the Fifth Auditor yelled out in undignified alarm. Fontoon took secret pleasure in the fact that, although he felt like he was having a heart attack, he had not shouted out in a panic. Mr. Pappy had not so much as blinked. He was, after all, as used to it as anyone could be. It happened with some regularity.

Certain birds were attracted by the light from the tower and would sometimes fly headlong through the windows. There was one particular flock of birds that seemed especially accident prone. Fontoon called them Muttering Blue Bellies because their bellies were bright blue, and because, walking around disoriented in the smashed-glass landscape, they emitted a sound that to Fontoon's ear sounded very much like 'goddamfrigginsonuvamutha' while he kicked at them and tried to shoo them back out through the broken window.

Fontoon cleared the room of birds and glass as Mr. Pappy took the Fifth Auditor to the watch room. When everything was tidy again Fontoon joined them there.

The watch room had a small library comprising an odd assortment of donated books. Some dealt with lighthouses and their history, but for the most part there was no particular unifying theme by which they could be sensibly organised. When Fontoon entered the room the Fifth Auditor was idly thumbing through a copy of *The Five Little Peppers and How They Grew*. Mr. Pappy had given him a cup of tea.

"Ah," said the Fifth Auditor, clearly embarrassed by what he considered his own girlish behaviour. "Well done. Well done. Do you get these little emergencies very often?"

"More often than you might think," said Fontoon.

"You must have nerves of steel," said the Fifth Auditor. "I'm afraid I nearly jumped out of my skin."

"It is a startling thing."

"Yes. In any case, I want to tell you that, upon further review, and taking into account Mr. Pappy's feelings on the matter, you will not in fact be dismissed from your position."

"I see. Thank you."

"You will be put on probationary status for three months. If there are no further lapses the matter will be expunged from your record entirely."

"Thank you. And thank you, Mr. Pappy."

Mr. Pappy nodded, and Fontoon shook the Fifth Auditor's hand.

Mr. Pappy escorted the Auditor to the exit and then retired to his own quarters. He generally stayed there until the end of Fontoon's shift, when he would return to tell Fontoon it was OK to leave. He would tell him not in words but by coming into the watch room with his hands in his pockets and nodding and then lighting a pipe. Fontoon would say 'all right, so long', and Mr. Pappy would nod again.

Left to his own thoughts then, with the major tasks completed and the light burning brightly, Fontoon sat down with a deck of cards for some solitaire and idle contemplation. The wind whistled in the lamp room through the broken window and the light slapping of cards on table resonated against the background noise of the rolling ocean.

There should be no better place for writing poetry than a lighthouse. The atmosphere. The free time. The view. Fontoon set aside his playing cards, grabbed a pencil and some scrap paper, and sat down near the window of the lamp room to view the sea. If anyone could have seen him just then, he thought, they would surely surmise: 'There. There, my friends, sits a poet.' And he wrote down some words.

> Beautiful strange commuter girl,
> stand proud like I'm
> not even allowed to talk to you.
> Angry about your acne scars?
> With eyes like stars from the planet Mars?
> You're beautiful,
> strange commuter girl.
> So beautiful.

At first he presumed he was just getting going, but then thought that perhaps he had better stop there before it took a turn for the worse. There. It's a poem, just as it is. Knowing when to stop, this is the essence of poetry.

When Mr. Pappy came in and nodded and lit his pipe, Fontoon nodded back and gathered his belongings. He took a look at the poem on the scrap of paper, crumpled it, and put it in the trash on his way out.

Piece of crap.

Chapter Key

"I want to thank you all for making time for this little presentation here today," said Mr. Bentley. "I know you're all very busy."

Mr. Bentley was nothing if not good at pretending to care about other people's time. He glanced at Shirley's breasts and made a mental note not to think about them.

"I'll get straight to the point," he continued. "As you know, we always try to recognise the Fontoon Wrecking Company Employee of the Month, but this month is even a little more special than usual."

The men seated around the conference table exchanged glances. So there was going to be a bit of a surprise. This was exciting. Who knew? Certainly not Weasby. Hornbottom was looking around eagerly as if to get some kind of clue. Was that a smug smile on Jenkins' face?

"This month's award goes to our man Jenkins," announced Bentley to a warm round of applause and surprised smiles. "But not even Jenkins knows why this month is special."

Jenkins basked in the acknowledgement of his hard work and the envy and resentment of his co-workers. He wondered why this month was so special.

"As most of you are no doubt well aware," continued Bentley, "Jenkins' team of researchers came up with the kind of innovation we dream about here at Fontoon Wrecking Company: disappearing keys. Jenkins, why don't you tell us a little bit about your discovery?"

"Well," said Jenkins, blushing with eagerness, "they're made of a highly unstable compound. For the most part they'll look and act like regular keys. They'll sound like regular keys when they jangle. But sooner or later, in the absence of light, such as when they're placed in a pocket, they'll disintegrate completely. I mean, they'll be gone. Poof."

The room broke out into appreciative chuckling.

"I mean, it won't happen every time, there's a random factor in there. We can't predict it ourselves, the exact timing of when it'll happen. But we do know one thing: sooner or later, it'll happen. That key's clock is ticking."

Jenkins received the murmured congratulations of his colleagues. Weasby reached over and gave him a firm pat on the back.

"Thank you," said Jenkins. "Thanks very much."

Mr. Bentley handed Jenkins the usual Employee of the Month certificate, and then he handed him something else: an envelope.

"What's this?" asked Jenkins.

"Why not have a look and see?" replied Mr. Bentley.

Jenkins opened the envelope and pulled out a cheque. He had been given a big fat bonus.

"Jeepers!" cried Jenkins. "That's a hefty cheque!"

Mr. Bentley smiled with a mixture of warmth towards a prized employee and hatred for underlings.

"I'll let Shirley explain. Shirl?"

Shirley sat up straighter in her chair. She had known in advance that she would be asked to explain why this month's Employee of the Month award would be a little extra special, and she had prepared for the occasion by writing down the reason and printing it out from the office printer. She glanced down now at that very piece of printer paper.

"We've gotten a lot of interest in these keys from other wrecking companies," she announced, nearly trembling with the excitement of making the announcement. She paused ever so slightly to breathe in. "They're selling like hot cakes!"

Laughter and applause filled the room along with a generalised gloating.

Nice tits, thought Mr. Bentley.

Chapter Neighbours

How many pens do you have? Please sit down. Chinese men have American pens, but American men do not have Chinese brushes. Do you have a table? Do you want a chair? Do you like strawberries? Let's have tea.

One Hundred. One Thousand. One Million.

One floor directly above Admiral Fontoon's apartment, Yan Peng was studying the English language from a book. Yan Peng and Fontoon were friendly acquaintances. Sometimes they would go out for coffee, and Fontoon would answer questions about English and pick up the odd Cantonese word. He would greet Yan Peng by saying *'Leih hou ma'*. When he left him, he would say *'Joigin'*, or sometimes 'Bye bye' after the Hong Kong manner. When Yan Peng asked him how he was doing, Fontoon would say 'Hou hou' unless he was feeling poorly, in which case he would say *'Gei hou'*.

Yan Peng had achieved a high level of proficiency at martial arts as senior pupil of Po Chi Leung, a famous master. One of Yan's arms had become famous in its own right and was called a Firebrand Arm. Nobody else had one; Yan's was the only Firebrand Arm.

Peter Gramlinson had killed Yan Peng's master using a dirty trick. Most people had never heard of Peter Gramlinson; he was one of those men who avoided the spotlight. Among those who did know his name to whisper it, there were several theories about who he really was. More than a financier, not an intelligence officer. He was rumoured to possess enormous political influence, but he was not a politician, nor a lobbyist. He seemed to move in interconnected but widely divergent circles: oil, minerals, currency trading, arms, commodities futures, satellite and communications technologies. He was as likely to be found in Beijing as Ankara or Moscow, not infrequently in New York, loved Paris, had a home in Azerbaijan.

Normally Po Chi Leung would have defeated Gramlinson in unarmed combat ten times out of ten. But whereas Po Chi Leung valued his honour above all else, Gramlinson felt no compunction about fighting dirty. He had weakened Po Chi Leung with slow poison for weeks, and then deprived him of his antidote on the day of the fight. As they fought, Po Chi Leung became increasingly sickly, even coughing blood between exchanges of blows. Soon he was uncommonly vulnerable to even a modest death strike to the middle chest, and Gramlinson was able to finish him off. Gramlinson's genuinely satisfying pleasures were few and far between, not least because he had a tendency to tarnish his own victories by cheating. Here too his attempt at achieving a delicious narcissistic pleasure by personally vanquishing an esteemed opponent left him feeling somewhat hollow.

The conflict between the men came about because one of Gramlinson's ventures involved uniting the Eight Clans. Seven of the Clans had eventually agreed to be united after a period of bribery and warfare, but the Eighth Clan belonged to Po Chi Leung who, in addition to having some serious reservations about Gramlinson's motives, did not want to see his Clan subsumed for any reason, full stop. To Peter Gramlinson, Po Chi Leung was an annoyance, with his stern warnings and his righteous jibber jabber, as well as a dangerous enemy.

In any case, Yan Peng now had to squeeze his English

lessons in around his plans to avenge his master's death.

Sometimes, however, there were distractions from even these important priorities; now was one of those times. The slight depression Yan Peng had noticed in his floor had gotten worse; it had unmistakably become an actual hole. Through it, he could see into Admiral Fontoon's apartment. This was as disturbing as it was embarrassing as it was dangerous. What a mess. Immediate action was required.

Yan Peng called down into the hole: "Hello! *Neih hou ma!*"

Fontoon was not home, so the thing to do was call Mr. Burgleman.

Hal Burgleman was the building's super. He was hard of hearing and deathly skinny, with dry, leathery skin. He walked without a cane but had a stiff, awkward way of moving that frightened Admiral Fontoon a little; his hips would jerk forward on one side and then the other, as if to throw his bony legs forward one at time, while he held his pointy elbows up and out, letting his gaunt, limp hands dangle and twitch. He had a habit of smacking his lips incessantly.

"What do you want?" shouted Burgleman over the phone.

"There's a hole in my floor in Fontoon's ceiling!" Yan Peng shouted too, because Burgleman was shouting. All conversations with Burgleman were shouted.

"What?"

"A hole! There's a hole in my floor!"

Bastids, thought Burgleman.

"All right!" shouted the super and hung up the phone, preventing Yan Peng from asking any questions about what would happen next and when.

Fontoon was just arriving back home from his shift at the lighthouse. The journey home had not been easy. A major office building downtown had lost its turgidity and spread like so much warm putty over several square blocks, oozing down subway vents and creating havoc for trains, cars, buses, and pedestrians alike. In a few hours the building would regain its structural rigour and rise once again to resume its slow oscillations. In the meantime people would just have to work around it.

Going through his own neighbourhood, Fontoon became a little depressed. It all seemed to be going to seed. The whole stretch along Grace Park now consisted of shuttered shops. For a while it had seemed like it was going the other way. Cafés had appeared. Attractive young people with good haircuts sat in them. But it seemed gentrification had run into the End of Western Civilisation. Antonio's Pizza, that natural products shop, Rose's Diner, Moon Candy on the corner of Sheldon and the Boulevard: all shuttered now. When Master Billiards disappeared, Fontoon had stood with everyone else across the street, watching the mist over the negative space, shaking his head. It all seemed inevitable in retrospect. Somehow, nail salons and locksmiths proved to be the survivors. There were dozens of them. What kind of a town was that?

Fontoon arrived back at last, exhausted, and reached into his pocket where he always kept his keys. They weren't there. He checked all his other pockets where he never kept his keys, and they weren't in any of those pockets either. It was particularly annoying because he made a special practice of jingling his key pocket each time he left anywhere for anywhere else. He distinctly remembered jingling as he left Wossafocken Point. So life was sometimes absolutely infuriating and these keys had simply disappeared.

There was nothing for it. He had to buzz Burgleman.

"What is it?" shouted Burgleman over the intercom.

"It's Fontoon!" shouted Fontoon back, "I'm locked out!"

"What?" came the return shout.
"I'm locked out! Please let me in!"
"Fontoon?" shouted Burgleman.
"Yes!"
"You lucked out? Like I care?"
"I'm locked out! No key! Please let me in!"
"Hang on! I'll let you in!"

While Admiral Fontoon waited and prepared to wince at the sight of the super's ungainly figure clattering towards him, Mr. Burgleman was muttering "bastids" to himself as he retrieved his giant ring of keys. Finally he emerged into view, smacking his lips. He jerked towards Fontoon, bones and keys all a-jangle.

"Fifty dolliz," he said as he let Fontoon inside.

"I know, I know," said Fontoon wearily, adding, without hope, "Can't you cut me a break for once?"

"What?" shouted Burgleman.

"I asked if you could cut me a break!"

"A break! Who's gonna cut *me* a break?" shouted Burgleman.

When they arrived at Fontoon's apartment, Yan Peng was there. He had come to put a note under the door to explain that he had not created the hole that now joined them, and that he did not mean to spy. The note explained that he was sorry for the hole anyway, and hoped that working together they could get it fixed and find a way to tolerate it and live in mutual respect until then. Yan Peng was pleased to see that Burgleman and Fontoon were together. It would seem to indicate progress.

"What are you coming down here for?" shouted Burgleman.

"I'm bringing a note," said Yan Peng.

"Get outta here! I said I'd fix it!"

"I know. The note is for the Admiral."

"Bastids," muttered Burgleman, opening the door.

All the shouting did not escape the notice of Marla Stankpool across the hall. She opened her door a crack, hoping to see what was going on without being noticed. However, all three men turned and saw her little eyes peering out when they heard the obvious sound of a door being opened. She opened the door a bit wider.

"Ah heard shoutin'," she said. "Is everyone all raht?"

"Yes," said Fontoon. "I got locked out is all."

"Oh," said Marla. She kept staring at the three of them and they kept staring at her until finally she closed her door and pressed her ear against it instead. She stayed there pressed against the door for a full five minutes even though the men had all gone inside Fontoon's apartment, where explanations and plans about holes in ceilings were made. Even though the conversation was shouted, she could barely hear a muffled thing. Eventually she walked away clucking.

Marla lived with her husband Ed and their young son, a quiet and reserved boy called Pig. Pig was eight years old and smart as a whip. He had done so well in school that he had skipped most grades and was now a senior in high school, where he was well hated. An eight-year-old high school senior is often a celebrity and rarely a chum. At home he barely spoke a word. Although he was articulate and possessed an agile mind, Pig found that nothing he might say could possibly rival for eloquence the timely emission of an anguished animal-like scream. These outbursts usually occurred during family dinners.

Stankpool dinners were contests for the moral high ground. Marla's favourite weapon was the frequent announcement of the early time she claimed to have gotten up that day. She would always claim to have been up since the crack of dawn, and would pepper her conversation with references to it, either as a reason why she was too tired for something, or to make it clear that she was in what she called 'no mood'; her real point was always simply that she had been the first one up.

Her claim was often repeated but never verified. Marla had her own separate room; nobody knew the precise moment her eyes opened each day or the position of the sun when foot first touched fluffy slipper. Marla would rarely emerge from her chamber earlier than mid-afternoon. She would announce that she had been reading important magazines all day, keeping informed, unlike ignorant Ed, who spent his work hours in an ersatz medical laboratory using canary shit to concoct buckets of a*lbum nigrum*, a long-discredited general-purpose internal and external remedy, for sale on the black market.

The fact of the matter was that Marla never got up in the morning, other than perhaps to slipper up and pad ostentatiously around the apartment for a minute or so, or in some other way announce her presence before returning to the welcoming warmth of her bed, where she would generally remain, napping and watching television, until nearly dinnertime. She made these early noises to provide a measure of evidence in support of her claim to having been up with the perky birds of daybreak, and also to provide herself with an internal justification – she had been up, technically – which would add a touch of realism to her self-righteous insinuations. It would help her wrap herself more tightly in her own personal blanket of comforting deceptions.

The thing that relentlessly drove Ed towards madness was not his awareness that she was lying, but his irritation that she would press this claim despite the fact that neither he nor Pig accepted it as a legitimate framework within which to establish moral superiority. Indeed, Ed loved sleeping and saw nothing but great benefit in doing it as much as possible; Pig got up in time for school without attaching any inherent worth to the act. One result of all this was that Marla experienced wholly unnecessary subconscious feelings of self-loathing because she failed to adhere to her own pointless principles.

Because of her secret personal feelings of failure, Marla was quite vulnerable to Ed's main method of attack, which was to call Marla a 'fat-ass bitch'.

When these forms of attack cancelled each other out, Ed and Marla would employ Phase Two tactics. Ed's Phase Two tactic was to pick apart and contradict details of whatever story Marla was in the midst of telling. Marla's Phase Two tactic, her ultimate weapon, was to rise from the table and declare, in as haughty a tone as she could muster, that she was 'going upstairs'. She meant she was going back to her bedroom, where she would ostensibly resume her important reading in a huff. There wasn't really an upstairs in the apartment, but part of it was raised slightly higher than the rest of it. A single step perhaps seven inches high separated the bedroom area from the living room and kitchenette. Going 'upstairs' would give Marla the all-important last word, leaving the others to stew, except that they were usually just relieved. Pig had no need of a Phase Two tactic; his anguished scream, if not overused, could be neither challenged nor followed.

As Fontoon bid Burgleman adieu and settled down to a cup of tea with Yan Peng, the Stankpools sat down at their own dinner table, where Marla was serving spaghetti. She had added a handsome pile of mistletoe berries to Ed's plate. Mistletoe berries were poisonous, but only in extremely large doses. Marla didn't want Ed dead; she wanted him on his toes. They had the following conversation:

"Ah was talkin' to that nahce Mr. Fontoon earlier t'day. He

wanted to know if ah wanted to head out bowlin' with him, well, ah had ta tell him ah was too tahrd. Ah been up since fahv ay em."

"Fat-ass bitch."

"Well isn't that pleasant at th'dinner table. Anyways, ah couldn't go but he was so nahce, but ah told him ah had a lot of readin' ta do and ah was tahrd from bein' up so long..."

"Yer lyin', Marla. You hates that Fontoon and he hates you."

"That's jest not true, Ed, ah never said that. Donchoo start with me. Ah've been up since fahv ay em."

"You have not."

"Ah've had it with you Eddie, ah really have. Ah don't have ta stand for this. Ah cain't take it, ah really cain't. Ah'm going upstairs!"

"Good riddance! You can take your poison spaghetti with you!"

"Aieeeaaagh!"

Across the hall, Yan Peng and Fontoon paused in their conversation and looked up.

"You can hear it very well from here," said Yan Peng.

"The screaming?"

"Yes."

"Yeah. Couple times a week anyway."

"I can hear it too, from upstairs. But not so well."

After some final words about covering the hole with plywood until Burgleman arranged to get the hole fixed properly, Yan Peng excused himself in order to go and continue his training. Fontoon was left to his reveries.

He thought about writing a poem called Screaming Boy. It could be a beautiful and politically important poem that might bring him great fame. It would deal with internal torment and the frustrations of expressing essentially non-verbal emotions. It would deal with how poorly we treat each other, how insensitive we can be, how foolish and cruel. It would be deeply personal and focused on one real boy, yet it would suggest abuses of power that could hardly fail to implicate the black tyrannical heart of even nominally democratic liberal regimes. He thought of young women moved to tears in their college dormitories as they read it wearing their free-and-easy, provocative clothing.

Fontoon found himself feeling physically restless, agitated, unable to concentrate. He admitted to himself that his honest instincts were to ignore any feelings of pity he might have towards Pig. He had no real wish to confront or change the Stankpools. He only wished their problems would be quieter. Fontoon enjoyed the honest feeling of acknowledging his own callousness. *Severe eyes,* he thought smugly. Now he wouldn't have to write that poem; he had no right. No, the truth was that he was only trying to compete for the moral high ground with his good friend Kent Peterson. Kent Peterson took an unashamedly interventionist approach to endangered children.

Kent worked for Eco-Child, a nonprofit organisation whose motto was Healthy Children for a Healthy Future. Kent had become concerned about Pig's welfare after overhearing an episode of screaming while visiting Fontoon. One question had led to another and Kent had ended by frowning. How could he stand by and do nothing? He'd be a hypocrite, he reckoned, if he just talked about child welfare in the abstract comfort of his little office and looked the other way when a real situation arose in his own life. Once he went so far as to speak to the boy when he saw him in the hallway. No big words. Just to let him know there was a guy there. A big brother figure. Somebody to whom he could turn.

"You know, kid," he had said, "if you ever feel like you're in trouble, you can come talk to me. You never know. Maybe I could help."

Admiral Fontoon had coped with Kent's behaviour by rolling his eyes behind his friend's back. But also, inside, Fontoon admired Kent. Not everyone can say idealistic things in an earnest fashion without a trace of irony, and those who make the attempt risk looking in the mirror one day and coming face to face with an insipid schlemiel. For those who know this to be the case, it takes a certain kind of strength to go ahead and speak that way anyway; the innocent courage shines through clearly somehow and tends to stop smirks in their half-formed tracks. People do get a little bit nervous when they suddenly think they've possibly gone too far in the direction of cynicism. Then they'll quietly wait to see if good things are possible after all, not sure what to hope for.

Fontoon considered that if anyone was looking through his window right now and seeing him all reflective in his apartment like that, they'd have to admit they were looking at one sensitive fellow. Real tears came to Fontoon's eyes as he considered the undeniability of his own poetic nature and how likely it was he would die unrecognised.

At that precise moment, Fontoon's front door came flying off its hinges and sailed across the apartment. Fontoon didn't have time even to shout in alarm before it knocked him off his chair and lodged in the wall behind him.

Speak of the devil. Kent Peterson had come to call.

Chapter Hurt

"I didn't mean to hurt you."

How many times had Kent Peterson had to say that in his life? When would it ever stop?

Unfortunately the world is simply not built for men as strong as Kent Peterson. Once, when he was barely a teenager, he threw a spaldeen up in the air so high and so fast that it would have gone into orbit if it hadn't burned up from friction within the atmosphere like a little pink backwards meteorite.

He was a one-man disaster area. Wine glasses, coffee cups, pens, tables. People's front doors. Nor was Kent some kind of sculpted muscleman. On the contrary, he was soft. Flabby. What was he supposed to do for exercise? Bench press freight trains? There was no plausible way for him to push himself to his limits.

Even as a child Kent realised that the physical dominance he easily established over his classmates gave him no satisfaction. He became disgusted with his own strength and with the fearful sycophants who called themselves his friends. Repudiating the use of violence to achieve his ends, Kent became introspective, serious. He did his best to hide his absurd strength. All he wanted was to fit in and live in harmony with people.

Therefore, even though he also had x-ray vision and an uncanny 'warning sense' that would alert him to impending danger, Kent was not inclined by disposition towards the hero's life, with all the fighting it would necessarily entail. Fighting crime and injustice would require a kind of moral certainty that Kent just didn't have. What was crime, really? What was injustice? Who was he to play vigilante judge and jury all the time? How could he in good conscience throw his lot in with the institutional forces that systematically oppressed the poor? Wasn't crime as much a social failing as an individual wrong? Would there be so much crime if there were economic and social justice, and reasons for people to believe in fair play and compassion? No, Kent would leave the superhero game to others. He'd leave it to Stickyman.

Stickyman was a local guy with a strong sense of right and wrong and some extremely sticky boots and gloves, which enabled him to cling to any surface. He only had regular strength and could barely peel himself off of a wall; he wasn't exactly a walking advertisement for the hero business.

"Jesus, Kent!" said Fontoon.

"Sorry. Are you all right?"

"By some miracle."

"Really sorry. I was just coming back from work. Wondered if you wanted to shoot some pool."

Kent understood that Admiral Fontoon always wanted to shoot some pool.

"You've completely destroyed my door. What is it with you?"

Neither Fontoon nor anyone else who knew Kent had ever quite been able to confront the facts and conclude that Kent was possessed of supernatural strength. They would see the incontestable evidence, but the necessary conclusion remained psychologically unacceptable and therefore unreachable. Instead they opted for outlandish denial and jokes and strings of crazy coincidences. Fortunately for Kent Peterson, there were a lot of people who had no problem simply shrugging their shoulders and moving on.

"Sorry man. It just... I mean... I don't know."

Kent hung his head. He had had a bad day of being too strong for some things and not strong enough for others.

"The Reward?" asked Fontoon, indicating the name of their preferred pool-shooting dive.

"Sounds good," said Kent Peterson.

"I'll have to call the super first though," said Fontoon, gesturing towards the flown door.

"Really sorry."

Fontoon called Mr. Burgleman for the second time that day and let him know what had happened.

Bastids, thought Burgleman as he hung up the phone.

Chapter Sticky

Stickyman always woke up to the radio because the peppy people on it made it easier to get up. There would be a little team of them and they'd always be talking about something, keeping up the banter, and somebody was always laughing. It created an energetic, positive effect. Somehow it kept you from feeling too down. It made you feel like life was normal.

Today was no exception. The hosts were mocking somebody, and it all seemed pretty funny to Stickyman and he started to feel peppy. Five minutes later he was getting out of bed and making some coffee. It was so great to have coffee in the morning, and Stickyman always made sure to remember to appreciate how great it was to have it. He made a nice piece of toast, and put some butter on it. Soon he was sitting at his breakfast table, looking out of his window at the city he had sworn to protect. His toast was nice. His coffee was fantastic.

There were his sticky boots in the corner; there were his sticky gloves. Stickyman took a hot burbling sip of coffee and felt resentful of his equipment. It ought to be effortless, but those sticky boots and gloves were just too sticky. It wasn't really his fault, but Stickyman couldn't help but feel he was always letting the city down. Some hero. He thought of all the criminals he had let get away, how so many of them had taken potshots at him with impunity. Fucking sticky boots and gloves!

Stickyman chewed up the last of his piece of toast. Should he make another? Hell with it. He was sick to death of feeling like some kind of peripheral character early in a film, just clinging to the hope he'd end up being important later. He knocked back the last of his coffee and got in the shower, where he began to think. He thought of giving himself a pep talk, and when he did that, he called himself buddy and soldier. What's with the negativity, buddy? You see another superhero out there busting his hump for this city? No? That's what I thought. So buck up now, soldier. You're going to put those boots and gloves on and you're going to go out there and you're going to do the best damn job you can, and that's all you can do and nobody can ask any more of you than that. Your time is coming. You're going to catch a criminal and you know what it's going to be? It's going to be sweet, that's what it's going to be. Oh yeah, it's going to be sweet as sugar. You hear me, buddy? Huh? You hear me? Get on out there, soldier, buck up and move!

Stickyman lifted up his arms and made sure he got all the soap to rinse out of his armpits, first one and then the other. He turned around and leaned forward and grabbed his butt cheeks and opened them up to let the water run down to make sure he rinsed all the soap out of his butt crack, then he turned back around and lifted up his wibblies to make sure all the soap was rinsed out from there as well. Then he gave himself one last turnaround until he was sure all the soap was off from everywhere on his body, because he didn't like the idea that some soap might remain on him and turn into dried soap. Soon he was out and dry and clean and slipping into his futuristic tight stretch-material Stickyman outfit. He stood over his boots and gloves with his hands on his hips, a figure of no small resolve.

He slipped on one boot, then stepped into the other. He pulled on his gloves, first one, then the other. Inhaling deeply, he spoke aloud to the room: "OK, hero. Let's get out there and patrol this crazy old city."

And with that, he struggled mightily to lift one foot off the floor and march right out of that door to face the new day.

Chapter Moustache

Don't lose track of your coin. Mosconi doesn't teach that but you learn it. People will always try to take advantage of any confusion to jump the queue, so if you want to play, stay sharp. Put your coin up and keep track of it. Tracking coin takes concentration away from other tasks, such as having conversations. Both Kent and Fontoon were poor listeners to begin with, and poor observers more generally.

Fontoon once had a moustache that suddenly began to bother him. He was at Kent's apartment when it happened, in the bathroom, looking in the mirror. *What the hell is this moustache?* He decided to shave it off there and then. He did one half first and then smiled. It was decided; he would emerge from the toilet with half a moustache. The idea was to cause general amusement; the idea failed.

It failed because Kent didn't notice. Fontoon had assumed the general amusement would be instantaneous, but instead he was forced to sit with one half of his face moustachioed and the other half clean, just waiting. A new game began: how long would it take Kent to notice?

Kent never noticed. Eventually Fontoon, after forgetting all about it himself for a time, pointed it out. Kent found himself with an indignant feeling and no words to say. Some weeks later he had grown a retaliatory sideburn that Fontoon didn't notice. They had achieved equilibrium, technically, although at a different and more mutually embittered level.

The order of pool-related procedures was well established

by long habit: enter together, then divide to conquer. One man secures queue position in the time-honoured fashion by slipping a coin onto the table edge; the other man goes after the pints.

"So what's new?" asked Kent, concentrating very hard on not smashing two beer glasses to smithereens with the merest excess of pressure from his mighty hands.

"I was arrested. Spent some time in jail."

"Cool, cool."

Fontoon registered the unfocused look in Kent's eyes and his under-responsive tone, and he decided to add lies.

"Yeah," he continued. "Lost a leg. Screwed it back on."

"That is awesome," said Kent.

Fontoon nodded. He was used to it. In any case, he was barely even listening to himself talk, so near was it to his turn at the table. The next shiny coin in line was his, so when the game ended he moved briskly over to the coin slot, loaded it up, and pushed. He closed his eyes, better to enjoy the exquisite sound of billiard balls falling, rolling, colliding, like a team of little clickety-clackety ballplayers jostling down a corridor from the locker room and eager to get back on the pitch.

Fontoon had noted how meticulously and incorrectly the reigning table champions had racked the previous game. They did it the way most bar players did it, which was to alternate stripes and solids around the perimeter of the rack. It was certainly an aesthetically defensible approach, but technically wrong according to the official rules of the Billiards Congress, which Fontoon had committed to memory and stored literally in his back pocket. A legal rack must meet two criteria: the eight-ball must be in the middle, and there must be a stripe in one back corner and a solid in the other. Everything else is art or folly.

Fontoon

Against a slapdash opponent, Fontoon would have taken punctilious aeons to rack the balls into a very precise arrangement of chromatic pairs. However, against such people as the present opponents, he simply dumped the balls into the triangle with *sprezzatura*, surreptitiously ensuring he had his eight ball and his corners right. Work against type and be strictly legal, that was his motto.

As he withdrew the triangle, Fontoon reminded himself of Mosconi's wise words: *You've got to hate the man you're playing, and he's got to hate you. If you don't, you can't play your best game.*

"Your break," he said.

Upon seeing Fontoon's rack, the opponents glanced at each other doubtfully. There was no careful alternation here. This could not be right. Fontoon smiled at Kent and Kent winked back. The two of them had worked this game many times and they knew what the opponents were thinking. The only question was whether they would actually say anything. Fontoon felt his back pocket. Yes. The Billiards Congress was in session.

The opponents remained silent. One of them walked uncertainly up to the table and chalked his cue with the slightest shrug.

Fontoon shot some air out of his nose with a force considerably greater than strictly necessary, then reflexively pinch-wiped the openings of his nostrils in case he had left anything to hang by the strength of his contempt. In fact, a small mucoid particle had been dislodged, and Fontoon freed it with his thumb, dared to look at it, held it momentarily by his side, then looked one way and flicked the other. He surveyed the room belatedly for witnesses. Not only had nobody apparently seen, but now a young woman was smiling in his direction. He winked at her before turning to his opponents.

Fontoon sank the three in the side by glancing it off the fourteen. As he began to line up his next shot, one of the opponents intervened with an objection.

"It went off our ball," said the opponent, whose name was Matty. He looked at his partner Louise. Louise nodded.

"And?" rejoined Fontoon, mindful of the weapon in his back pocket.

"You can't go off our ball," said Matty. He had not expected to be forced to state the obvious.

"Untrue," said Fontoon, resuming his shooting posture.

The opponents conferred by way of a glance. Could they be wrong?

"You can but you have to call it," said Louise.

At this, Fontoon stepped back out of his shooting posture in dramatic dissatisfaction and placed the butt end of his cue down on the ground with a sigh.

"Actually," said Fontoon, "you just have to call the ball and the pocket. That's the actual rule." Kent Peterson looked decently at the ground.

"No it isn't," said Louise, on her third pint and feeling reckless, as Matty felt unaccountably ashamed.

The crumpled rule book was produced.

"You carry around the rule book?" asked Louise scornfully and imagined poking Fontoon in the eye with her finger.

"I do," said Fontoon.

Before anyone could read standard rule 3.6 of the eight-ball regulations modifying rule 1.6 of the billiards general rules, Matty called out to the bartender.

"BJ!" called Matty.

"Yo!" said BJ.

"Can he shoot off my ball?"

"No!" said BJ.

House rules trump everything. Fontoon yielded the table and play continued with suppressed hostility until the eight-ball shot. There it hung on the lip of the side pocket like a ripe Kentucky plum, as unmissable a shot as there has ever been in the history of the game. Matty had just failed on a perfectly straightforward attempt to sink his last ball and felt himself sink in what he guessed was Louise's estimation of him as a man. Fontoon turned and made an apologetic glance at his opponents, with mingled feelings of shame and vengeance. Everyone involved felt cheated in this game for one reason or another or none.

Matty and Louise were already putting their cues down in disgust with themselves and the world around them. Fontoon drew a deep breath, shook his shoulders loose, sized up the eight-ball, leaned into his stance, focused on the object ball, drew his cue back, and took a few warm-up strokes. He knew he had to hit it low, so the ball would stop or come back a little. If he hit it too high, the cue ball would follow the eight into the hole. He knew this. He aimed low. He drew back one final time and shot sharply.

The cue ball hopped clean over the eight and into the hole. Game over.

Fontoon winked at his opponents as if to suggest he had done it intentionally out of some sort of grandiosity, even while cursing himself inwardly. There were many coins now between him and his next game. There was nothing for it. He and Kent would have to converse. When they had settled against a wall with their pints and their remorse, Fontoon broke the ice with space facts. It was the one area in which they could maintain mutual concentration.

"Guess how much a teaspoon full of neutron star would

weigh."

"One teaspoon?" said Kent.

"One teaspoon."

"You sure you don't mean tablespoon?"

"The little one. Teaspoon. One teaspoon."

"Level?"

"Come on. If it's rounded it's not a teaspoon. Apothecaries. Level."

"No idea. A lot."

"Go on. Guess."

"I don't know. A ton."

"Wrong."

"Two tons."

"Warmer."

"Ten tons. A hundred tons."

"A hundred and twelve million."

"Hundred and twelve million tons? One teaspoon?"

"That's how dense a neutron star is. Hundred and twelve million tons. One teaspoon."

Kent secretly wondered whether he'd be able to lift that teaspoon.

"That's a lot of tons."

"Stars in the galaxy?"

"Two hundred billion."

"Good. Number you can see at night under the best possible conditions?"

"Three thousand."

"Impressive. How did you know that?"

"You've used that one recently."

"Oh. Well; well remembered. And it's such a paltry number because?"

"Something about the universe expanding."

"Yeah, and red shift."

"Right."

Fontoon fell into scientific reverie and considered how unlikely and amazing everything was. Life? Out of gas and dust and gravity and time? Why bother?

He had been in love once, a decade ago now. She was called Madeleine. She did not even dump him; it was Fontoon who broke her heart, for all the usual banal reasons and with all the usual lies. He moved on. After the tumult Madeleine forgave him and they became friends. She once told him she would always love him, and if he ever wanted to come back, she would have him. She wanted him to know it. She set pride aside. She told him just the once, in an actual whisper, and then didn't say another word about it. By now the light from that relationship was already 58,781,714,785,651.79 miles away. She had had other boyfriends and was now married. Fontoon assumed she had long ago rescinded her theoretical willingness to have him back. But it wasn't so! Hundreds of trillions of light miles later, both of them old and squinty, she will think about him and silently still beautifully rue. Still feeling it in her little beating heart. Still so sad, so wistful, just in one little well-managed compartment. Still in love, but very disciplined, very strong. Still in love!

Fontoon's coin marched along. He and Kent played again and reigned as table champions for three games. Later that night, a star that had previously been barely visible from earth disappeared forever from the night sky due to the implications of Olber's Paradox.

Chapter Family

Madeleine was crying the beautiful tears of sad and unutterable joy. In this light, her ninety-two-year-old face recaptured its youthful prettiness and she was at once old and young, as if time had flattened. Alternate Admiral Fontoon was crying too. His time had come. He was old and he could feel it. He felt lucky to have the opportunity to sense it in advance. That was only one small thing among many he felt lucky about.

"Thank you," he said to Madeleine, his eyes welling once again. "You..."

"Stop," said Madeleine, laughing her special gentle laugh and wiping her tears away. "You don't have to say anything. I already know everything."

"I want to say it," said Fontoon, his heart bursting with gratitude and love and exquisitely painful joy. "I want to thank you. To think that I almost... that we might never have..."

"I know, my darling, I know."

"I was such a fool when I was young."

"Well. You came around."

"Thank god. I mean, not God, you know, but..."

"I know, I know."

"OK you two, you're going to get all of us crying if you don't cut it out." It was the five children of Madeleine and Fontoon, and their twenty grandchildren, and their three great grandchildren, all of them in fact already in beautiful, sad tears sitting respectfully in the corner of the hospice room where Admiral Fontoon lay dying. Everyone laughed at their tension-cutting little joke. If people get too sad or too earnest, somebody is always making a little tension-cutting joke to keep life tolerable.

"I love you," said Fontoon, "all of you. I love you all so much..." And then he was gone. Madeleine closed her eyes and a tear rolled all the way down her cheek as she held his hand tightly and began at last to let him go. *À bientôt,* she thought, allowing herself this secret wish. Only little Timmy checked his watch, and that's only because he was really very young, and they had after all been in the room for over an hour.

Chapter Diary

Mikako was always shy and secretive. She never married. Her parents had died when she was quite young. She and her little brother Takashi were reluctantly looked after by an aunt from the time they were twelve and ten, respectively. Takashi kept to himself. Mikako always felt that she drifted through life very much alone; she couldn't think of a single person who knew her well. Her private observations of other people's foibles were a primary source of amusement in her life. Perhaps because of her own secretive instincts, she was drawn to the secret moments of others. She loved to observe people when they were unaware, when they felt alone.

Mikako would never actively intrude into another person's privacy, such as by peering into their windows or opening any drawers or letters or that sort of thing. Rather, what amused her most was how often people felt alone in the company of others, in full public view. In libraries, bars, restaurants, on city streets, in parks, on trains – once you noticed it – it was astonishing how freely people acted as if there were nobody else in the world. They would chew their food loudly. Pick their teeth. Scratch themselves anywhere. Spit. Mikako watched them all with bemused horror. These sightings became a special subject of fascination for Mikako; she began to document them in her diary.

One day when she got home from the pub, she opened her front door, ran into her apartment, and went straight to grab her diary from where she had left it on the kitchen table. She was dying for a wee at the time so she took the diary into the bathroom with her, sat down, and opened to a fresh page.

She never showed the diary to anyone and nobody ever saw it. Sixty years later when the elderly Mikako died of natural causes peacefully in her sleep, it was up to Takashi to clear her things out of her house. The attic was the worst. There was just no going through every single thing. It would have taken an enormous amount of time and effort and frankly, it wouldn't have been worth it. Not to Takashi. He was old himself and time and energy were precious and Mikako, bless her, had a lot of silly things that were of no interest to Takashi, not that he didn't love his sister.

He never saw the actual diary. It was in a box of other papers. When Takashi lifted the lid of the box and saw that it was full of papers and none of them appeared to have any bearing on financial matters, he put the lid back on and put the box with the other things that he was throwing out. The box was put out by the road, where it was picked up by the rubbish men and taken down to the landfill, where it was theoretically supposed to decompose, but it didn't. It was compacted, spread out with other rubbish in thin layers, and covered with synthetic foam, eliminating practically all of the oxygen and suffocating the aerobic bacteria that were supposed to do the recycling work. If anyone had gone and dug in there, they could have seen mummified hot dogs and bananas, and read ancient newspapers and entries from Mikako's diary such as:

Dear Diary: Disgusting! Tonight I saw a man by the pool table at the pub blatantly pick his nose in front of everybody. He dug his thumb right up into his nostril, pulled out a bogey, looked right at it, and flicked it right onto the floor. Then he tried to act casual, like it was normal or hadn't happened. His face said normal but his finger said weird. I stared right at him when he looked around the room to see if anyone was watching him. He was shit at pool and he blew it on the eight-ball, and his bogey is somewhere on the floor of that bar. Who knows how long it will be there? Who knows what else is on the floor? Know what I feel like doing? Cleaning my shoes. I wish I could float.

Chapter Tits

> One day
> Sad to say
> I'll be dead and gone
> Cry for joy
> A little boy
> A son to carry on

It was a poem that occurred to Admiral Fontoon as he watched a family waiting for a subway train. Although it suffered from rhymes, the poem made Fontoon quite tearful when he thought it up, and he marvelled at how beautifully sensitive he was. He planned to write it down at his earliest opportunity but then he forgot because he was hungry. The poem is now lost forever.

Fontoon went to his favourite street vendor and ordered his usual: a bacon, egg, and cheese sandwich on a roll with a cup of coffee, regular. He paid in small change.

Change accumulates as inevitably as gravitational collapse in a Bok globule. What is one to do? Admiral Fontoon employed strategies. First, he tried to contain the coins physically using a small basket that he kept on his dresser. Second, each day he would count out a quantity of them, emphasising those of lower value and including as many pennies as his conscience would allow. He would go forth into the world with these in his trouser pocket. They were to be discharged as completely as possible.

Besides keeping the accumulation to a minimum,

purchasing things in this way was somehow akin to using free money, psychologically speaking. It reduced the amount of paper money that had to be sacrificed. Two fifty became effectively two. An item costing one twenty-five might be gotten for nothing using only nuisance coins. Fontoon found that getting rid of as much change as possible was not only efficient but quietly exhilarating.

However, there were certain intangibles that complicated things. Is it entirely free from peculiarity, one might ask, to present Beautiful Vendor Lady with a meticulously counted-out stack of three dimes, three nickels, and five pennies, and moreover to do it on a regular basis? And sometimes to have it involve eight nickels and ten pennies? Occasionally to be so shameless as to employ fifteen or twenty pennies at once? Would this be any way to impress somebody with whom one's romantic vulnerabilities were all entangled?

She would smile at Fontoon, this coffee-slinging seductress; she'd give him quite a special smile. It was a knowing smile, a bewitching, flirtatious, glad-to-see-you-again smile, and he would coyly smile back in kind. The act of approaching her mobile vending unit was enough to give him certain tingles.

He stood now in the queue, having counted out his coins and secured them in his anxious little fist. He watched dreamily as she dispensed coffees and pastries to all comers in a businesslike fashion. She had an easy way with people. She was born for this kind of work. Soon it was his turn; their eyes met. The businesslike façade fell away and out came the smile. The world around them slowed and became blurry background. All sound became music. He told her what he wanted in a way that somehow suggested unspecified rakishness. She acknowledged the order in turn with that lingerie smile. Had she winked?

She turned to work her machines and then extended her tender hand, her delicate pale white fingers lightly gripping his regular coffee, her tattoo of a rabbit smoking a cigarette just visible extending from the arm of her T-shirt. He handed her a carefully prepared exactitude of assorted change with a kind of embarrassed shrug meant to suggest unlikely, even magical, coincidences. And then he walked away, feeling a kind of burning, wondering as always whether she truly loved him or perhaps thought him strange. That smile. Could he really have intrigued her, or was he some sort of amusing eccentric? What secrets, he mused, lay behind those enigmatic lips?

It so happens she thought of him as Mister Pennies. When he came up to her and made his order, she could hardly keep a smile off her face as she thought of it, here he comes, Mister Pennies. She would see his hands there, clutching his exact monies, and then she would tell him the price, which he obviously already knew, and she would think: here they come, here come the pennies. And then they would come and she would smile. She did feel more or less warmly towards him because of his obvious flaws, but not in any way that would ever have her kissing him in a thousand years, this chubby fellow and his little piles of ridiculous change. The change itself was nothing to her, since after all, receiving exact change meant less work, no math to do, nothing to give back, especially since she took his word for it and didn't even bother to count. Nevertheless it was annoying somehow, him and his punctilious coinage. It was in no way a sexy thing to do. Still, she didn't mind being worshipped. It suited her.

Fontoon sat down on a nearby bench to savour the moment and his treats. A handsome silver-haired man in a suit emerged seemingly from the bushes behind him and sat down next to him.

"Women," said the man, and winked, and began pretending to read his newspaper. It was one of those days when a ray of sunlight or a particular smell or something we'll never know causes a deep memory to surface unexpectedly. Fontoon felt a rush of embarrassment.

It was true that Fontoon had tried to feel Franny Baminelli's tits, and that tits was the word he generally used for women's breasts when he thought about them, but the whole thing had all been arranged through third parties. If it weren't for meddling and insinuation, Fontoon wouldn't have been anywhere near Franny Baminelli's tits.

Franny had told her friend Ellen to tell Fontoon's friend Eric to tell Fontoon that she was interested in him and would not be averse to being asked out on a date. All this was many years ago when Fontoon was scarcely more than a child, a junior high-school boy. So he had been told by his friend that Franny's friend had given instructions that he was to be told that Franny liked him. Fontoon was very frightened to receive the information, because there wasn't anything not to like about Franny Baminelli.

Fontoon was willing but wanted to take his time about his approach so as to make it sound natural and not a case of obeying instructions. Maybe he'd see her around and would slide in a question about whether she might like to go out some time, smooth as you please. The important thing was not to sound like he was doing someone else's bidding. Franny's friend Ellen on the other hand was one feisty tamale who expected quick and decisive action from her red hot tip.

When two days had passed following the transmission of the message, an agitated meeting occurred between Franny and Ellen. Nothing had happened. What the hell was Fontoon doing? Leaving Franny dangling like that? Was it some kind of insult? Was he squandering this priceless opportunity? Franny and her friend dissected the situation and examined its viscera from every conceivable angle. A new message was passed. Fontoon's friend Eric called up Fontoon on the telephone.

"Why haven't you called Franny?"

"What?"

"Why haven't you called Franny?"

"I'm gonna."

"Franny's apparently wondering why you haven't called. Is there a problem?"

"No man, there's no problem. You just told me about it like yesterday!"

"It was two days ago."

"What is there, a rush? I didn't want to make it seem so obvious. I figured I'd see her pretty soon, and then I'd ask her out."

"Jesus."

"What?"

"So you do like her?"

"Yeah I like her."

"OK. You do like her."

"Yes. I like her."

"So you'll call her. You're planning on calling her."

"I'll call her."

"You should call her soon, man. She wants you to call her."

"I will. I'll call her."

"Good."

Eric passed the message to Ellen who told Franny that Fontoon definitely did like her, and would call her soon, and that he was just waiting a little while so as not to appear too obvious. So Franny and Ellen began to wait, more or less patiently but with their arms somehow crossed, since now they knew there was to be a planned waiting period, and that once it was over, Fontoon would call and not appear obvious. Fontoon now knew, however, that this was the case, that they now knew his whole strategy, that there was no longer any point in waiting because it was now stupid. He didn't know it from any new messages passed along, but by his own realisation, wordlessly, thanks to the invisible omni-connecting tendrils of the all-feeling universe. He called Franny that night.

She answered the phone too quickly, not letting him warm up to the fact that the phone was ringing and that she might answer it. He asked her how she was doing and she said good. Just the one word, and then the expectant silence. In that one word he could sense a sort of blush, and a sort of impatience, and a sort of annoyance. He wasn't much on small talk anyway, and she didn't seem to be in the mood for any, so he just asked her if she'd like to go out and she quickly said yes. He asked it with a tone of voice that said, 'So I hear you want to go out with me and I'm supposed to call you so here I am', and she answered in a tone that said, 'So you finally fucking called yes jesus christ I'll go already'. And they set a time and a date and so the business was arranged. They were going to the movies.

When they got to the movies and got into their seats, and the lights went down and the movie started, Fontoon let a few minutes go by and then he slipped his left arm around her shoulders. That was all fine. She accommodated herself to his arm and they were cosy. A little bit more time passed and then he leaned over, lips first. That was fine, too. She didn't turn cheek at him or anything. She turned and offered lips and they kissed. She really did like him after all. They kissed more and more until they were really kissing, Fontoon's left arm still around her shoulder. Fontoon's right hand began to do a little exploring, from knee to side of thigh, up to her elbow and upper arm and shoulder, just wandering and rubbing and trying to wander across to where she kept her breasts.

He tried to come across the side and onto her left one, but ran into some sort of clever shoulder block. He tried the other one and was stymied by a strategic body turn. He attempted to come up from underneath but ran into stiff resistance from a well-poised elbow. She was so good at blocking that it seemed as if she wasn't blocking at all. It seemed more like he was just naturally running into obstacles, like a wind-up toy on a messy table. So he kept trying until he was blocked so often that he realised they must have been blocks all along. And then he stopped. All in all, he probably made five or six gentle attempts, and was gently rebuffed as many times. They remained cosy, and they enjoyed the movie, and everything was fine, or so thought Fontoon. He went home feeling great. He had gone out on a date with Franny Baminelli and they had had a nice time. He had kissed a girl.

"Ellen says you tried to feel Franny's tits."

It was the next day. Eric was laying out the report.

"What? What the hell? What is this?"

"Is it true?"

"It's not a question of whether it's true or not, it's a question of what the fuck, that's what it's a question of."

"I'm just saying, I heard you tried to feel her tits."

"Well, I did try to feel them. So what? Is she mad at me?"

"No, I don't think she's mad at you. She said you were very creative at trying. But I don't think you do that on the first date."

"I was creative at trying? Well she was creative at blocking. You can go back and tell her I thought she was very impressive."

"I'm not passing messages for you guys, I'm just trying to talk to you as a friend."

Fontoon

Eric told Ellen that Fontoon thought Franny was very good at blocking and that he was impressed. Franny thought that was funny. She didn't want Fontoon to get the impression that she was the sort of girl whose tits were easy to feel, but she liked him, and she sent out the message that she would like Fontoon to ask her out on a second date, where, implicitly, her tits would be made available. Fontoon was told he should call her up again and he obeyed, quickly this time and feeling bullied.

In Franny's opinion the second date was a good time to take things to a slightly more intimate level. She set it all up strategically. Fontoon would meet her at her parents' house. Her parents would not be home. They would be alone. However, she would be locked out. They would have to sit outside the house in her backyard. Outside and alone in the warm spring air. They could get quite intimate, but not third date intimate. The rules in Franny's mind were clear and businesslike: she expected her breasts to be felt; bra removal was negotiable; buttock grasping outside the jeans would be permissible but front bum and panties were off the table.

Fontoon showed up for the date like he was supposed to, and sat with Franny on the bench in her backyard, where she acted surprised that they were locked out. She gave him the story that was supposed to give him all the information he needed, that her parents weren't home, that they wouldn't be home for about an hour, that they would have to wait outside alone together in the warm spring air.

"I guess we'll just have to sit here and see if we can think of anything to do," said Franny, flipping her hair back and letting her loose T-shirt slip off of one of her freckled shoulders.

"Yes," said Fontoon.

All Fontoon could think of was to sit and indulge in feeling resentful and stubborn. The way he saw it, all his choices were unsatisfactory. He could either play the part of manipulated little pawn, doing what he was told, or he could refuse and thereby deny himself certain pleasures. Either way it would all be reported on and analysed by the chess-masters, but at least by refusing he could exercise his own volition, go against expectations, and achieve a measure of wounded dignity. Looking back on it, Fontoon couldn't quite remember whether he literally sat on his hands, but he thought he might have. He would be nobody's fool this afternoon. Franny and her breasts waited impatiently to no avail as the afternoon passed uncomfortably.

Apart from one further scolding from Eric about expectations and stepping up and appropriate times, nobody ever said anything about it again, at least not as far as Fontoon knew. There were no more dates with Franny Baminelli. He was on the one hand glad he hadn't played along with the game, glad that he hadn't robotically followed instructions like a nincompoop. Then again, he guessed it would probably have been fun. Perhaps he had over-thought himself into a strange little hole. If Franny's tits had been there now, he would have been more than glad to feel them, reportage be damned.

It's terrible. Life being so short and opportunities being wasted and all. No, but it was good that he didn't. But ahh, what a shame! Oh, what the hell did it matter? This is how he thought about it now, as he slowly chewed the last of the bits of bacon in his bacon, egg and cheese sandwich.

"Did you know," said the man on the bench next to him, "the sun is so hot that if a tiny piece of it the size of a pinhead could be captured and put in the centre of the city of Boston, the entire city and all the Boston Celtics would be incinerated?"

"Seriously?"

"Oh yes," the man continued. "If they were home at the time. In fact, you would have to travel at least as far as Northampton in the west before you would be safe."

"So then... Martha's Vineyard?"

"Toast. The whole Cape, really. Nantucket would just about survive."

The men nodded in comradely silence for a few moments, pondering the power of a star.

"It's quite a ball of fire," offered Fontoon at last, wiping his fingers on his greasy little napkin.

"It really is," said the man. They sat for a few more silent moments.

"Chase Krugley," said the man suddenly, holding out his hand.

"Ad..." began Fontoon, but he was interrupted.

"Admiral Fontoon," said Krugley. "I know. May I tell you something?"

"Go on."

"I don't want to frighten you."

"I don't scare easy, mister."

"Good. The thing is, I've been watching you."

"Watching me?"

"Yes, for some time now."

"Why would you do that?"

"It's kind of my job."

"Really. Spying on people."

"Watching them. Looking for certain things."

"What kind of things?"

"Potential."

"Oh yeah?"

"Yeah. And I'll tell you something else."

"What's that?"

"I'm impressed."

"By what?"

"You."

"Well, I am pretty impressive."

"Don't joke. You really are."

"What's impressive about me?"

Fontoon was trying to sound hard-bitten, but to his dismay his eyelashes involuntarily fluttered.

"You have one hell of a poetic disposition," Krugley began.

Had he actually just said that, thought Fontoon. Damn these eyelashes!

"Furthermore," continued Krugley, "your firm grounding in amazing space facts gives you a sense of perspective that can only be called enviable."

"I do try to take the cosmic view," admitted Fontoon.

"On the other hand, you're constrained by your circumstances. Do you feel that?"

"Well, frankly, at times, yes."

"You're damn right you do. It's like you're walking around in a goddamned straitjacket. Is it your fault you don't happen to have priceless connections to the publishing industry and fancy degrees from universities that only look at your breeding and your bank account? And how exactly is a person of a poetic disposition supposed to negotiate the ruthless world of modern media? Answer me that!"

"I don't know."

"Exactly. Well that's where I come in. I look at you and I see a fellow bursting with creative possibilities, a fellow with thoughts worth sharing, worth knowing. I think of this fellow being allowed to drift along in obscurity until he dies alone and uncounted, his potential wasted, and I see not just a personal tragedy. No. That would be your own business. What

I see is a world robbed of a resource. That's what I see. Well let me tell you something. That's *my* business. That's all of our business."

"You sure talk a good game, mister." Fontoon silently kicked himself for using the word 'mister' twice in one conversation.

"Oh, I'm not all talk. Have you ever heard of Buhongo?"

"Nope."

"No one has. They like to stay out of the news. I'd like to offer you a residency there. Buhongo will give you exactly the kind of platform you need."

"Yeah, but what is it?"

"It's a place where things become possible."

"And what does Buhongo want from me?"

"If you mean money, no, nothing. This isn't a scam. You don't need to trust me. Come and check it out. Will you?"

"Not sure."

"There's a pool table there and a rack of Balabushkas. Ever played with one?"

"No."

"How would you like one with your name on it?"

Krugley gave him a business card to look at. By the time Fontoon looked up, Krugley was gone.

Chapter Snap

"Sir! Sir!"

Mr. Bentley sighed and looked up from his desk.

"Yes, what is it, Hornbottom?" said Mr. Bentley, adding *you little prick* inside the privacy of his own head.

Hornbottom worked hard enough, true. Still. Mr. Bentley didn't like the cut of the man's jib. Sometimes a fellow just doesn't need a reason not to like somebody. Besides, Mr. Bentley was in the middle of some important pondering of his secretary Shirley's new blouse. Shirley's new blouse was quite sheer. Quite sheer. As boss of the outfit, he was entitled to some extracurricular daydreaming. Nobody could tell him he wasn't. Few things were as irritating as underlings intruding and suddenly making you feel self-conscious about something to which you were perfectly entitled. So what if Bentley's father had pulled a few strings in the Wrecking Company network to get him this particular plum position. Did a fellow have to justify his own existence every minute of every day now, and to underlings? *People should be more sensitive,* thought Mr. Bentley. Anybody with an ounce of sensitivity could have seen that Mr. Bentley wasn't in the mood to be disturbed. Why had he hired this lurching buffoon and put him in charge of horizons?

"It's Fontoon, sir," said Hornbottom, breathing hard with excitement.

"You don't say," said Mr. Bentley, summoning his most withering tone of voice. "News about Fontoon, here? Here at the Fontoon Wrecking Company? How bizarre."

You little prick, thought Hornbottom, keeping his wide-eyed innocent stare and nodding his head earnestly.

"Yes, sir," he said. "Remember how I reported he was being watched? Well they've made a move. We know who they are. They've sent a man out to him."

"What man?"

"It's Krugley, sir."

"Buhongo."

"I'm afraid so, sir."

Shit, thought Bentley. *Why is everyone always trying to make my life harder?*

"Chin up, Hornbottom," said Bentley. "Is he still capturing the products of his egestion in a wonderful collection of glass jars, thanks to this firm's legendary work on him in early infancy?"

"Yes, sir."

"Fine. And is he still wary of women, thanks in no small part to this firm's manipulation of communications in the Baminelli incident?"

"Absolutely, sir."

"I see. And are you still sending him pamphlets, tempting him towards a graduate degree in poetry?"

"Sent him one this morning, sir."

Mr. Bentley sat back and consciously exuded eminent satisfaction. He picked up a pencil and fondled it absently, looking at the way his fingers held it rather than at Hornbottom. Finally he did look up at Hornbottom, and he smiled. He smiled because he planned to snap the pencil dramatically if Hornbottom was in any way impudent.

"Well," said Bentley. "Thank you for bringing me this important information." He had found the perfect midpoint between courteous dismissal and outright sarcasm.

"He'll have opportunities there, sir," said Hornbottom, momentarily biting his lower lip. "At Buhongo, I mean. It's not completely out of the question that he might realise some of his potential."

Mr. Bentley suddenly snapped his pencil in half and let his smile fade by half. Hornbottom's breath became quicker and shallower.

"Do you know what I think?" he said calmly to his inferior.

"What?"

"I think he'll screw it up."

"He might, sir, he might. On the other hand..."

"He'll screw it up!" shouted Mr. Bentley.

"Yes, sir," said Hornbottom, bowing slightly as he left the boss's office.

Mr. Bentley pressed his intercom buzzer. Outside his office, his secretary Shirley pressed the button that allowed her to respond.

"Yes, Mr. Bentley?"

"Shirley, would you come in here for a moment please? I'd like to see you."

"Right away, Mr. Bentley."

Shirley got up immediately without so much as shuffling any papers and entered Mr. Bentley's office.

"What is it, Mr. Bentley?" she said.

"Would you mind telling Weasby I'd like a progress report about the trick pool-cue project on my desk by this Friday COB?"

One of the small pleasures of Bentley's job was using the acronym COB to indicate that he wanted something by 'close of business'.

"Sure thing, Mr. Bentley," said Shirley.

"And tell him I want to see him next week. Schedule something for us in the small conference room, Tuesday, Wednesday at the latest. Mid-morning, I think. Would you do that for me?"

"I sure will, Mr. Bentley."

"Oh, and one more thing, Shirley."

"Yes, Mr. Bentley?"

"Is that a new blouse?"

"Why, yes it is Mr. Bentley."

"It's wonderful."

"Why thank you, Mr. Bentley."

"That's all. Just in case nobody else told you. Please ensure I'm not disturbed for the next ninety minutes."

"Yes, Mr. Bentley."

He'll definitely screw it up, thought the big man.

Chapter Quit

"You see, Mr. Pappy, I've got this new opportunity..."

"Mr. Pappy, there's something I want to tell you..."

"Mr. Pappy, have you ever heard of Buhongo?"

"Sir, I'm tendering my resignation. It's all here in this letter."

Nah.

Fontoon busied himself with the final tasks before the lighting of the second-order Fresnel lens. He had done all the pleasantly mindless dusting, had polished the lens, and had filled the lamp with oil and wiped it all down. All he had to do now was dust the housing one last time and trim the wicks, and it would be time to fire up the beast. Then he could settle in for some peaceful monotony with the sounds of seagulls and waves. He would miss it, the old lighthouse at Wossafocken Point. Funny, that.

How was he going to break it to Mr. Pappy?

Would the old man even care? Why should this be so difficult? Should he do it now? Should he have done it immediately upon arrival? Should he wait until the end of his shift?

Of course, he'd be willing to give his two weeks' notice, or longer if Mr. Pappy wanted it. But it seemed just as likely that Mr. Pappy would kick him out immediately.

Fontoon set the lamp aflame and stood back. Sheets of brilliant white light pealed out across the ocean for miles and miles. Beautiful.

Fontoon

He'd miss the crush of the subway riders too and the Boingy Boingy Man. He nearly even spoke to the astonishing woman with the voice like twin faeries that morning, before catching himself. The change in circumstances provided a conversational opportunity, but he let it slip.

"Hey," he could have said. "Just wanted to say goodbye. I won't be coming through this way any more." She wouldn't have had any idea what he was talking about, but from that distance he could have smelled her hair at last. One sniff like that could last a man a lifetime. It was worth any risk, except it's very difficult actually to say things.

He'd miss Andy, the leader of the bus-stop community. Maybe on his actual last day, he'd bring cupcakes for the bus-stop people. He could give them to Andy, and Andy could pass them around. No no, he could just hand them around himself. He would hand Andy one first. If Andy took one, everyone would take one.

It was all sad, like changes were always sad, like life is sad, but it was good. There could obviously be no question of not leaving the useless dead-end job for the opportunity of a lifetime. Mr. Krugley had made it clear that the Buhongo gig was a live-in deal. He could keep his apartment in the city. Buhongo would even pay for it. But day to day, he'd be living at the estate. It would probably take a day and a half before he never even thought about this part of his life again. If that long.

Fontoon grabbed a pack of cards and dealt out a hand of solitaire. Maybe those birds would come crashing in tonight.

Time was stalling, but eventually Fontoon's shift ended. He knew it because Mr. Pappy came in with his hands in his pockets and nodded at him. Fontoon cleared his throat as Mr. Pappy took his hands out and began to light his pipe.

"Good night, Mr. Pappy," said Fontoon, and then after the

slightest hesitation: "Actually, can I talk to you?"

Mr. Pappy looked hard at Fontoon's face. The corners of his mouth pulled back slightly and the creases around his eyes multiplied, betraying what would pass for a smile.

"Quitting," said Mr. Pappy, pointing at Fontoon with the end of his pipe.

"Quitting," said Admiral Fontoon.

Chapter Enclave

Deep in the recesses of his headquarters complex, Peter Gramlinson sat in his courtyard and looked at his unexpected visitor. He stroked his long white beard and laughed his Two Voices Laugh. The Two Voices Laugh was so called because both a deep, manly roar of a laugh and a chillingly high-pitched and haughty woman's laugh could be discerned within its overall range of vibrations. Gramlinson didn't have to laugh like that, but he knew how to, and if anything he was in danger of overdoing it.

"I do not fear your Two Voices Laugh, Mr. Gramlinson."

The serene young man in simple robes who spoke so bravely stood at the entrance to the courtyard directly across from Mr. Gramlinson. It was Yan Peng, Fontoon's neighbour and top pupil of Po Chi Leung.

"Reason I'm here," said Yan Peng, "I'm here to avenge Master Po."

Yan Peng's Firebrand Arm started glowing as he ran across the courtyard with the obvious intention of punching Peter Gramlinson. Gramlinson instantly rose thirty feet in the air, spinning like a top, his colourful robes whirling around him, and he hovered there, his eyes sparkling, his face impossibly youthful surrounded by his wild mass of long white hair. He cleared his throat to prepare to use his Legion Voices, which was a voice he knew how to make that sounded like several voices of varying registers in slightly imperfect unison with a few closely echoing whispers.

"Pulsing Palm of Firebrand Arm?" he said, using the special voice. "You dare come so poorly prepared for the leader of the Eight Clans?" He threw in a Two Voices Laugh as small bolts of lightning began to crackle around his long, crooked fingers.

Yan Peng calmly swept his robes behind him with one hand to free his legs for motion. With his other hand held out palm upwards towards Mr. Gramlinson, he made a beckoning motion with his fingertips, inviting his opponent to do his worst. The two men locked eyes, and the battle was on.

Chapter Buhongo

"But how could he possibly stay sober? He's a nihilist."

Irina was in her bath, extravagantly lifting her soapy and diminutive foot out of the suds so it could be admired. It was a stunningly dainty and perfect little foot – they both were. She almost never wore shoes. Her body frequently got people talking: her impossibly slight frame and waspish waist, her carelessly artistic fingers, her taut, slappable behind. Above all it was those marvellous delicate feet, together with the unapologetically forthright way she would use words like 'fuck' and 'cock', tilting her head back slightly and adding the subtlest possible amount of extra emphasis, that made her irresistible to men and women alike. She was rumoured once to have eaten human flesh while investigating cannibal tribes in Borneo; she had shot elephants.

"Well, he's supposed to, apparently," countered Northrop Hindlips, the amply proportioned and perpetually red-faced man who had nothing to do and once walked from the Cape of Good Hope to Cairo. "He's determined to try."

"But how dreary!"

It was all true: Alyosha Ilyvich Razumikhin was a nihilist, he was trying to stay sober, and it was dreary. Alyosha was an intelligent man, a man of some experience, a man whose heart had broken seeing friends go by the wayside. Therefore he could not help but acknowledge that, no matter how hard he tried, he might fail. People failed all the time from trying. They went into dark tunnels and didn't always come out. The truth is Alyosha always knew he was doomed.

Alyosha Ilyvich Razumikhin had had a bad childhood. Upon reaching his early twenties nine years ago he had, in an unreality of extreme intoxication, experienced a burst of exploding rage. Late one night beneath a bridge, he had provoked a man into threatening him with a shovel. Alyosha had calmed the man down. He had convinced the man to hand over the shovel. Then Alyosha had grabbed the shovel by the handle and swung it hard, simultaneously screaming and crying, the dreaminess of it breaking apart into chunks of wet reality only when the man fell, his head at a grotesque angle, just shy of entirely separated from his body. Had it really just happened? Sounds faded back in. The man's terrified friends backed away, yelling:

"Policia! Policia!"

Alyosha's own companions laughed in astonishment and went running, running fast away. And so he staggered after them.

It was never in the newspapers and the police never cared what went on under bridges. It was murder – there was no way around that – and he had gotten away with it. It turns out that getting away with murder isn't that rare.

For a long time, somehow, it didn't really bother him. It was always there, but it could be pushed into a corner and ignored. It could be filed under japes and capers. The dead man wasn't much. He had lived under a bridge. He was probably undocumented. His prospects were dismal in every category, to say the least. He was no great loss. Still, Alyosha never got entirely comfortable with the facts, which sat in his mind patiently with their nightmarish hands folded and their faces twisted into ugly smiles.

The fact that the man was and would always remain

nameless began to bother him. Nameless horrors are the worst kind. Why couldn't it have been in the papers? Just a small notice would have sufficed, naming the victim, noting the crime. The man should have a name. The world should mark his death. This was a human being, who had once been somebody's little baby boy. The whole thing began to fester after a while, right there from the corner of his mind where it had been pushed, and began to suck everything else into it, distorting what it could not consume.

Alyosha began to have certain dreams in which he found himself with an infant he did not mean to have and did not want. He would throw it into a rubbish bin and cover it with garbage, push it down to muffle the sound of it wailing. He would walk away but would always come back to see if it was dead yet. The baby was always still alive. It looked up and ate garbage and grew. It would smile.

Probably Buhongo was not the best choice of places to attempt sobriety, everything else being equal. Buhongo residents were chiefly aristocratic types who had long since become *mal vue* in society for their excesses, and they occasionally welcomed artistic outsiders if they were the right sort.

Irina Crandemere was their leader; it was she who established the house rules. Drinking would start in the morning, well before lunch, usually with Pink Gins. In the afternoon towards teatime, the traditional choice was Gin Fizzes in the shade, followed by Bronxes or White Ladies at sundown. After that it was whisky, cocaine, champagne, morphine, and Mother Bailey's Quieting Syrup until six in the morning, sometimes followed by rousing matches of croquet.

Alyosha Ilyvich had been there nearly two years. Buhongo had accepted him based on certain family connections to the tsar and his status as the former singer for a seminal art metal band from Prague. His job was to add glamour and presence; his suitability for the task was now in some doubt.

"It may be dreary," offered Marilyn de Ponze from the corner of the room, picking some fluff out of her corduroy trousers, "but I think we should all give him our support." Marilyn had been consumptive since birth and was afflicted with what her doctors called 'the madness of the 1920s'.

"Good god," exclaimed Dizzie Dezzaro, whose grandfather had been friendly with Theodore Roosevelt. "What can you mean?"

"Oh relax, Diz," countered Marilyn. "I'm not suggesting we should all give up with him."

"Well thank god for that." Dizzie had been genuinely alarmed. "Then what?"

"I don't know," said Marilyn irritably, flicking the fluff in Dizzie's general direction.

"Well, there's no harm in sort of wishing him well I suppose," mused Hindlips. "I think I could manage the odd clap on the back, the odd 'good man', the occasional 'attaboy'."

"How dreary," sighed Irina, putting the one foot back into the bath water and dangling the other one daintily over the side of the tub.

Just then Ali, the servant in charge of doors and announcements, appeared at the entrance to Irina's bath. There were servants for each of the many necessary chores – looking after guests, making whisky and sodas, tending the dogs, starting the generator, hunting buck, shuffling cards.

"Excuse me, madame," announced Ali. "There is a new arrival."

"Good god," exclaimed Dizzie Dezzaro.

"Admiral Fontoon?" said Irina, visibly brightened. She had

been thoroughly briefed by Chase Krugley and was full of plans and anticipation.

"The very same."

"Wonderful. Bring him to me at once."

Irina's favourite way of greeting visitors was to do so while emerging from the bath. Mixing nudity and strangers is thrilling, the more so when everyone pretends that it isn't.

Earlier that day Fontoon had climbed into the passenger seat of the Hispano-Suiza that Chase Krugley had arranged for him, and as Fetu, the driver, set off it had started to rain, gently at first and then harder. The terrain had quickly become unfamiliar as the city streets gave way to a rift valley punctuated by extinct volcanoes. They had negotiated an escarpment in a torrent along a precipice in some terrible mud, Fetu behind the wheel never losing his seemingly permanent grin. Finally the car had gotten hopelessly stuck in the roiling gloop outside the grounds of Buhongo. Fetu held up his favourite umbrella, which had a long history full of fascinating yet ultimately meaningless coincidences, and kissed it before bequeathing it to Fontoon.

Fontoon felt lonely as he got out of the Hispano-Suiza and opened his new umbrella. Fetu pushed his car out of the mud, refusing Fontoon's half-hearted offers of help, and drove away happily. Fontoon made his way through the extensive gardens that comprised the grounds of Buhongo. Alyosha Ilyvich thoughtfully watched him walking in the rain from his vantage point at his bedroom window.

The garden through which Fontoon strode weaved together scarlet canna, frangipani, bougainvillea, tender English roses, long-stemmed lilies and fuchsias, and long avenues of jacaranda, Nandi flame, and eucalyptus trees. Before knocking on the door, Fontoon stopped, closed his eyes, and breathed in deeply. Jasmine. Mimosa. *Nice garden,* he thought.

The door opened. Ali invited him in and asked him to wait while he announced his arrival. Fontoon put his hands in his pockets and whistled while he looked around: enormous place, expensive furniture, lots of paintings. Then Ali came back and Fontoon was ushered right into a bathroom, where instead of just one person having a bath, there was an entire social gathering.

"Ah, come in come in come in!" said Irina. "Admiral Fontoon, isn't it? Not a navy admiral though, not a military man at all, thank goodness for that. You're some other sort of admiral entirely. I think it's fantastic. There. Now you know a good deal about how I feel and I know nothing about you. You're a poet, everyone knows that, and you've come to inspire us. We think it is wonderful, don't we? Well come in, don't be shy, let's have a look at you."

Irina smiled as she languidly emerged from her bath. She kept her towel and her dressing gown on the other side of the bathroom so she would have to glide naked across the tiles quite slowly in front of all her guests. She hated dressing alone.

Fontoon took another step into the bathroom, nodding at Northrop Hindlips, at Dizzie Dezzaro, at Marilyn de Ponze, looking anywhere but at the naked lady who addressed him. The others looked at him, amused. He wondered if he should say something, but there hadn't actually been a question, and he couldn't quite think of anything appropriate. He thought he should probably say something about being delighted. He was formulating the required words when Irina spoke again as she reached for her towel.

"You're not going to be shy, are you, because that would be unbearable. I hate shy men. You can look at me you know. I'm perfectly at ease. I know perfectly well I'm naked. You're a poet, you mustn't dislike naked women. You're called Admiral, you should be bold."

Irina towelled off her back so that her small, perfectly formed breasts jiggled vigorously at Admiral Fontoon.

"Delightful," said Fontoon. "I mean, I'm delighted. To be here."

"Please come fully into the room and meet everyone, we've all been dying to meet you. Come in, turn around, let's get a good look at you. Please relax, my goodness, I'm not asking to see your cock." She tilted her head back slightly and emphasised the word.

"Not yet anyway," tossed in Lord Hindlips.

"Good god," exclaimed Dizzie Dezzaro.

"Unless you'd care to show us, of course," added Marilyn de Ponze.

"Perhaps not just at the moment," rejoined Fontoon, trying to assume a jaunty attitude, not wanting to appear the least bit inhibited.

"Be good," Irina playfully warned her friends as she wrapped her dark hair in her towel. "Let's not frighten our new guest away, that would be a terrible shame."

Fontoon's eyes met Marilyn's. She looked at him with an uncommon directness and a little half-smile. She was idly imagining Admiral Fontoon circumcised, and then not, without actually caring either way. Fontoon looked away.

"We've heard of you, of course," Irina continued, shimmying her way into a bright red thong. "We understand you are a fantastic poet. We think it's marvellous. It takes a poet to negotiate a place like this properly, a man with enormous vision and a real artistic sensibility about him. There's no hope otherwise. The best thing in the world is great poetry, and of course there's nothing worse than bad poetry. And if it isn't truly great, then it is awful. There is no in between. I think you're terribly brave."

Irina admired herself openly in the mirror, running her hand along the graceful curve of her bottom.

Salim, the servant in charge of Gin Fizzes, appeared in the doorway with a tray full of them.

"Thank god," said Dizzie Dezzaro, arising. "I thought you were never coming."

The drinks were handed round. Fontoon studied the glass in his hand and, unsure as to its contents, decided to ask. He was generally always grateful in any case to have thought up something to say in a conversation.

"What are we drinking?" he said, trying to sound like the last thing in the world he cared about was what they were drinking.

"Gin Fizz, of course," said Irina.

"Is there anything else for afternoons?" asked Marilyn, genuinely surprised.

"Absolutely not," declared Dizzie Dezzaro. "Gin Fizzes are just the thing."

"Never had one," said Fontoon, trying to make it sound like it was some kind of miracle that he, of all worldly people, had never had such an ordinary drink. The others looked at each other, silently appalled. They loved being appalled.

"I imagine the Admiral probably steeps his verse in absinthe," mused Irina, putting on, but not fastening, her dressing gown.

"Tell me, Admiral," said Northrop Hindlips.

"Yes?"

"Do people buy much poetry these days?"

Admiral Fontoon had no idea whether people bought much poetry these days. He didn't imagine that they did, but he felt that as a poet he should probably have some clearer sense of the market. His hesitation in answering was misinterpreted as offence by Marilyn de Ponze, who intervened on his behalf.

"Oh, who cares, Northrop. What a question. As if a great poet is going to be concerned with money."

Northrop Hindlips found himself uncomfortably on the defensive. He had been cast in the unflattering light of one who perhaps believed that the only activities worth pursuing in life were those that returned hard cash, one who was unable to appreciate beauty for its own sake. It was an intolerable insinuation, particularly among the aristocracy. Nobody could prove he felt that way.

"Yes, of course, poetry is poetry and all that," he said a bit too hurriedly, cursing his own face for blushing. "Certainly can't put a price on it, for god's sake. Still, one gets published, doesn't one?"

"Christ, Northrop," said Marilyn, stirring her Gin Fizz impatiently. Dizzie Dezzaro was leaning forward attentively, earnestly trying to follow Hindlips' argument. Irina, sitting at her make-up mirror, lifted one of her feet and began to draw circles in the air with her toes.

"Well, I just wondered," continued Hindlips, "these artefacts, these publications, I wonder if people are buying many of them."

"It's a good question," Fontoon said. "I've wondered if there's money in it myself. All I can tell you is none has rained down on me so far."

Everyone laughed and social equilibrium was restored. Fontoon's perceived value increased by the precise amount that Hindlips' was reduced, as if they were attached to opposite ends of a mobile.

"Perhaps we could have a reading one evening," said Irina,

slipping off her dressing gown and wriggling into a tight black dress. "Wouldn't that be ducky? Don't you think it would be ducky, Marilyn?"

"It would," agreed Marilyn. "It would be extremely ducky."

"Could we? Would you mind terribly doing a reading for us one evening Admiral?"

Fontoon had been afraid of this moment or some moment very much like it ever since he had declared himself a poet. Eventually someone was bound to want to hear his poetry, to see some example of it. The time had come to say something plausible.

"Oh, I didn't come here to bore you all with my poetry," he said with a small wave of his hand. "Anyway, my poems, I never feel like they're truly finished."

"Now Admiral, you know what I told you about shy men," countered Irina. "It simply won't do. Fortune favours the bold, Admiral. Come here. Zip me up. Say you'll do a reading."

Irina turned her exposed back to Fontoon. He admired her fine shoulder blades as he zipped her tight black dress.

"If you insist," he said, realising that the future was nothing if not full of potential excuses.

"I do," said Irina, turning to face him forthrightly.

"Listen to him, he's such a dear," said Marilyn de Ponze.

"Good god," said Dizzie Dezzaro.

"You see, darling," said Irina, "they love you already. We all do. Do you know what I think?"

"I hope it's what I'm thinking," said Northrop Hindlips.

"Pink Ladies," said Irina. "Ali?"

Ali appeared at just that moment with a tray full of new drinks, to hurrahs and some applause. Fontoon shrugged, took a drink, and pretended to feel comfortable.

Upstairs in his room, Alyosha Ilyvich Razumikhin was

thinking about a man whose name he never knew. He looked darkly out at the rain and wished that one of those extinct volcanoes would just once prove everyone wrong and explode, and the nearer the better. It's not so much that he wanted to die, but what a glorious last thing to see that would be.

Chapter Miguel

Alejandro is working hard, scooping the pulpy sediment out of the maguey stem to create a hollow into which the *agua miel* will flow. When Alejandro finds enough of the juice collected in the stem, he uses a hollowed gourd to extract it into his sheepskin bag. Already his bag is half full of the sweet cactus milk. He resists the temptation to drink some of it immediately, although the day is hot.

Alejandro smiles. The brown tassles on the tall maize stalks tell him that the plant is fully grown now and the ears of corn have formed. The corn silk shows that the kernels are forming on the cob. The crop is good. The winter will be all right.

His mother comes out of their house and the children run up to kiss her hand. She is on her way to the cistern to draw some water for the washing.

"Mama!" yells Alejandro, holding up his bag of *agua miel*. His mother waves him off. Alejandro smiles.

Later that night the family relaxes together at the fiesta. Nobody misses the fiesta, neither young nor old. Even if they don't want to dance, they go to enjoy the music and to watch the dancers, to enjoy the courtship rituals and the laughter, in short to absorb and exude the joy of life. Everybody goes.

Alejandro's mother never speaks of Miguel any more, but Alejandro often wonders about what might have happened to his brother. Miguel had left the country and gone north many years ago, on his own. He had heard that life was better up there. Perhaps he could make a lot of money, maybe even earn enough to send some back home to his family.

At first, Miguel had written some letters. He had managed to wire some money back home. Alejandro had felt envious of his brother's adventures. He imagined Miguel in fine clothes, dancing in the big-city nightclubs with big-shot friends and beautiful women in swirly dresses. Ah, but that was not for Alejandro anyway. He dismissed his feelings of envy and felt bad for any touch of resentment over his brother's success. Miguel was Miguel. Alejandro was Alejandro. This is the way it was.

Alejandro looks at his mother. She is laughing, watching some of the children dance to the music at the fiesta. He wants to ask her about Miguel, but he stops himself. If she had heard anything, she would have told him. Her silence means that she has heard nothing. His question would only make her sad.

It had been many years now. The letters had stopped. The money had stopped. Had Miguel fallen on hard times? Could something bad have happened to him? Or had he become so successful that he could no longer think of his family back home? Could he have forgotten?

Miguel had not forgotten. Something bad had happened to him – a series of bad things. He had lost the job he had found and become poor. That led to many other bad things. His money was bad. His health was bad. He had bad habits. Bad friends. Bad ideas. Finally there was the bad thing with the shovel.

Miguel is in Heaven now and is coping fine. He hopes to meet God one day but so far, no. Miguel doesn't mind. He recognises that God must be insanely busy. At least he was in Heaven; he couldn't complain. Finding yourself in Heaven, well, you keep your mouth shut and try to blend in.

Miguel thinks about his family quite a bit, and wonders if they're all right. He gets impressions of them up there, and feels that they are all right, but then he wonders if it's all in his mind or if the information is actually reliable. In any case, he hopes they're all right. He misses them. What a fiasco it had all been. Given a do-over, he'd never have left.

Or would he have? Miguel thought about everything that had happened to him, about the screaming man who killed him. He had mixed feelings. Naturally he had gone through a period of posthumous anger and resentment, and more than that an overwhelming feeling of general tragedy about the human condition. It was so sad, life. So violent. So arbitrary. He reckoned he had had a lot more living to do. Yes, he felt cheated. No matter that he was down and out, a man likes to live! It's not as if he had lost all hope. He'd had comrades. They'd had their laughs. It was a life, after all, a human life, and that's no cheap thing, not to a human being, not when it's his own.

Eventually, however, one resigns oneself to history. It even begins to look inevitable. With time and distance come objectivity and detachment. None of it really mattered. That was the funny thing. Details, details. He had lived. He had died. Happens to the best of them. From this vantage point, Miguel could look at it all quite fondly, like a broken doll from an ancient childhood.

He even thought up a poem for the screaming man, for whom he felt now only sympathy.

> *Mi hermano, mi hermano en el dolor*
> *Castigado al no castigo*
> *este castigo de revivir*
> *mientras yo he hallado paz*

Fontoon

Olas de amor que me llegan desde los cielos
Hermano, te doy lo que no te permites a tu mismo:
¡Yo te eximo! ¡Te absuelvo! ¡Te perdono![1]

Well, thought Miguel, you can't criticise a dead man's poem. He smiled.

As the fiesta drew to a close, his mother looked at Alejandro, who was carrying one of the little ones, asleep on his shoulder. She smiled. He was a good man. A good boy. They all were.

---

1 My brother, my brother in pain; you suffer the punishment of no punishment, the punishment of reliving, while I have found peace.
In waves of love from high above, I give you what you cannot give yourself:
I hereby release you! I absolve you! I forgive you!

Chapter Influence

"Good evening everyone, and welcome to Public Debate. I'm George Stephanopoulos, here as always with Zbigniew Brzezinski, Henry Kissinger, Tony Blair, and supermodel Heidi Klum. Tonight we also welcome a very special guest, poet extraordinaire Admiral Fontoon. If you've been living on the moon or someplace and you haven't heard this man talk about space, well, buckle your seat belts, ladies and gentlemen and count down for lift off. You are in for a treat."

Chapter Tick

There exists in this world a certain special tiny sound. It is a sound so small and humble that it would likely go unnoticed in the virtual silence of a quiet field on a warm, windless day. Amid the shouts and laughter and music of a large room full of Dionysian revellers, however, this same small sound has the power to freeze the entire crowd at once, instantaneously, if only for a fleeting yet somehow eternal moment. Everything pauses, like a momentary voltage dip when the lights blink dark. Heads turn slightly. Glances are dared. A wave of communal shame mixed with derision passes swiftly through the room. And then the world powers up again with a hum and life continues as before.

This unique sound is produced by a miscue on the break – the feeble tick of pool cue just barely glancing off cue ball, sending it in a slow diagonal forward spin like a little imp reeling towards a chair because it is about to faint.

"Damn," whispered Fontoon, before looking up and trying to project a breezy lack of concern.

It wasn't the first time it had ever happened to him. Indeed he had made a special effort to address the issue both mentally and physically. He would make sure his cue was aimed dead straight through the centre of the cue ball. He would make a few practice strokes, being sure to relax his shoulders and free his hips. He would ensure that he was exhaling smoothly as he plunged his cue straight forward. He would keep his eye on the ball.

Still, somehow, at the last moment, it was as if his brain would seize up. His shoulders would tighten; his eyes would involuntarily close. He fizzed suddenly into radio static and his mind jangled. Just now it had happened again. Throughout Buhongo, even in distant rooms, everyone momentarily froze.

Fontoon watched the cue ball roll forward weakly, barely troubling the assembled rack. The object balls, instead of exploding around the table in all directions, wandered off in a kind of slow daze, like old people who had been assembled for a photograph and then had forgotten what they were standing there for.

"That," said Chase Krugley, entering the room all smiles and handshakes, "was ugly. Happens to the best of them. How are you liking that Balabushka?"

"It's gorgeous. I really don't know how to thank you."

"I can think of one thing."

"What?"

"Never break like that again. That was ugly! I'm teasing you. Happens to the best of them."

"Well, it's a beautiful cue."

"1973, from a Szamboti straight-grained maple blank. One of the last ones old George made personally. They're not that easy to get ahold of, you know."

"I know."

"I know you know. That's why I got you one. I knew I had to do something special to impress you. Are you settling in all right?"

"Fine."

"Interesting crowd, right?"

"Definitely."

"Listen, Admiral," said Krugley in lower and more confidential tones. "I'm not here to waste your time and I'm sure as hell not here to waste mine. Are you feeling ready for anything today?"

"Sure."

"That's what I like to hear. You know what we call that where I come from?"

"Tell me."

"Gumption. I love it. Listen. Your media appearances are huge. I mean they're enormous. People are responding to you. Do you know what I'm saying, Admiral? I'm saying they love you. And they listen to you, I mean really listen. Do you know that after you went on that rant about how expensive razor blades are and how it didn't make any sense, razor blade prices across the board dropped by seventy-four percent within the week? Do you know what that means?"

"What does it mean?"

"It means I'm a genius. I mean, I'm a goddamned genius. Can I spot them? Can I? Admiral, I'm asking you a question."

"You seem to be very good at your job."

"I seem to be very good at my job. I love this guy. You know what you are? Do you?"

"What am I?"

"Magic. Pure magic. Which is why you're going on the radio tonight."

"Whose show?"

"Yours."

"Mine?"

"I love the way your eyelashes flutter when you say stuff like that. Part of your charm. You know what it's called? You're going to love this. Tell me if you hate it. We can change it but it would be a pain. Fontoonery. Do you love it?"

"It's got a kind of a ring to it."

"Kind of a ring to it. I love this guy."

"What'll I talk about?"

"Admiral, I'm going to say something now and I want you to listen very carefully."

"OK."

"Are you listening?"

"Yes."

"Are you sure?"

"I'm listening."

"You asked me what you should talk about. Is that right?"

"Yes."

"Are you still listening?"

"Yes."

"Here's your answer: Anything you damn well feel like. Think you can do that?"

"I think so."

"You're damn right you can."

Their conversation was interrupted by one of the servants, who entered the room quietly and then knocked firmly on the open door. He was holding a tray with two drinks on it.

"Excuse me, gentlemen," said the servant.

"Qu'est-ce que c'est?" said Chase Krugley.

"Bronxes," replied the servant.

"Repeat after me, Admiral," said Krugley. "Hell yes."

Chapter Sun

Hello everybody out in radio land and thanks a lot for listening. There's something I'd like you to think about today, and that's the sun and exactly how far away it is. The short answer is that it's far away but not all that far away.

Look at all the other stars, at night of course, tiny little dots, and then think, as morning rolls around, that you're about to see one of them real close up. It makes you feel pretty lucky. And then we roll around to it and the sky gets orange and purple and then boom, there it is, orange ball of fire, and it's just another star, but it's our star and it's so close that it just lights everything up. Now. How far is it? We all know this one right? Ninety-three million miles away.

Think of it. Ninety-three million miles. OK? It's a long way, but it's not the same as infinity. It's a finite number. It's a certain distance. We're still using miles, for one thing, not light years. Let's try to imagine it in a way that we can feel. So we can really try to grasp that distance, so it's not meaningless. This is crucial for a sense of real perspective.

First think about one block. You know how long a block is, not that long. You can easily walk a block without any trouble. Five blocks. Ten blocks. You can walk ten blocks, you understand that type of distance. Twenty blocks, that's about one mile. Again, that's walkable. Union Square to Soho. It's not that long, one mile, you can hold it in your mind and get a real feel for it. Now you imagine that ten times. A one-mile stretch, laid end-to-end ten times. Can you feel that? Ten miles, two hundred blocks. It's not that long, you can do that.

OK, now just keep doing that. Ninety-three million miles is one billion eight hundred and sixty million blocks. Not even two billion blocks. OK, so you can't really exactly feel that, but it's finite. The distance can be measured in blocks. You know we're pretty close because we can not only see that thing really well, we can feel the heat coming off it. Imagine that!

Chapter Music

Good evening everybody and thanks once again for listening. Sometimes people ask me things, like what about music? Is music important? You bet it is. Music is one of the best things about being human. That reminds me of a story. One time I played some really cool music for a girl, and she listened to it for about thirty seconds, and she not only didn't like it, she hated it so much that she suddenly started laughing uncontrollably and she just couldn't stop. She went helpless with laughter. She laughed her head off. I had to sit there and watch her. Finally she just said, as best she could, still laughing:

"I just don't understand why anyone would listen to this."

Chapter Magic

The world is full of so much magic that we don't even really notice it most of the time. Once you do notice it, it's pretty obvious. Let me tell you a little story.

I'm heading into the city, only there's a problem with the subway. It's not running. Everybody's annoyed. Bunch of annoyed people go off in a mob to wait in line for the bus. The bus takes forever to come, and when it comes, there's no room. I'm at the end of the line and I'm as annoyed as anyone. Looks like I'm at least three buses away from getting a ride. I decide to walk to another stop further from the subway station.

I walk a good while and find another stop and wait another twenty minutes. The whole time, remember, I'm annoyed. And sure enough, when the bus comes, it's full, and I can't get on. The world and me, we're at odds, right? I'm annoyed and the world is fighting me. But the driver, seeing me throw my hands up, actually slows down and opens his door in front of me just to apologise. He smiles at me and says there's nothing he can do, and obviously he's right. He suggests a better place to wait, where there's more buses. It's a good idea and I thank him.

At this point, I start to loosen up. Am I in a huge hurry? Not really. And there's nothing I can do about it anyway. I decide to take my time and not care how long anything takes. I get to the next stop and a bus comes. It's still full, but this time I smile at the driver and say it's no problem. The bus is full of old ladies and they all smile at me. A few of them wave. Now

I'm feeling pretty good. I'm ready to walk the whole way into town, but then another bus pulls up right away, and this time I can get on. I'm already feeling like things are going my way now, and then the driver just waves me on without taking my fare. He says it's on him. No reason.

Relax into things and the world works with you. That's what I'm talking about. Magic.

Chapter Gravity

I wanted us all to take a moment tonight and think about gravity a little bit. Gravity is nature's most ridiculous force. Now, I can understand how gravity keeps us all stuck to the earth. The earth is huge compared to us, and we're right here, literally touching it. That makes a certain amount of sense. It's still abstract, in the sense that I don't think we have a great answer for why there should be gravity, why everything pulls on everything else just by existing and having mass, but it does behave in a predictable way and it explains a lot of things. So, we have to accept it, gravity exists. We jump; we come back down. We're stuck here. That's gravity we can understand.

But now consider Pluto, which used to be one of the planets. I still like to think of Pluto as a planet. There are two things about Pluto I'd like us all to think about right now. First, it's small. It's not quite fifteen hundred miles across. That's much smaller than the moon. And it's less dense than the moon, so in terms of mass, Pluto has only eighteen percent of the mass of the moon. So we're talking about a pretty flimsy object.

The second thing I wanted to note about Pluto is how far away from the sun it is. It's really far from the sun. It ranges from less than three billion to over four and a half billion miles from the sun. Now, what does that mean? It means that if the sun were the size of a basketball, Pluto would be a speck the size of a single grain of salt, and it would be more than a kilometre away. Let's call it twelve and a half blocks away. If you're shooting baskets at Tompkins, your grain of salt is down on Delancey heading for the bridge. Just think about that. These objects are supposed to feel each other somehow? But that's what we're expected to believe about Pluto, that this grain of salt in space is going around and around a basketball a kilometre away, because of this thing we call gravity. They say gravity is the weakest of the four fundamental forces, but I call that freaky strong.

I'll tell you something else about gravity. I've looked this up. Don't think that Pluto is some kind of extreme case, a tiny grain of salt circling at four and a half billion miles, because that's not even close to the limits of gravity's range. You know what gravity's range is? Infinity. You heard me. It doesn't have a limit. If a thing is in the universe, it's pulling on you right now. And you're pulling on it. No matter how far. No matter how small.

It's all completely preposterous, but it's true.

Chapter Poetry

"So!" came a loud voice from behind Fontoon. "The great poet, am I right? Admiral Fontoon? Eh?"

It was Lord Burrell, the Earl of Vermilucci, a man who had been much praised ever since Eton for his charm and devastating good looks. His two passions were croquet – he was a tournament-class player – and sleeping with other men's wives.

"That's me," said Fontoon.

"Burrell," said Burrell without extending his hand. He was rifling through the refrigerator.

"A pleasure," said Fontoon. It sounded like the sort of thing Buhongo people might say.

"Hell's bastard bollocks!" yelled Burrell.

"What's the matter?" asked Fontoon.

"I had a brace of partridges in here and they're gone. Damn it to hell. Bastards. They were in my box with my name on it. It's bloody inconsiderate. I'm going to put a note on the board."

Lord Burrell strode past Fontoon to the erasable notice board, grabbed the red marker, and began to scribble in an angry hand. His note said: 'To the anonymous thief: Please stop stealing other people's food! One brace of partridges this week, a kilo of cured ham last week – it's bloody inconsiderate! Grow up!'

Having vented his spleen in this manner, Lord Burrell was in a much brighter mood when he set the marker down.

"So!" he practically shouted at Fontoon. "What abominable weather. Can't be helped. It's all a man can do to keep in stroke under these conditions."

"Keep in stroke?" said Fontoon.

"Croquet," said Burrell. "That's my game. I don't suppose I'm too bad a shot. Used to play on the national team before I had to leave the country."

"England?"

"That's the one."

"Why'd you have to leave?"

"Well, 'have to' is putting it a bit strongly. Thought it best. Got into a bit of a situation when an MP's wife and chief constable's wife got together and figured things out, and an even worse situation when the MP and the constable caught on themselves. The constable showed up at my door with a horsewhip one day and laid it about me as best he could, chasing me around my rooms – not the first time I'd tasted horsewhip I'm afraid, nor the last – and word was that the MP had been going on somewhat alarmingly about pistols. All quite overdramatic if you ask me. Can you imagine making that much fuss about women?"

"Well, that's people for you."

"Exactly. Exactly. Well said. I say, you're not still nursing a Gin Fizz are you? Christ, man, it's after six. Bronxes or White Ladies, maybe a Trinity, that's the custom, but if you want my advice, take plenty of wine as soon as the sun goes down. More especially, burgundy – even better, port. They enrich the blood, you see. There's nothing better as a prophylactic. You can add as many gin cocktails as you like around the edges, but lay off once the evening deepens. From ten o'clock onwards it's best to stick to whisky and champagne, at least as far as drink is concerned."

"Just thought I'd finish this one up and see how I feel," Fontoon said by way of self defence.

"See how you feel! Ho! Ho, that's rich, I like that. See how you feel! Ho ho ho! That is good. I can see I'm going to have to keep my eye on you! Yes, by all means, you do exactly as you like, understand me, exactly as you like, and see how you feel. Ho!"

Nobody had any idea what was so hilarious about that. Even Burrell would have been hard pressed to explain. He simply expected people to be witty, and generally to be witty in ways he wouldn't understand. So he was always at the ready with a hearty laugh in case anything sounded remotely like a quip. This was as much courtesy on Burrell's part as fear of being thought slow.

"Another hilarious joke, Burrell? I'm so sorry to have missed it."

Alyosha Ilyvich had slipped into the kitchen unnoticed. He lit an unfiltered cigarette and blew the smoke disdainfully into the centre of the room.

"Ah," said Lord Burrell. "Alyosha Ilyvich Razumikhin, Admiral Fontoon. Or have you already met?"

"Nope. Nice to meet you." Fontoon extended his hand and Alyosha Ilyvich looked at it and blew some more smoke. Fontoon retracted his hand.

"I keep to myself mostly, I'm afraid," said Alyosha Ilyvich.

"Keeps to himself! Ho ho!" Lord Burrell's eyes sparkled with merriment.

Alyosha Ilyvich didn't respond. He opened the refrigerator and scanned the contents for unmarked foods. Someone would inevitably leave some fruit or milk or a yogurt in there without remembering to mark it with their initials. Sure enough, a ripe Cox's Pippin sat on the lower shelf, like a baby rabbit unaware of a hungry kestrel circling overhead. Alyosha Ilyvich snatched it immediately.

"Unmarked," he said, clearly gloating. "Fair game." He wasn't even hungry, but this was one of his favourite pastimes.

Lord Burrell could not object. There was something distinctly unfair about it – one knows perfectly well whether even an unmarked food item is one's own or not – but Burrell had done the same thing himself on many occasions. He had even helped himself to a bit of milk now and again from somebody's clearly marked container. Once or twice he had gone so far as to finish the last drop, when he wanted it very badly for his tea. Still it made him uncomfortable to see someone else do it, and not even bothering to be surreptitious about it. He picked up a black marker from the counter top and began to mark his pantry box with skulls and cross bones.

Irina came gliding in with Dizzie Dezzaro just as Alyosha Ilyvich had tossed his apple core into the rubbish bin. Dezzaro was just finishing one of his anecdotes about his grandfather's friend, the late Theodore Roosevelt.

"...and the beast's head hangs on a wall at the old estate to this very day, if you can believe it," he was saying.

"I can, darling, I can," said Irina. "So this is where everyone's been hiding. I should have known. The kitchen is always the best room to be in during a party."

"Unless a bedroom is available," countered Burrell.

"Naughty man," she replied, giving him a little kiss. "Where on earth is Lishan?"

"Right here, Memsahib."

Lishan was the servant in charge of sundowners. He walked into the kitchen behind a rolling cart whose stock included gin, sweet and dry vermouths, triple sec, bitters, an array of juices, plus a few bottles of burgundy and some port.

"Thank god," said Dizzie Dezzaro, moving towards the cart. "I thought I was going to faint. What'll it be, everyone? Bronxes?"

There was general agreement on this point and Lishan quickly set about the task of mixing a two-litre pitcher full of the requested cocktail.

"And a little port for the Admiral," interjected Lord Burrell, giving Fontoon a little elbow and adding confidentially, "to enrich the blood, you see, at least until you've acclimatised." Thus Fontoon found himself with a Bronx in one hand and a glass of port in the other. He downed the port in one go, mainly so he could set the glass down and be a normal, one-drink person, then held up his Bronx, and spoke:

"Cheers," he said.

"That's the ticket," said Burrell, and everyone but Alyosha Ilyvich raised their glasses and drank.

"Good god," said Dizzie Dezzaro, after he had nearly finished his Bronx in one huge gulp. "Then it's true!" He was looking right at Alyosha Ilyvich.

"Oh come on, Diz," replied the Russian. "Haven't you ever seen anyone not drink before?"

"Not that I can remember – although my memory's not what it used to be."

"Ho ho!" laughed Lord Burrell.

"Well I think it's marvellous that he's not drinking," said Irina. "I think it's *sexy*." She emphasised the word and tilted her head back slightly.

"You think everything is sexy," said Alyosha Ilyvich. "So it doesn't really count."

"Ho ho! Touché!" said Burrell.

Dizzie Dezzaro opened the refrigerator as Alyosha Ilyvich lit another cigarette. "Dammit!" exclaimed Dezzaro. "I'm sure

I had a Cox's Pippin in here!"

"Maybe you ate it," said Alyosha Ilyvich.

Dizzie Dezzaro eyed the Russian suspiciously. "It was new this afternoon."

"Maybe you've forgotten," said Alyosha Ilyvich, with a sly wink in Fontoon's direction. Fontoon allowed a wry smile and scratched his nose innocently.

Dizzie Dezzaro looked around the room with petulant impotence.

"Ho!" cried Lord Burrell. "Ho ho!"

"I think we should move out to the verandah at once," said Irina. "I love the colour of the sky at this hour. Anyway, Hindlips and Marilyn are out there alone. If we leave them any longer they'll probably end up *fucking*, and then they'll be knackered for the rest of the evening, and we can't have that!"

Fontoon couldn't help but admire her forthrightness. What small feet she had. What a tiny waist. What an extraordinary bottom.

Such was Irina's command over the proceedings within Buhongo that everyone dutifully followed her straight out to the verandah. The sky was all deepening purples and blues, with a fierce bright arc of orange low on the western horizon, and broad violet stripes emanated eastward like an awning in front of some cosmic barbershop. Venus shone out so brightly that it seemed obviously three dimensional and spherical, more like a tiny version of the moon than a brighter version of a star. It seemed that if one had a net on a long enough stick, it would be possible to scoop the little planet right out of the sky. The only thing left to do then would be to put it in a special velvet box.

Fontoon refilled his Bronx from the pitcher and strode out a few paces into the garden to reflect. The air was moist with jasmine and mimosa, and Fontoon allowed himself the drunkenly poetic notion that these fragrances were the cause of his intoxication. He was just drunk enough to love everyone and to be glad of everything. He was particularly happy about the moon and how much sense it made, lit up in precisely the way you'd think it should be. Moon here, sun there: perfect.

Alyosha Ilyvich was also gazing into the heavens. He had climbed onto the roof as the others gathered on the verandah, and now he lay there on his back smoking another unfiltered cigarette, his eyes fixed on the stars. Everything was intensely disappointing. The universe. Himself. Drugs and alcohol. Relationships. The nothingness behind everything.

"Hey!" he shouted. "Poet!"

It was dark. The others had gotten bored on the verandah and gone running to the sitting room, where they were already opening bottles of champagne and pouring glasses of whisky. Fontoon had been left out in the garden, where he had thought he was alone.

"Who, me?" he said, looking around.

"So I am told," came the voice from above.

"Where are you?" asked Fontoon.

"I'll come down."

Alyosha Ilyvich swung down from the roof, hanging by his hands for a few moments before letting go and landing in front of the verandah. He got up and brushed himself off. His body language said 'so what' and he had an air of dignity.

"Drink something for me," he commanded Fontoon. "Drink something for me or so help me I'll have to drink it myself. That would be a real pity on my first day of sobriety."

"I've been drinking plenty already," said Fontoon.

"I insist. You must drink more. You must drink one for me."

"OK then," said Fontoon, raising his glass. "Here's to you."

"No!" said Alyosha Ilyvich, angrily, grabbing the glass out of Fontoon's hand. "I said *for me*, not *to me*. We'll have to start again. This drink is no good. It's tainted. It isn't mine."

Alyosha Ilyvich threw the contents of the glass out across the garden. Looking around almost desperately, he spied the pitcher on the verandah, which still contained a good half litre of Bronxes. He strode over to it in big long strides of his thin legs, grabbed it, and filled the glass, spilling a good deal of drink onto the verandah in the process. He strode back in long thin strides to where Fontoon stood and handed him the glass.

"There. This is my drink." He pointed at Fontoon with his long index finger. "Drink!"

Fontoon wasn't sure in what spirit the command was intended, and he wasn't altogether certain there wasn't an insult in it somehow. And if there wasn't an insult, then there was likely something else unpleasant about it. He suspected that somehow he was being dragged into someone else's self-loathing. However, he had lost half his drink across the garden and had been issued a replacement, so he reckoned there was no more than the usual harm in drinking it. The Russian could have his drama; Fontoon would have his gin. He took a sip and gave Alyosha Ilyvich a look that said 'OK?'

"I think it's better if you drink all of it."

"I will."

"I mean all of it at once. Right away."

"I don't know. I'm really more of a sipper."

"But I'm not, and that's my drink. If you let it lie around it will continue to tempt me, to torture me. Kill it for me. Finish it off."

"Yeah but..."

"I beg you. My friend. You must understand, you're a poet."

"Very well." Fontoon drained the glass as the Russian

looked on, wide eyed.

"Excellent. That really hit the spot. Thank you, my friend. You have done me a real service. Allow me to pour you your own drink. I'll be all right for a while."

"I'm probably good actually."

"Nonsense. I threw your drink away – atrocious behaviour – you must allow me to replace it."

"You already..."

"No no. Your own drink, your very own. I beg you." He was already pouring out another Bronx into Fontoon's glass.

"Thanks."

"A pleasure. Write me a poem."

"Hah!"

"Don't laugh. I'm serious."

"Oh. OK. Well. All right. I'll write you one and it'll be in my book."

"That would be wonderful. When will you write it?"

"Oh, I don't know, I actually need to get writing. I'm kind of waiting for the right mood to strike. A poet must..."

"You haven't written any poems."

"Well, I..."

"I apologise. I am impertinent."

"No, it's just..."

"You've written them, but you've burned them. You've written reams, and then in a brilliant fit of artistic pique you've burned the lot of them, thrown them into the fire."

"No. I've written nothing."

"Nonsense. I'll tell you what you must do. You must write it at once."

"Write what?"

"My poem, of course. Right now. This is how things get done. Later we can burn it. Have you anything else to do? Of course you haven't. I will help you. Let's get started. What's the first line?"

"Wait. I do have something to do."

"What."

"I have to take a piss."

"No! Impossible! Not until the poem is finished. You must hold it until the poem is complete. It's perfect. You'll have a sense of urgency. The piss can be your reward."

"No, honestly, I couldn't possibly concentrate, I ..."

"First the poem!"

"No."

"I must insist!"

"Honestly."

Fontoon said it slowly and deliberately and put his hand on Alyosha Ilyvich's shoulder. The thin Russian tensed up for battle and then relaxed in defeat.

"All right. Have your piss."

Fontoon walked further out into the garden and relieved himself against a eucalyptus tree, pleased with himself for winning a battle and gaining a touch of upper hand.

"But it's like eating dessert first," called the Russian after him.

"So be it!" rejoined Fontoon.

By the time Fontoon returned, Alyosha Ilyvich had produced a pad of paper and a pencil and was sitting expectantly on the grass.

"I'll write it down for you," said Alyosha Ilyvich. "All you have to do is say the words as they come to you."

"Right."

"And Admiral. Admiral, Admiral."

"Yes."

"I need this to be a good poem. Let's not have just any

doggerel. When we burn it, its ashes must be beautiful."

"OK. A good poem. Coming right up. Let's see."

"Poetry is the only thing left. It's all there is."

Several minutes went by in silence. Fontoon paced around as Alyosha Ilyvich sat patiently with his pen poised above the paper.

"I like it very much so far," said Alyosha Ilyvich.

"Smart ass."

"No no, I mean it. There's a stillness about it. Good things will come."

After several more minutes of beautiful stillness, the young Russian spoke again.

"I'll help. I'll do the first line. You can change it later if you want. How about: 'O', just the letter 'o' with no 'h'? You can only do that in poems, so we might as well take advantage of it. What do you think? Almost anything can follow that too, so we're leaving all our options open."

"All right. Let's start with 'O'."

"Excellent. I'll write it down."

Alyosha wrote it down and smiled. He tapped the paper several times with his pen, proudly, as if to indicate that they were onto something special. Several minutes went by in shared silence.

"I have another idea," said Alyosha.

"Very well," said Fontoon. "I'm certainly willing to hear it."

"The poem shouldn't be very happy. It should be about betrayal. It is natural as the daylight fades that we should use the metaphor of the evening."

"That seems reasonable to me. I agree."

"Excellent. How about this: 'O foul night, you beautiful traitor' – what do you think – 'you empty temptress' – I like that, empty temptress, it has a ring and it's meaningful – and something about what a bitch she is – 'your gaudy'...something black, what's black?"

"Coal?"

"Hm. No. Cobalt. Cobalt is black, isn't it? If it isn't we can change it later. 'Your gaudy cobalt shine that I once thought was mine is no more.' What about that? I'll read it back. 'O foul night, you beautiful traitor, you empty temptress, your gaudy cobalt shine that I once thought was mine is no more.' That's not bad, is it? What do you think?"

"It strikes me as rather good, I think."

"Me too. And you see how it rhymes shine and mine, but not at the end of a line – my goodness, now I can't stop rhyming – I think it's good to have those little sorts of sub-rhymes. But the very ends of the verses should rhyme, shouldn't they? I think they should. Poems should rhyme, shouldn't they, Admiral? 'The Drunken Boat' rhymes, in French of course. I thought it didn't for the longest time, because I was reading a translation. But then I saw the original. It rhymes, Admiral. What do you think?"

Fontoon reckoned there were poems that rhymed and poems that didn't; he wasn't really sure but he thought that must be the case. Maybe the ones that didn't rhyme were cooler – or maybe not. Certainly they shouldn't be too regular and nursery rhymey or they wouldn't be very good. But they could rhyme, other than that, if the rhyming was clever. Anyway, this poem was for Alyosha Ilyvich, and if he thought it ought to rhyme, then Fontoon had no objection.

"Poems can rhyme," Fontoon answered in as sage a voice as he could muster, "as long as they're not too rhymey, if you know what I mean."

"I think I do, yes. I agree completely. So you'll make this

one rhyme, then?"

"Yes."

"Excellent. I'd like it to rhyme."

Fontoon stared at the moon, and Alyosha Ilyvich stared at Fontoon, and several more minutes passed in silence.

"Let me help just a little," said Alyosha Ilyvich. "I have a small bit of an idea. Of course you'll want to change it all later."

"Go on, please. It's no problem. I've always thought..."

"Yes, good, very well, if you insist. How about this – we're on the second verse now I think, aren't we?"

"Ummmm, yes."

"Excellent. How about 'screams of anguish' – no – 'a billion screams of anguish' – that's better isn't it – 'and the laughter' – no, no – 'a billion screams of anguished laughter' – oh, I like that, 'anguished laughter', and it captures a meaning, too, there's always pain behind laughter and vice versa – and we have to be careful here, I think, because at the end it has to rhyme with 'no more', remember. Let's see. 'A billion screams of anguished laughter, into your' – I don't know, something ominous, a flirtatious demon – 'into your beckoning, silent doom' – is that over the top? It's just like the night, isn't it? You have to be fearless in writing poetry, don't you? I mean, it's no good to be afraid to write poetry if you want to be a poet, is it? You tell me."

"I think it's all right. 'Silent doom'. 'Beckoning'. I don't think that's corny, I mean, 'doom' is a funny word, but then there's no other word for it, is there? And I think 'silent' saves it. If there was any doubt. Let's go with it."

"Shall we?"

"Let's."

"We can scrap it."

"No no. It's evocative. It's evocative as hell."

"All right. You'll want to change it all later anyway. Now tell me. What rhymes with 'more'?"

"Shore. Poor. Bore. Lore. Door."

"My god. We've ended up with a good word at the end of our verse. We're spoiled for choice here. I have it. What about 'a room of eternal windows and no door'? That's good isn't it? Notice 'doom' and 'room', plus 'no more' and 'no door' of course. Not too obvious?"

"Not bad at all."

"I'll be damned. You really are a poet. Don't stop here. It's too short isn't it, just two short verses? I mean, it could stop there, if you thought it was right. It's balanced, isn't it? What do you think?"

"Well..."

"Too short?"

"Yeah. A little too short, I think."

"Very good. Make it longer. Work your magic. Remember, this poem is very important to me."

On they worked in exactly this way, with long silences punctuated by suggestions from Alyosha Ilyvich, always approved by Admiral Fontoon. Finally they had doubled the length of the poem and were down to the task of finding an ending line.

"'No more?' Oh, we've used that one."

"First verse. But you're right, it's exactly what we need. It should end with 'no more'. That's obvious. Of course! We can change the first one and use 'no more' at the end! You've done it! You're a genius! Let me just scribble something down here, tell me what you think."

Alyosha Ilyvich scribbled down another line, one with which to bring the poem to a close. He presented the finished piece to Fontoon for his scrutiny.

"Read it out loud," asked Alyosha Ilyvich, and Fontoon did. When he was finished, the Russian's eyes were brimming with tears and he breathed a loud sigh.

"Beautiful," he said quietly. "Thank you."

"It's not bad, is it?" said Fontoon.

"It's phenomenal. You've really outdone yourself. I hardly know what to say."

"Well, I mean, you helped..."

"Pah. I tossed out the odd phrase. You had all the responsibility. You're the poet, Admiral, not me."

"I don't know..."

"Enough. False humility is disgusting. Don't let's ruin it. Shall we burn it now?"

"I was actually thinking we might wait a bit."

"Are you certain? I have some matches."

"No no, let's wait. We can always burn it later."

"Very well. Let's go in, shall we?"

"Let's."

Chapter Strongman

"That's a lot of blocks," muttered Strongman Simms, the nation's president, reaching over to turn off his radio. "You heard this guy? That's a hell of a lot of blocks."

"But not an infinite amount," said the Chairman of the Joint Chiefs of Staff significantly.

"Exactly," said the Strongman, pointing his finger at the Chairman of the Joint Chiefs of Staff. "It's a certain length."

"Still," said the Secretary of Defence. "It's a hell of a long way."

"Nobody's saying it isn't, Secretary," put in the Secretary of Energy.

"Good, because the Secretary of Defence is correct," said the Strongman. "It is a long distance to think about. But once you start imagining it..."

"You get kind of a feel for it," said the Director of Homeland Security, leaning back in his chair with a faraway look in his eye. "You can't exactly grasp it, but somehow... it starts to seem real."

"That's it!" shouted the Strongman, slamming his hand forcefully on the big oak table. "You realise you have a connection to it! I want us all to continue imagining it for a few minutes right now. I don't want to lose this moment."

All the Strongman's advisors and cabinet members closed their eyes and relaxed their facial muscles and just thought about exactly how far away the sun was and wasn't. The room was silent for six minutes except for the innocent clearing of the occasional throat.

"Amazing," the Strongman said finally, as eyes opened all around the big oak table and warm glances were exchanged around the room. "And the light hits us from there, and you can still feel its heat."

"Feel its heat?" said the Secretary of State suddenly. "You don't have your factor thirty on it'll burn your ass!"

Everyone laughed.

"I have to tell you," said the Strongman, "the guy makes a good point. The guy makes a good point."

"The sun is so far away and no further," said the Secretary of the Interior, in a tone of voice that said 'I'm summing everything up'.

"I'm not talking about the sun any more, Mr. Secretary," barked the Strongman.

"Oh," said the Secretary of the Interior.

"I'm talking about some of that other stuff. This guy, Futon..."

"Fontoon, sir," said the Secretary of Commerce.

"I don't give a wax canary what his name is, Mr. Secretary," barked the Strongman. "His words have moved me. What he said about war the other day..."

"That it was bad?" guessed the Attorney General.

"Worse than bad, Skeezles." The Strongman had known the Attorney General for many years and called him by his nickname 'Skeezles'. "He kind of went right to the core of what we've been about around here. It's like he could see right through us. He said we were like a gang, like the mafia, running the whole world like a big protection racket for the private benefit of a small elite class and using the military to bully our way around."

"Nothing wrong with that," said the Secretary of Defence,

looking slightly wounded. "Survival of the fittest."

The Strongman looked at him.

"Two weeks ago I would have agreed with you," he said. "But you know what? He's right. What we're doing is selfish and wrong."

The Secretary of Defence scowled.

"Come on," said the Strongman, "you know it and I know it. Who'd we give all the re-building contracts to when we invaded what's-its-face?"

"Our friends," said the Secretary of Defence, looking down.

"And why'd we go in there in the first place, I mean why did we go in really? Did we really give a rat's ass about anybody's democracy? Did we?"

"No," said the Secretary of Defence, uncomfortably.

"Why'd we go in there?" demanded the Strongman. "Why?!"

"Make a lot of money," mumbled the Secretary of Defence.

"What?"

"To make a lot of money, sir," repeated the Secretary, more firmly.

"Who for?"

"Ourselves and our friends."

"I can't hear you!"

"Ourselves and our friends, sir!" shouted the Secretary of Defence.

"Ourselves and our friends. That's right. Thank you, Mr. Secretary. And what else for?"

Nobody spoke.

"What else!?" the Strongman demanded.

"Power," said the Secretary of Intelligence meekly.

"That's right! Power! Pure geostrategic positioning as a hedge against resistance and future resource scarcity! We've become power-mad bastards! And did any of us think about how many lives would have to be lost? Did any of us think of that for a half a second? Did we lose any sleep over it?"

"No," said the Secretary of Defence, glumly, and everyone else also muttered the word 'no'.

"What?"

"No, we didn't lose any sleep, sir!" everyone shouted at once.

"That's right," said the Strongman. "I tell you, this radio fellow has really opened my eyes. This war, it sickens me to think what we've done – and it's not just the war either. It's our whole outlook. The war is just a symptom. Without us really realising it, we've been totally consumed by greed and lies and violence. Freedom indeed. Do we even know what the word 'freedom' means?"

"I thought we did," said the Secretary of the Interior uncertainly. The Secretary of Defence snorted with scorn.

"But I, I guess we don't," retracted the Secretary of the Interior in a tone of voice that said never mind.

"You're goddamn right we don't. We've been making a goddamned mockery of the word is what we've been doing. Well all that's about to change. I'm issuing an executive order to disband the military."

"What?!" cried the Secretary of Defence and the Chairman of the Joint Chiefs of Staff.

"And the intelligence agencies. Goddammit, gentlemen, you know as well as I do that it's the right thing to do. Don't you? Don't you?"

"Yes," said the Secretary of Defence, glumly.

"Yes," said the Chairman of the Joint Chiefs of Staff and the Secretary of Intelligence, hanging their heads.

"We all know it, in our heart of hearts," said Strongman

Simms. "Well I'm disbanding the military and putting all that manpower, all that money, and all that ingenuity into projects that ensure a decent, safe life for all peoples. Once other governments see we've done that, I expect they'll all follow suit."

"What about our enemies?" put in the Director of Homeland Security, meekly.

"Enemies," spat the Strongman with forceful contempt. "Enemies my ass. We invented them, we'll uninvent them."

"But, but, but," began the Secretary of State, "but what about the economy?"

"Good question, Secretary," said the Strongman. "Have my 'little s' secretary get our corporate masters on the phone. And get the shadowy financial elites, media lapdogs, and mob kingpins on as well. Let's have us a conference call right here and now. Pronto!"

The Strongman's personal secretary made it happen in a hurry.

"Mr. X, Green Man, Carlo, thanks for joining us," said the Strongman. They all said variations on 'it's a pleasure' and 'thanks for having us'. The Strongman decided to start them off with a joke.

"Gentlemen, why do women fake orgasms?"

The corporate masters, shadowy financial elites, media lapdogs, and mob kingpins didn't know.

"Because they think we care."

There was a pretty good amount of laughter.

"Listen," broke in Mr. X when he was done laughing and had let a decent few seconds pass while everybody's chuckles died out, "I think I know why you've called."

"Me too," put in the Green Man. "Have you guys been listening to that radio boy?"

"Hoo boy have I," said Mr. X. The Strongman said he had too.

"You know I have," put in the owner of the mainstream media.

"His thing about the difference between measuring well-being as opposed to measuring growth had me doing a little soul-searching," said the Green Man, "and I gotta tell you: I didn't like much of what I found."

"Yep, yep, yep," agreed Mr. X. "And his whole thing about how fleeting our time here has been compared to a million years of success for Australopithecus really gave me a sense of perspective."

"Two million years of Australopithecus," corrected the Strongman.

"I'm pretty sure it was one million, Mr. Strongman," said Mr. X with non-specific threatening undertones.

The Strongman didn't like to contradict Mr. X, but he was certain that Admiral Fontoon had put the length of time of the reign of Australopithecus at no less than two million years. He hesitated.

"Well, you probably know," said the Strongman. "I guess it depends on when you date it back to."

"The Strongman is right," said Carlo, a mafia kingpin. "Two million years."

"Two million," conceded Mr. X. "Even better."

"So are you guys thinking what I'm thinking?" asked the Strongman.

"I believe so," said Mr. X. "Our whole focus on artificial measures of short-term growth is distorting our understanding of wealth. Real, true wealth. That's clean air and water, good food to eat. All our incentive structures are just plain screwy."

"And healthy lifestyles, health care, and education," put in the Green Man. "There's simply no good reason for us all to work so damn much. This infinite-growth consumer-culture monster we've created is ruining life for everybody."

"All the crime and violence has made a pretty swell mess for a lot of people," said Carlo, shaking his head, although nobody could see that on the phone.

"What the hell were we thinking?" wondered Mr. X out loud.

"I don't know," said the Green Man, and everyone could tell, even on the phone, that he was shaking his head ruefully. "But I do know this: we're going to have to work together to change things around. And I'll tell you something else for nothing: we're going to succeed."

"You bet we are," said Mr. X. "If we can't do it, I gotta ask you: who the hell can?"

"So, you want us to report the truth from now on?" said the media monopolist, still unsure if he could believe his ears.

"You're damn right I do. Dammit, gentleman," said the Strongman, slamming his hands on his big oak table, "this world is going to be such a beautiful place!"

"You're goddamn right it is," said Carlo.

"Hear hear!" said the group as one.

Chapter Spat

"Excuse me, Memsahib," said Ali to Irina in the sitting room as she filled Lord Burrell's glass with more champagne. "There are new arrivals."

"Ah!" exclaimed Irina. "And me not in my bath. Still, it's terribly exciting. Tell me, Ali, who are they?"

"Hugh Grogan, the third Baron Weldamere, Lord Glossworth, the Earl of Ennismidgen, and their wives."

"That is too wonderful," said Irina. "Send them in immediately and call up some more servants."

It was only moments before the Grogan party came bustling into Lady Irina's sitting room to join the already festive scene within.

"Hell's teeth!" exclaimed the baron on entering. "What good mischief have we stumbled into here?"

"Hughey darling," said Irina, kissing both his cheeks and taking him by both hands. "How good of you to drop by."

"Hadn't strictly intended it," confided Grogan amid the general hubbub of cheeks being kissed and hands being taken. "We'd piled into the old Bugatti and were making our way across the escarpment when the dratted thing got hopelessly stuck in the mud. Imagine our relief when we realised we were right out front of Buhongo, so we thought we'd just stick our noses in to see if anything was on."

"Of course something's always on at Buhongo, isn't it?" said Gwladys Glossworth, whose name was pronounced just like Gladys but was spelled with an extra 'w'. "You must meet my new husband James."

"The Earl of Ennismidgen," said Irina. "Charmed."

"The pleasure is mine, Lady Irina. I've heard so much about you and Buhongo."

"Well then you can't say you haven't been warned," came a voice from behind. It was Alyosha Ilyvich Razumikhin, who had just walked in with Admiral Fontoon.

"Alyosha Ilyvich," said Irina sternly but with playful, flashing eyes. "Cheeky monkey."

"At your service," said Alyosha Ilyvich, with a deep bow.

"And this is a very hot new poet, Admiral Fontoon," continued Irina, putting extra emphasis on the word 'hot' and tilting her head back slightly. "We are so pleased to have him."

"You haven't had him yet, Irina."

"Alyosha Ilyvich is in rare form this evening," observed Irina for the benefit of her guests.

"It's true," agreed the Russian. "I've discovered a new way of drinking. I can drink as much as I like and not a drop passes my lips. It's fantastic, I should have thought of it years ago. Speaking of which, I'm parched. Let's have that whisky, Admiral. We must drink to your new poem."

Berhanu, the servant in charge of whiskies and champagne, was prompt as ever when the call was heard, and two drinks were at hand virtually before Alyosha Ilyvich had stopped speaking. Lord Burrell took Gwladys Glossworth by the elbow and escorted her to the nearest sofa.

"You must be dreadfully thirsty after your journey," he was saying, "and we have so much to catch up on. Come chat with me."

"Has the Admiral written a new poem?" asked Marilyn de Ponze from her corner chair. She kept to shadows, mostly, making her pale and delicate skin appear even paler and more delicate, her high cheekbones seem even higher and more bony.

"He has," said Alyosha Ilyvich. "A gorgeously dark little affair about nothingness. To your poem."

Admiral Fontoon had an impulse to say 'our poem' in acknowledgement of the generous assistance he had received during its creation. However, inasmuch as several of the guests now stood beholding him with something akin to admiration, he was able to convince himself in an instant that there was no need to belabour any behind-the-scenes details, which in any case would surely only embarrass Alyosha Ilyvich and ruin his moment of magnanimity. Fontoon contented himself therefore with a bashful "You are too kind," as Alyosha Ilyvich, with a strange twitching of his lips, watched him down his whisky.

"Now mine," said Alyosha Ilyvich.

"Your new method of drinking is going to kill me," said Fontoon, but took the second glass and drank it on his friend's behalf. "But hey. It's a party."

"I want to hear the Admiral's new poem," said Marilyn, coyly sipping her champagne and crossing her legs at the ankles.

A general hue and cry was raised demanding to hear the new poem, but Irina's voice rose above the others and quieted the crowd.

"We must of course hear the new poem this evening," she began. "But let's not spoil the effect by just rushing into it headlong. Auspicious occasions like this do not happen every day, and I think at least a tiny bit of ceremony is called for. I propose that the Admiral gracc us with a reading as a sort of opening ceremony before the feather game."

Irina's proposal was greeted with enormous enthusiasm among those who knew what the feather game was. Fontoon didn't know and didn't care; he was pleased to have a reprieve from his first public reading. Only Lord Glossworth was troubled by any sense of dissatisfaction. He couldn't stand being excluded from the cognoscenti and his irritation could be heard in his voice.

"But what's this feather game?" he cried out.

"You'll find out," said Alyosha Ilyvich, who had taken against the Earl without having a particular reason why.

"Woo-oo-oo!" came the sound of somebody imitating the steam whistle of a locomotive, and everyone turned around. They knew who it was going to be, but they couldn't see him yet. All they could see so far was the first few of a long line of chairs entering by way of the ballroom.

"Oogachaka oogachaka oogachaka oogachaka," came the voice. The train lengthened as more chairs emerged from the ballroom. People began to howl their enthusiastic encouragement, clapping their hands and whistling.

"Woo-oo woooo!" came the voice again as the man himself, the engine behind the train, at last appeared, pushing for all he was worth. It was Dizzie Dezzaro, tricked out in pink swallowtails and a top hat, and this was his almost-nightly ritual. He would make the servants line up as many chairs as he felt up to pushing, and he would have himself a game of choo-choo trains, pushing the chairs from room to room until he had gotten a satisfactory amount of attention. After that, generally speaking, it was time for musical chairs. Buhongo boasted an old phonograph with a tulip horn, and an enormous number of vintage 45s and 78s.

Dizzie Dezzaro, with what breath he had left, imitated the last dying groans of a locomotive on its last legs, then pulled the rear chair out, spun it around once on one of its back legs with a good deal of flair, and finally flopped into it, exhausted.

For his performance he received his customary standing ovation and a few catcalls.

"Champagne!" cried Dezzaro as desperately as he could, fanning himself with one hand and clutching at his throat with the other. "I need champagne! Quickly!"

Champagne was quickly brought by Berhanu, and once Dezzaro was taken care of, it was offered around to everyone else as well. After several more glasses of bubbly had been demolished, the group sprang into action unbidden, as though controlled by a single hive mind, and began arranging the chairs in a large oval for musical chairs. Fontoon looked on with great amusement. He was just about as drunk as he had ever been in his life, but even though he was now drinking for two, he was sure the others had easily managed to outstrip his own pace. Yet while Fontoon could barely stand, the Buhongo regulars remained sprightly and surprisingly coherent, if increasingly boisterous. Fontoon smiled to himself because he realised they had set up at least thirty chairs for the game, and there were still fewer than twenty players. They had played three games so far without noticing that anything was wrong. The music would stop, everyone would flop into a chair, or across two or three chairs, after a few moments they'd shout 'hurrah!' and they'd get up and start again.

"Excuse me, Memsahib," said the dignified Ali to Irina, who was controlling the phonograph. "There are new arrivals."

"Oh, but that's wonderful, Ali," said Lady Irina. "Who are they?"

"Prince Eugen of Bavaria," responded Ali, "and a small entourage."

"That is absolutely delightful," said Irina. "Thank you, Ali. Do send them straight in."

Prince Eugen was the hereditary Grand Duke of Splechen,

one of the largest spending men in Europe. The scene he encountered upon entering the large sitting room did not surprise him; he was a frequent visitor to Buhongo. The musical chairists had either realised that there were too many chairs for musical chairs, or had decided there were too many chairs for some other, possibly aesthetic, reason, or had simply been seized by an idea for a new game. Whatever the impetus, several of their number had taken to hurling chairs gleefully from the sitting room into the ballroom, where several more of them had taken just as gleefully to picking them up and hurling them out of the window.

"We were just driving in the neighbourhood along the escarpment," said the prince, "and I'm afraid our reconditioned Model T just wasn't up to handling the mud! Stuck. Hopelessly stuck. Stroke of luck we were practically in front of Buhongo at the time. Good to see people up and about in the old place, I must say." Salim, the servant in charge of mud on the escarpment, smiled the special proud little smile of a man who is impeccable in his job and knows it.

"Is that Prince Eugen?" shouted Northrop Hindlips just before grunting loudly as he sent a chair sailing a good twenty feet through the doorway into the ballroom. "Good evening, sweet prince!"

"I can see," said the prince, smiling, to Irina, "that I've got a little catching up to do. I've brought you a gift."

"You darling man."

The prince snapped his fingers and Habib, who was always the prince's servant at Buhongo, appeared with a crate of ornate bottles.

"Absinthe!" exclaimed Irina.

"Makes the heart grow fonder, as they say," said the prince, bowing slightly with an ironic expression.

"Do come and join us over here," called Marilyn de Ponze from where she sat in a corner languidly cutting up some five grams of cocaine into a pattern of lines on a glass table.

"Delighted," said the prince, deftly plucking a bottle of absinthe from the crate and opening it as he strolled in Marilyn's direction.

It was perhaps two hours later that Admiral Fontoon found himself being grabbed and hurled to the ground with some force by Northrop Hindlips, the effect of the impact not lessened by the fact that Hindlips himself had landed on top of him. Fontoon had never played rugby before, but he had picked up the rules readily enough. It was a simple matter of tossing a cushion around randomly, occasionally running with it around the ballroom, overturning as many pieces of furniture as possible along the way, variously piling on top of someone or getting piled upon, and starting again. It was a fine game, thought Fontoon, who at the moment was not the least bit concerned with physical pain. He stood up with some difficulty, tossed the cushion in the general direction of one of the prince's entourage, and set off to chase him round the ballroom. If he had been asked, Fontoon would have had to admit that he hadn't had quite so much untroubled fun in a very long time.

Fontoon eventually found himself in the beautiful sobbing phase of drunkenness where his indescribable sensitivity could only be expressed through the free flow of tears. So as not to make a spectacle of himself, he decided to recover his equanimity from the comfort of an isolated chair in a corner of the ballroom. As he watched everyone, his head felt suddenly cavernous. It was an odd but not unpleasant sensation. His head had become an enormous thing, like the inside of a huge cathedral, or bigger, the inside of a hollowed-out moon.

Fontoon

He moved it left, he moved it right, and it rotated in all its immensity, light as a ping-pong ball. His head was so big that the party, all of Buhongo, had to move inside it, where it became tiny. Tiny little chairs and tables, tiny little people. Their voices sounded far away now, even though their tiny little bodies were very close, as if seen through backwards binoculars. Fontoon felt that if he shook his head, everything would probably snap back to normal, so he made sure not to shake his head. He liked everyone tiny and quiet.

He tried to breathe very smoothly, so as not to disturb himself. Everyone certainly seemed to be having a good time. Everyone certainly seemed very comfortable. They all seemed to be friends, the best of friends. Fontoon wondered what they wanted out of life. Was it this? Buhongo? Had they achieved it? Would it last? Was it enough? Would he ever feel like they were his friends too? Did he want that? Did they ever feel like they were wasting time? What did they feel about the black hole problem at the centre of the galaxy? They had seemed so big at first, but look at them. They were just itty bitty little things who could hardly make any noise. Suddenly Fontoon felt protective of them, and forgave them all their sins, whatever they were. Would they be scared of him when they realised the size of his head on the inside? Ahhhh, and where oh where was the girl from the subway and her beautiful acne-scarred face, and what oh what did she sound like when she made sound?

Alyosha Ilyvich had seemed like potential friend material, but he had gone off sulking after Fontoon had drawn the line at heroin. He had done his drinking, smoked his opium, snorted his cocaine, but he wasn't having any needles. As a matter of fact Alyosha Ilyvich had not seemed appreciative enough – not nearly appreciative enough. He'd say thank you each time, and then he'd stand there and keep looking at Fontoon, like he was waiting for something that wasn't coming. He'd give Fontoon a phased smile. At first it was an innocent smile, but the sense of waiting gave it a dissatisfied air after the first few milliseconds. Shortly thereafter the smile would look like strained patience, then a desperate plea. It would become enigmatic just before going flat and breaking off bitterly at the end. The smile went through all these phases in the space of a few seconds.

Fontoon had weathered it perhaps a dozen times that day. He couldn't imagine what sort of satisfaction Alyosha Ilyvich had hoped for from their arrangement beyond the simple joke of it and what bonds of friendship it helped forge. He didn't imagine that there was anything else to squeeze out of it, and he felt somewhat wounded by Alyosha Ilyvich's disappointment. Hadn't Fontoon been valiant? Shouldn't they be sharing a sense of soaring triumph? Hadn't they conspired in a witty little performance piece together? Did they not stand shoulder to shoulder in the sacred circle of art? Wasn't that enough?

Didn't people overdose on heroin and die? Wasn't it reasonable to refuse – wasn't it unreasonable even to ask? Wasn't it only OK to request unreasonable indulgences if reasonable refusals were accepted with grace and good humour? But when Fontoon had refused – apologetically refused – to inject an unspecified quantity of heroin into his veins for Alyosha Ilyvich, the young Russian had been affronted. He had urged and begged and cajoled and finally he had shouted, shouted in real anger at Admiral Fontoon for not being a good sport, and he had insulted Fontoon and even spat – spat! – in disgust as he walked away. Who were these people? What was he doing here?

Fontoon looked around the room and the first thing he

noticed was that everything sounded normal again. Then he realised that all the people were full-sized and that his own head seemed more or less about the size of a basketball once again. His pleasant trance was broken, and he heard the sound of a human being energetically imitating the screeching of a chimpanzee. The sound came from directly over his head. Admiral Fontoon looked up and his eyes met the eyes of the human being who had made the sound. The two of them looked at each other. They were both normal sized.

It was Dizzie Dezzaro. He was hanging by his arms from the rafters. He made the chimpanzee sound again, and then he was off, climbing his way along the rafters with his arms.

Actually fairly impressive, thought Fontoon, and then he thought: *Is there anything in this life that isn't heartbreaking?*

He stood up, stretched, and made his way to the billiards room. A little respite from the madness. It was quiet in there. Somehow the muffled sounds of the party made it seem even more quiet than if there had been absolute silence.

First, the rack. He took some time with it, adhering to his little chromatic formula and ensuring that each ball was in solid contact with all its neighbours. When he was satisfied with the tightness of his rack, Fontoon picked up his Balabushka from the wall rack and examined it. A good weight; a beautiful cue.

He approached the table with the centre of his belly as an old player called Gus once taught him to do. He knew he had to be relaxed, that was the first thing, and he had to concentrate. Giving his shoulders a good shimmy to remove all tension, Fontoon set his sights on the front-most ball of the rack that lay before him like an arrangement of candy-coloured jewels. They were so beautiful. The lighting was perfect: a dark room, the table glowing from the overhead hanging lights, appearing to be suspended in space, or in water. Fontoon made a few practice strokes, and then inhaled and began to exhale slowly. He made sure his hips were free, so he could move easily and add body weight to the stroke. At last, still exhaling, his eyes on the rack, his mind as one with his body, his concentration penetrating well through the target, he made his quickest stroke, trying to feel he was running an enemy through with a spear. He nearly missed the cue ball entirely.

Tick.

The ball rolled slowly forward and well to the right of the rack.

Oops, thought Fontoon. "If people didn't miss," old Gus had said, "there wouldn't be pool." He tried again and made a very decent break of it. He re-racked again and again, just practising his break. On quite a few occasions he made a very satisfying cracking sound and sent the balls scattering to all four corners of the table.

I can do this, thought Admiral Fontoon. *There's nothing wrong with me.*

Out in the ballroom, a few people had begun to dance amidst all the wrecked and upturned furniture. Lord Burrell danced with Gwladys Glossworth, and Prince Eugen with the wife of the third Baron Weldamere. As Fontoon continued his practice, there came the muffled noise of gasps, laughter, and clapping. From another direction – through the window, it seemed – came the sounds of clattering and skidding vinyl. Fontoon didn't care what it was about, he just wanted to master his own concentration and tune out all distractions. It was only the prince, in an impudent rage, tossing records out of the window and insisting they were 'the wrong kind', aided cheerfully by the Baron's wife as the Baron himself drank whisky and made sullen faces. Burrell and Lady Glossworth danced on, regardless.

Suddenly the door to the billiard room flew open. There stood Northrop Hindlips, Marilyn de Ponze, and Irina herself.

"There you are!" exclaimed Irina with exaggerated relief.

"We thought perhaps you'd run off!" added Hindlips, although no one had really thought so.

"Hey, you can't get rid of me that easily," joked Fontoon, assuming once again what he had begun to think of as his Buhongo identity as wry comment-maker.

"It's almost time for the feather game!" said Irina in a stage whisper, her eyes flashing with coy mischief.

"You must read your new poem," said Marilyn, "for ceremonial purposes."

"Well," began Fontoon, feeling anxious out of a desire not to appear anxious, "why not?"

"Hurrah!" said Irina. "Come out and join us in the ballroom. You've been all right? I mean, you're enjoying the party? You haven't been in here sulking or anything?"

"No no," said Fontoon. "I'm just a little crazy for pool tables. I absolutely can't resist them." Fontoon noted to himself that he never used the word 'absolutely' in this manner, and felt a measure of self-contempt for becoming such a big phony already.

"I do like a gamesman," said Hindlips. "I hope you'll join us at croquet in the morning."

"Morning schmorning," said Marilyn. "Tonight, let there be poetry."

Fontoon followed the others out to the main ballroom, where everyone had gathered for Irina's feather game. There were now perhaps forty people in all. Guests had continued to arrive as Hispano-Suizas, Bugattis, and Model Ts continued to accumulate helplessly in the mud on the escarpment outside the grounds of Buhongo. Aristocrats and heiresses mingled with artists and academics, their hushed conversations and bright-eyed expressions creating an atmosphere vivid with anticipation. Fontoon's nerves suddenly tried to curl him up; he fought it as best he could.

Irina stepped onto a low platform with her exquisitely small bare feet, lifting her ball gown slightly to display and free them. The murmuring in the crowd grew louder with the increased excitement as Irina stood looking over them, smiling beneficently. She had only to clear her delicate throat, emitting the gentlest of half-coughs, for the eager hush to fall. Her guests began to nudge each other and widen their eyes. Only Lord Glossworth seemed bemused by the spectacle, and grew once again impatient at the sense of exclusion from the cognoscenti.

"I'd like to know what all the fuss is about," he muttered to nobody in particular, but in the general direction of Prince Eugen, who looked away and pretended not to have heard. Glossworth scanned the room for his wife and soon found her across the room sharing an intimate laugh with Lord Burrell, who had his arm draped over her shoulders, rather inappropriately, Glossworth thought. She must be a bit drunk, reckoned Glossworth, who was a bit drunk himself, and he resolved to inflict cold indifferences upon her throughout the foreseeable future.

"Dear friends and honoured guests," spoke Irina at last, bringing the hall to utter attentive silence, except for a small choked-off groan from Admiral Fontoon, who stood nearby holding his stomach and bending forward slightly. "We have the great good fortune this evening of a very special treat indeed. Poet. Thinker. Man of Action. Billiards champion. Here to open the feather game ceremonies personally, our own Admiral Fontoon is going to favour us with a reading of his newest work, written this very evening on these very grounds. Welcome him."

Taking funny little duck steps, Fontoon stepped onto the platform to the welcoming applause. So this was it; this would be his public debut as an actual poet; it was really happening. Fontoon bent his efforts toward the task of appearing literary, running his fingers once through his apparently careless hair in what he hoped was more or less a professorial fashion.

The people were in a mood for laughing; they therefore hoped the poetry would be bad, and would bias themselves as far as possible in that direction before hearing it. It was nothing personal, but good poetry might impose a certain spiritual quietude that would compete in an unwelcome way with the unbridled merriment that was desired.

Fontoon cleared his throat and thanked the assembled guests, casting a quick glance at the farthest corner where Alyosha Ilyvich sat with his arms crossed and his legs folded. The instinct to flee came upon him, but he was able to look at himself severely enough and with strict enough eyes to stay put. He took a deep breath, surveyed the crowd, and did his best to smile.

Chapter Feather

"The poem is called 'O Foul Night'," announced Fontoon, as Alyosha Ilyvich closed his eyes and prepared to receive.

"Aah-eeyah, eeyahhh-eyah-eeyahhh," came a sudden jungle Tarzan scream, shattering the patient stillness, as the figure of a man in leopard print underpants swung through the ballroom on a vine made of tied-together bedsheets.

It was Dizzie Dezzaro. He let go of his bedsheet vine and sailed into an armchair at the back of the ballroom, knocking it over and landing in an ungraceful heap. A smattering of applause greeted him as he stood up behind the toppled chair. He surveyed the room, obviously confused.

"Good god," he said. "Please do continue."

Fontoon read the poem, needing to pause only twice to double over with the terrible nervous cringe. When he finished, there was a moment of what could be called poetic silence. The general sense of the audience was that the poem had been rather good, and had created that certain quieting of the spirit, which, while unwanted, was after all not unpleasant once it had come. Heads nodded and then the clapping came – warm and energetic. True, the enthusiasm was fuelled in part by the excitement over the now-imminent feather game, but it was genuine nonetheless. Clapping longer and louder than anyone was Alyosha Ilyvich Razumikhin, who quietly said "Bravo" as real tears rolled down his pale cheeks.

"Not bloody bad," said Lord Burrell, putting an avuncular arm around Fontoon's shoulder as he left the platform.

"Sounds to me like you've been spending entirely too much time with Alyosha Ilyvich," put in Northrop Hindlips. "But well done all the same."

"Wonderful, wonderful, magnificent! It is a gorgeous paean to all the sadness in the world!" Irina was saying from the platform. "I love sadness. I wish I could *fuck* it. And now – are you ready? Shall we play the feather game? What do you think?"

Irina's subjects burst with hoohoos and hurrahs, giggling themselves up like champagne bubbles, popping with claps of their little hands. Admiral Fontoon smiled and basked in his success. He couldn't see Alyosha Ilyvich anywhere because Alyosha Ilyvich had left the room. There was no time to think much about that because a line of servants was entering the room carrying an enormous embroidered cloth. Everyone cleared out a space in the centre of the ballroom, where the servants unrolled the special tapestry, which was really an ordinary tapestry made special by its role in the feather game and the name that Irina had given it. It was known as the Wuhu Cloth.

"Make a circle, make a circle!" instructed Irina, although everyone was already doing that owing to human beings' circle-forming instinct, which is evident whenever there is an occurrence around which a circle ought to be formed, such as a fistfight or a canny salesman demonstrating potato peelers from Switzerland in a public square.

"All right, all right," continued Irina when the circle had been formed. "Everyone pick up an edge of the Wuhu Cloth, and when I say lift, lift it up off the ground. OK? Has everyone got an edge? Make room for the prince..."

"Which one?" shouted the wag Dizzie Dezzaro, to cries of 'ho ho ho'.

"Prince Eugen, Prince Eugen," laughed Irina, noticing that she had taken to saying everything twice. "OK OK! Everyone's in? Everyone's in?" Now she was doing it half on purpose. "Ready? Is everyone ready?"

The room was in a frenzy. They loved this game.

"Lift the Wuhu!" cried Irina, throwing her head back and imagining how pretty she looked.

Everyone lifted their edge of the Wuhu Cloth until the whole mass of it fluttered at chest level. Fontoon held onto his edge and looked out at all the upturned faces gazing breathlessly at the supremely calm figure of Irina. Next to Fontoon was Lord Glossworth, who elbowed Fontoon and offered him a look of impatient disgust. Fontoon declined the invitation to join in a conspiracy of disdain and took a one-inch sideways step away from his irritable neighbour.

Irina nodded at the servant in charge of music, who began with four of his colleagues to bang a wildly sensual rhythm out of some bongo drums. Irina began to move gently to the beat in a sort of slow-motion writhe, casting her eyes on one onlooker after another, smiling all the while. She reached behind herself and undid a crucial hook, and began gradually to slither her way entirely out of her dress, leaving her wearing only her red thong. The mesmerised crowd murmured its approval.

"Extraordinary," muttered Lord Glossworth.

Irina slowly and dramatically waved her arms around, like eels in a pool of honey, eventually bringing one closed hand to the front and pausing there to let a mischievous gleam appear in her wide eyes. Many of the gathered assemblage were now bouncing on their tiptoes with almost uncontrollable excitement.

All at once and with great flair Irina opened her hand. There between her thumb and middle finger she had somehow magically produced a beautiful blue three-inch feather. The people roared; the drums became louder, more insistent. She brought the feather to her lips and kissed it, still rolling like a slow wave to the rhythm. She lightly brushed the feather on her face, across her shoulders, her breasts. She stroked it down her flat stomach, along her thighs, between her legs, slowly slowly. Fontoon realised something: this was all getting pretty sexy.

Finally Irina drew her hand back across her body, like a ballerina, and then unfurled it slowly and released the feather, which lilted and lolled through the air above the Wuhu Cloth. Now everyone's concentration was on the feather. When it came near anyone they blew at it for all they were worth to keep it floating and gently flipping through the air. If it threatened to land in the centre, beyond the reach of their collective lung capacity, they would jiggle the Wuhu to send it again sailing upwards. Hypnotically they dedicated themselves to this task, but eventually despite their efforts the feather managed to land. The very moment it touched the Wuhu, Irina clapped her hands once and the drumming abruptly ceased. Irina, the high priestess, her hands still pressed together, closed her eyes and began to divine. The gathering was now completely silent, although more than a few people continued to bounce on the balls of their feet. Irina was no longer smiling, but serene and still, and stood as if trying to balance an egg on each of her delicate shoulders. At last her eyes opened, and she spoke.

"Lord Burrell," she began, "and Lady Glossworth."

Excited whispers and giggles rippled through the room but were quickly muted.

"What?" said Lord Glossworth.

"Prince Eugen," she continued, "and Marilyn de Ponze. Lady Weldamere... and Dizzie Dezzaro."

She continued in this manner, announcing pairs of names until all the names of everyone present were used up, except two.

"Myself," she declared grandly in her finale, "and Admiral Fontoon."

With that, a great cheering arose, Irina nodded to the music servant, who put on some 1920s jazz, and people began to seek out their designated partners. Irina's eyes fixed immediately on Admiral Fontoon, and her lips slowly spread into the naughtiest smile Fontoon had ever seen. She closed her eyes and danced her way towards him in slow motion.

She stopped only when their bodies were touching, then opened her eyes and looked up at Fontoon, as if understanding exactly how much of him was real and how much made up. She smiled at him and ran her indescribably tiny finger down his sternum.

"Did you enjoy the feather game, Admiral?" she asked.

"It was amazing," said Fontoon.

"I get the feeling you don't really understand it," she said in a seductive tone.

"That is possible," said Fontoon.

"I don't understand it, I can tell you that!" said Lord Glossworth as he stormed across the floor towards them. "What do you mean by sending my wife off with another man?"

"Well," said Irina, "what does she mean by going? Where's yours?"

"But, but," said Lord Glossworth, turning purple, "I, I..."

"Ah, there she is," said Irina. "Princess Annabelle. She's starting to look forlorn. Do go to her."

"I'll do no such thing!"

"Irina!" came a forlorn little cry from nearby. "Irina, darling!"

It was Constantina van den Hoogle, and she was pouting. The young heiress had been unable to locate her designated partner. "I can't find Alyosha Ilyvich anywhere!"

"Hmm," said Irina. "He's been awfully sober. I do hope he's all right. I'll tell you what you do. Go with Annabelle. She's been stood up as well."

"Hurrah!" said Constantina, hurrying off. "It's like Christmas!"

"Gwladys!" cried Lord Glossworth, not sure which way to run. "Gwladys!"

The pairs of people Irina had put together were now floating out of the ballroom arm in arm towards separate areas of the mansion. So it was not a question of dancing. Fontoon looked back at Irina, his eyes a bit wider than he wanted them.

"I think somebody's starting to get it," said Irina.

Fontoon had gotten it: Irina Crandemere intended to have sex with him. There was no other way to interpret it now. She meant to harass the general on the southern flank. He and his mild paunch were going to be confronted with her lithe forthrightness.

"This is all very modern," said Fontoon, trying to be ironic. "Very forward thinking."

"Well, Admiral," said Irina. "Shall we?" She moved her hips slightly forward and tilted her head slightly back on the word 'shall'.

"Let's," said Fontoon, taking her by the arm. They walked off together, Fontoon's gait a bit ducklike, because he was getting the nervous cringe again.

A closed window is a most confounding thing to a fly. He can see his way clear to the outside, can see it a hundred times clear with his compound eyes, yet when he races towards the glorious outdoors at full speed: wham! There's this incomprehensible – what? – in the way. He shakes off his dizziness, races around the room, and – hah! – there it is again! The outside world! Well he'll make sure not to miss it this time. I don't know what went wrong last time but here I go, there's no mistaking it this time: wham! Christ! What the hell happened? I must have missed it again somehow. There seems to be this something, this nothing in the way. Better race around the room crazily and shake off this dizziness. Ah. Well, whatever it was it's gone now, there's the outside, clear as a hundred bells. I can see nothing between me and those shrubs. Off I go! To the outside! Wham! Christ!

Irina opened the door to her bedroom and a dizzy fly whizzed out, although neither she nor Admiral Fontoon paid it any notice. They proceeded to Irina's imposing four-poster bed, flopped onto it, and started nuzzling. No sooner had Irina undone the first two buttons of Fontoon's shirt than the bedroom door banged open, and a tall, thin figure came lurching through. He grabbed onto the nearest object, which was Irina's wardrobe, and swayed unsteadily.

"I'm terribly sorry about this," said Alyosha Ilyvich Razumikhin in a slurred voice, "but I'm afraid..."

And with that, the pale Russian fell to the floor in a heap, unconscious. An empty pill bottle came loose from his flaccid hand and rolled onto the carpet.

Chapter Wreck

"All right, all right, everybody settle down," said Mr. Bentley to his assembled staff. He had to calm them down because they were laughing so hard and chattering to each other and giving each other high fives. Even Mr. Bentley could hardly suppress his own smile.

"Sorry, JB," said Jenkins, still beaming unabashedly. "But that was a thing of beauty. You have to admit!"

Mr. Bentley's personal secretary Shirley looked at the big man to see how he would react. She might have to go fetch an employee behaviour report form. But no, Bentley's eyes twinkled, and he was smiling.

"That was a fine bit of work," admitted Mr. Bentley. Everyone looked at Weasby, who was blushing. "I've seen aborted intercourse before, but this – this was dramatic."

Jenkins allowed himself the liberty of slapping Weasby hard on the back.

"Weasby," continued Mr. Bentley. "Why don't you tell us a little bit about your technique?"

"Well, you know," said Weasby, emanating humility, "just putting certain probabilities in motion and, well – sometimes things work out."

"It certainly looked like our man was going to get himself some there for a minute," said Mr. Bentley, casting an ashamed glance at Shirley, who looked down decently.

"It did," said Weasby. "It certainly did."

"And then wham!" said Jenkins, nearly shouting. Everyone

broke out into hearty chuckles once more.

"I'll be writing up an official commendation, Weasby," said Mr. Bentley importantly, turning everybody quite serious.

"Thank you, sir," said Weasby, blushing proudly.

Under the table, Shirley touched Weasby's shoe with hers.

Chapter Brothers

"So how's your brother?"

Margaret asked this question about Nastasya's brother because it was an excellent entrée into the subject she really wanted to talk about: her own brother. She was well prepared to sit through a bit of blah blah blah about Nastasya's brother in exchange for the opportunity to take centre stage with her sorrows.

"Not good," sighed Nastasya, automatically assuming the faraway hurt look she had perfected for these kinds of conversations. It had become an instinct, a switch. The brother conversation allowed her to exude a certain gravitas and thereby to attain a certain importance and to receive a certain sympathy, all of which she deeply relished. Her own life was not devoid of accomplishments, but was thin on real theatre. Her brother's tragedies could be dined out upon indefinitely, conferring upon her an aura of mysterious pain, the value of which could scarcely be overestimated in the artsy circles within which she moved.

"He's still doing quite a lot of drugs, it seems. I know for certain of two recent relapses. He destroyed some furniture in the house where he lives. He..." She paused here to purse her lips slightly and inhale just a little bit louder than was strictly necessary. "I guess he threatened his housemates with violence. He's just been a little crazy."

"Wow," said Margaret, who knew how to turn a nascent feeling of competitive disadvantage into a seemingly sympathetic look of concern. "That's a drag. Have you talked to him?"

"Yeah," Nastasya lied. "We talk all the time. I think he's suicidal again."

"Oh my god, really?" Margaret resented the way Nastasya was obviously lording it over her with her intense talk about suicide.

"Yeah," Nastasya sighed. "He ate a bottle of pills or something. They had to pump his stomach." Nastasya felt that ought surely to do it for now, so she added: "So how's your brother doing?"

Margaret sat ever so slightly more forward in her chair and affected a sort of worried pout.

"Well, he's in therapy, thank god."

"Mine too." It was a lie. Alyosha was in anything but therapy. Nastasya had instinctively jumped on the therapy train so as not to be left out.

Margaret shot a stern, silencing glance at the selfish interruption.

"Yeah, I guess he calls in sick a lot and he's missed a lot of work, and they're starting to get pretty pissed off at him. I think he might lose his job, and then I just don't like to think what would happen to him. He's just so depressed already."

"Mm hm, mm hm," came Nastasya's knowing assent. Been there, heard that a million times. "What about his relationship?" She knew the relationship story was coming, and she knew the value of being perceived as a good listener who paid attention and remembered things from one session to the next.

"Well, Anna Maria is gone. She'd had enough of his bullshit apparently."

"Oh, that's a shame though. I thought she sounded quite cool."

"In a way, but then she was also not the best influence on him. She was a total coke-head and all she ever wanted to do was party. She's like, twelve years younger than him."

"Right. I just thought, she also sounded, I don't know, intelligent and all."

"It's true, but..."

"Yeah."

"They weren't a good match."

"Right."

"So he's got this new chick now."

"Really?"

"Yeah, she's, you know, again, about ten years younger than him, a real party animal. She's called Annie."

"Annie?"

"Yeah."

"Wow."

"I know. Anna, Annie. He's going to get them mixed up."

"But she might not notice."

"True. She's extremely into Vicodin. Anyway, it's like he refuses to act his age, I mean, he's thirty-five now... thirty-six, and what used to just come naturally is now like something he has to prove. He's just not happy. He's not a happy camper."

But he's not suicidal, is he? thought Nastasya. *I win.*

"The poor thing," sighed Nastasya. "I wish he would just find a nice girl and, you know, settle down. Be happy. Find peace."

Yeah you would like that, wouldn't you, bitch.

Chapter Recovery

Alyosha did not die. Discreet doctors were brought in. They looked after him; he got better. However, he kept to his rooms even more than usual, nursing bottles of sparkling water that he insisted on calling *l'eau petulant*.

The Buhongo crowd varied in their reactions to his sickly presence, which was not in keeping with the overall *esprit de corps* they tried to maintain. On the one hand, they were delighted that he had abandoned sobriety. On the other hand there was recognition that taking it to the verge of death was uncalled for. People who can't handle their drugs and alcohol are nearly as unwelcome as teetotallers. Such people can be tolerated briefly but are ultimately insufferable.

Irina was the most sympathetic towards him because she had personal elegance. Dizzie Dezzaro was the least sympathetic because he had no stomach for anything serious. Hindlips wasn't sure what to think because he lived in a constant state of mild confusion. All of them to one extent or another thought of Alyosha as The Thing Upstairs. Alyosha felt this way about himself as well.

Fontoon had been very frightened by the episode. He was a grown man who ought to know what his own feelings were on any subject, yet he found himself in his alarm looking around the room to get a general sense of the prevailing mood. Were other people upset? How upset? Was this a thing to be laughed off, or a thing to be taken very seriously? Or a thing to be taken very seriously while strategically laughing it off for all appearances? Or was the opposite true?

"Hey," said Fontoon, poking his head into Alyosha's room after hovering outside uncertainly for long minutes. Alyosha was sitting in an armchair and staring out of the window.

"Poet," said Alyosha, moving his head a few degrees in Fontoon's direction and then back again.

"That's my story," said Fontoon, "and I'm sticking with it."

Alyosha continued staring out of the window and did not respond.

"It's the weirdest thing," said Fontoon.

"What?" asked Alyosha.

"How often do you cut your toenails?"

"God," said Alyosha. "I don't know. Not very often. They don't grow very fast. Every few months I suppose."

"Right! Way slower than fingernails. That's normal, right? Well mine are suddenly growing faster."

Alyosha turned his whole chair around to face Admiral Fontoon.

"Really?" he said. "How much faster?"

"I don't know. I have to cut them all the time now. It's like, every ten days."

"Are you over-cutting? Is this a mania?"

"No! I mean, I'm not cutting short little nubs here. I'm talking about long toenails. I cut them probably twice, three times for every time I have to cut my fingernails."

"How odd."

"Right? It drives me insane."

"It does sound maddening."

"It is. This morning I looked down and they needed cutting again. I'll tell you something. I actually threw a chair."

"People throw chairs here all the time."

"No, but I was sober. I was just mad. I threw it. It was the nearest thing to hand. I sometimes think I'm losing my mind."

Alyosha pursed his lips and looked at Fontoon from under his brow.

"Well," he said. "I wouldn't know anything about that."

They looked at each other for a few moments and then burst out laughing.

Chapter Jar

Fontoon had a favourite bathroom at Buhongo, large and elegant. Everything was marble and shiny brass and clean. The shower got nice and hot, and had intense water volume and pressure. The toilet itself seemed royal; it was like sitting on a real throne. Of all the places Fontoon had indulged his fondness for putting a fresh BM into a jar, this was certainly the most luxurious. It even had a powerful extractor fan, which worked wonders on the smell.

Fontoon had made a very bad smell, directly onto a piece of wax paper, squatting next to the royal toilet. The wax paper innovation eliminated the need for any fishing out, with all the dripping it entailed. He held up the wax paper and examined his prize in the light, half holding his breath, half sneaking the odd sniff, half repelled, half fascinated, half amused, half ashamed. Finally he flooped it into its jar, which he had brought along especially for the purpose, set it down, put the lid on, and tightened it. Next he carefully rinsed the wax paper and put it in the waste paper basket, and washed his fingers thoroughly. Now that the thing was hermetically sealed and safe, it was time to take a moment to admire it in its oddness. BM. What a funny thing to call it.

What a peculiar thing I do, mused Fontoon, and not for the first time. *But how fascinating. How fascinating.*

He smiled and felt dirty. Well. Well well well. All that remained was to covertly transport his private wonder through the building and into his special hidey-hole in the basement.

Fontoon

He put a towel over his jar-holding hand in a way that he hoped would pass as casually draped, although to be honest he couldn't help but be aware that it looked suspiciously just like a towel that had been carefully placed over something quite obviously shameful. Well. That was surely just the paranoia of the guilty man, whereas any innocent bystander was likely to think nothing of it at all. All he had to do was saunter casually through the big house as he would any other time when he had nothing in his hands at all, and no throbbing aura of degradation.

Fontoon left the bathroom, jar in hand, towel over jar, attitude fixed. He was prepared to wink at anyone he saw – at everyone if need be. In the absolute worst case scenario – say everybody in the house was there and they decided to make some sort of game out of finding out what Fontoon had under his towel – he was prepared to sprint through them full force, knocking over anyone who got in his way, yelling cowabunga or something like it so as to indicate he was just playing the game that they themselves had started. Then he would bust straight out of the house and keep going to the nearest cliff, where he would hurl the jar as far as he could so they would have no hope of ever finding it.

But these would be desperate gambits for low-probability situations. The likely thing is that nothing would happen, so he left the bathroom with a reasonable amount of sneaky confidence. His step looked more jerky than jaunty, partly because he couldn't decide whether to whistle or not, so he just made his mouth into a small 'o', sucked air into it, and pushed it back out in a shallow way. He did have some sweat on his upper lip. Almost immediately upon entering the corridor, he saw Northrop Hindlips leaning against the wall with an exaggeratedly pained expression on his face. He had been waiting for the bathroom.

"At last," was all he said, but he looked Fontoon up and down with a faintly ironic expression, seeming to linger just slightly on the towel-draped arm. Fontoon, his mouth still in its indecisive 'o' position, raised his eyebrows and ducked his head around playfully, as if dodging imaginary punches. He winked at Hindlips, worrying nevertheless that the older man's gaze seemed to fall once again on the suspicious towel. What's the matter? Never seen a towel before, never seen an arm? Never seen someone carry something out of a bathroom before? Unable to mind your own business? Nothing better to do than stare suspiciously at what everyone else does? How dare you stare at my arm, you lunatic. I ought to bash you over the head.

Perhaps it was just his nerves betraying him. He changed his suddenly ridiculous 'o' shape into a thin, cold smile and walked hurriedly past Hindlips toward the basement door. Was Hindlips actually pausing there now, there by the bathroom door? Spying? Waiting to see where he was going? Thinking there was something fishy about his towel-draped arm? Deciding there might be something in it, something amusing, something dirty? Northrop Hindlips was a busybody and a bastard. But no, Fontoon decided as he walked through the sitting room; this was paranoia. Mustn't give any credence to this kind of thinking or it would turn into full-blown rage and then incipient madness, thence into burgeoning... no, no, must stomp such ideas down into the dirt before they can sprout. Their unfurling little green heads might...

"Admiral, Admiral!" came Irina's voice from up the stairs. What now? What did she want? Why now?

"Just a moment, darling."

Had he really said that? He could never pull off the word

'darling' that way. Anyone could hear that, it would be painfully obvious. Everyone must despise him. What was he doing here among these wolverines anyway?

"There you are, Admiral," said Irina, gracefully appearing at the bottom of the stairs. "Honestly! Where can you be going? What are you doing?"

"Nothing," said Fontoon. "Just going about my business, I'm in the middle of something, would you like a full report? What is it?"

"This must be your poetic temperament at work," said Irina. "Touchy touchy. I just wanted some help dressing. Could you zip me up dear?"

She turned her unzipped back to him, all bra strap and little black dress. There was no conceivable way to say no, yet no conceivable way to do it with only one hand. He would have to put the jar and towel down.

"Of course," he said, feigning relaxation. He placed the jar, still wrapped tightly in the towel, down between his own two feet. He gripped the package tightly with his ankles and helped Irina with her zipper.

"Thank you, darling," she said, and she knew how to use the word. "You're a little highly strung. Shall I arrange some gin?"

"No thank you. Not just now."

"Come smoke a cigarette with me."

"I can't."

"Don't be silly, of course you can."

"No!" he said, too loudly, picking up his towel bundle jealously. He called over his shoulder as he hurried away, "I've got something to do... something poetic!"

That went well, thought Fontoon, as he hustled through the ballroom, where he caught the eye of Dizzie Dezzaro. Dezzaro was lying down in the middle of the grand carpet.

"Admiral, Admiral!" cried Dezzaro weakly. "Please help me!"

Damn. Perhaps Dezzaro could be ignored. But what if he was seriously injured? There seemed to be nobody else within earshot. Fontoon looked wildly around for Irina, but she had retreated back up the stairs. What if only he could help? What if it was a matter of life and death?

"Erm," said Fontoon quietly, "are you all right, Dizzie?"

"No," replied Dezzaro. "Help me. I beg you."

Fontoon sighed, and ventured reluctantly closer to the fallen aristocrat.

"What's the matter?" he inquired.

"The drapes ripped," said Dezzaro, who had been swinging on them. "I'm sure I've twisted my ankle."

"Are you sure?" said Fontoon, inching away again and tightening his grip on his towel-wrapped jar. "Give it a little shake. Try to walk it off."

"Impossible," said Dezzaro. "I'm completely crippled. I need some sort of bandage, something to wrap it up tightly with."

"OK," said Fontoon. "I'll go have a look around."

"That towel!" said Dezzaro. "It's perfect. Please. Let me have it."

"Impossible," said Fontoon, his knuckles whitening around his bundle. "It's filthy."

"It doesn't look that bad," said Dezzaro, squinting at the towel.

Fontoon's mind raced. Obviously people in dire need of help had to take precedence over hiding jars of personal shame. Yet there had to be a way out.

"Oh dear me," came Irina's voice from behind. "What's all

this?"

"Trouble?" added Northrop Hindlips, sauntering up.

"The Admiral won't give me his towel," said Dezzaro, sounding as if his feelings had been hurt.

A veritable crowd of Buhongo regulars was assembling behind Admiral Fontoon, all Gin Fizzes and ironic half smiles and casual leanings against walls. Two things were clear: Dezzaro had hurt himself, and Fontoon was in charge. The others were content to watch the drama unfold, so they made themselves comfortable.

Fontoon began visibly to sweat. He told himself to get serious, that a man in pain needed his help. This was a crucial, decisive moment, in which he had to act like an idealised, manly version of himself and cast aside petty personal humiliations. These are the moments that define a life, he told himself. Action moments. These moments ought to be embraced, one ought to have prepared for them.

He stood up. In a few seconds many thoughts bounced around his head like tiny grasshoppers. He thought about starting right out then and there in his gravest voice with 'Look, what I have here is a jar of somebody's shit' or 'For god's sake, somebody take this horrid jar, this man is seriously injured', as if it were everyone else's fault that Dezzaro was injured and it had something to do with them being somehow irresponsible about the jar. It also flashed through his mind that if anyone asked any questions about it he would brush them aside with an impatient 'not now' as if they had a lot of growing up to do, asking questions about crap when human health was at stake before their very eyes.

Or maybe somehow in the confusion he could somehow quietly suggest that it was Dezzaro's jar, but that nobody should mention it ever again so as not to embarrass the injured and obviously mentally impaired man.

Maybe he could suggest that, although Dezzaro might not even realise it himself, he had been poisoned and this repulsive jar contained his last desperate hope. Fontoon had hoped to spare Dezzaro the embarrassment, but he strongly felt that clues to finding the proper antidote could only be discovered by an expert analysis of this stool sample, which Fontoon had managed to obtain, and he'd prefer not to go into the details if everyone didn't mind. Fontoon shuddered as he imagined the part of the story where the scientist looked up and said, 'But this is not the BM of an Italian man!' No, this was all getting too elaborate.

"Of course the Admiral will give you the towel, Dizzie," said Irina. "Admiral, I think your towel would make poor Dizzie feel so much better. You don't mind do you?"

He still didn't know what he was going to say as he inhaled, but by the time he exhaled he knew what to do and it came out naturally.

"My good men," he said to the two nearest servants, frowning imperiously, inwardly marvelling at how authoritative he had managed to sound already. "This man is grievously injured and towels aren't going to help him. Take him to the couch and lay him there. Do it gently. One of you get some fresh water; the other, a cold compress. Everyone else, as you were, don't crowd him. Make way, I know exactly what he needs. Wait for me in the sitting room."

With that Fontoon shouldered his way through everybody, holding his bundle like extruding intestines, turned down a short corridor, and disappeared down into the basement. Proceeding at once to a certain spot on the back wall, he quickly uncovered a hole behind some loose bricks and pushed his jar into its furthest recesses. He wanted to take a few moments to admire the other jars there but he fought off the urge. That, surely, would be excessive. It was out of the question. He replaced the bricks and patted them, enjoying their cold flat feel and his own feeling of supreme relief.

He looked around quickly for any object that might serve as the thing that he said he knew Dezzaro needed. Anything remotely plausible would do. Something vaguely medical would be ideal of course, if there happened to be a stethoscope lying around. A thermometer. Perhaps an old Erlenmeyer flask. But there wasn't much time. Not the dusty drill. Not the sticky empty liquor bottles. Nothing in the laundry pile. Not a brick or some nails or a can of paint thinner. No. Nothing here at all. He would hope that nobody would remember that he had said he would bring exactly what Dezzaro needed, and if anyone brought it up he would say quite simply that he could not find what he was after. If pressed to identify the thing by some nosy buttinsky posing as someone who wanted to help, he would smile distantly in a haughty way, invoking unquestionable superiority, and say that it didn't matter.

Meanwhile, the others paused a moment to marvel at Fontoon's projected sense of command, and then they did as they were told. This was the Fontoon they had always really wanted without realising it themselves – Admiral Fontoon, Fontoon the Leader. Everyone couldn't help but smile. The servants briskly got after their assignments. Irina smiled her forthright smile, well pleased by Fontoon's behaviour, and led everyone behind the servants into the sitting room where they could assume poses around the wounded man at discreet and elegant distances.

"OK, where are we?" said Fontoon, returning. "Water? Good, excellent. Cold compress, very good, very good. So, you've all had a good look at him, what do you think of our patient?" Fontoon momentarily fancied himself a rather grand doctor from another century, the sort that would have a pocket watch.

"Did you find what you were looking for?" It was Marilyn de Ponze. What an annoying, terrible woman.

"Doesn't exist," said Fontoon, affecting a certain careless impatience, maintaining his airs. "Let's have a closer look at him."

Fontoon sat on the arm of the couch upon which Dizzie Dezzaro lay and put his hand gently on the man's forehead. Dezzaro moaned. Everyone's attention became more focused and some leaned physically forward. Fontoon rolled up Dezzaro's trouser leg and frowned at his ankle. He had kept the towel.

"Did you really think this would help you?" said Fontoon with mock severity, shaking the towel at Dezzaro's head.

"Well, I..." began Dezzaro, confused. "I, I don't know, I..."

"There's nothing wrong with this man," declared Fontoon suddenly, standing up. "Not physically. Get up, man. Walk!"

"Really?" said Dezzaro, looking at all the pleased faces staring at him from around the room. "I don't know..."

"He'll walk all right," said Fontoon. "When he's good and ready. *In his mind.*"

With that, Fontoon strode out of the room and towards his quarters, to the sound of spontaneous applause. There followed in his wake a moment of 'what now', only natural after such an unusual disturbance. Nobody could quite remember what they would ordinarily be doing at that time of day. It was loose ends all around as the room teetered on the edge of the void.

"Pink Ladies?" offered Northrop Hindlips.

"A beautiful idea," agreed Irina.

Within the hour, everyone was delightfully inebriated and

Dizzie Dezzaro had found the inner resolve to get up and dance around the room to great acclaim. He didn't have a twisted ankle after all; Fontoon had accidentally been right. However, Dezzaro was exhausted by the very notion of physical injury, and soon fell into a chair and thoughtful reverie, pondering the events of the day. Fontoon and that towel, there was something odd about it. Hmm. The room was spinning a bit, and Dezzaro shook his head to ward it off.

"Are you all right, love?" asked Marilyn de Ponze.

Dezzaro inhaled and exhaled dramatically. "Ahhh, yes, yes, yes," he said, smiling lazily and openly admiring the bony chest of Marilyn de Ponze. "I'm absolutely grand."

His smile spreading into something of a grin, Dizzie Dezzaro stood up and bowed deeply.

"If you'll excuse me," he said. Then he turned, walked out of the room, proceeded down the short corridor, opened a certain door, and descended giddily into the basement. Just for a bit of a peek round. No particular reason. An intuitive sort of thing.

Chapter Doreen

Bob and Emily Perkins and their daughter Doreen had pulled up chairs to sit around the radio, as was their habit. Bob had taken on the job of always getting the snacks ready; they had to have snacks at radio time. Tonight everybody got their own little bowl of strawberries – Bob had his drenched in cream – and two little squares of organic chocolate. After that, if anyone was still hungry, Bob would get back up and make some toast with optional jam. He'd always cut the crusts off for Doreen; she still didn't like crusts. Bob distributed the treats and settled into his seat just as the theme music got underway. 'Fontoonery' was about to begin. The Perkins family never missed it.

Doreen was eleven years old. She was plump, wore unfortunate glasses, and was slightly knock-kneed. Her mousy brown hair hung straight down around her head. She looked out at the world from her little brown eyes and felt timid, and she spoke timidly. She had one friend at school but mostly she got made fun of. One of the boys was particularly cruel. He called her names and made a round puffed-out-cheek face when he looked at her. A few people always laughed when he did it, and Doreen's face always went red and she felt like a great big nothing.

By the time they got to their toast – Bob had his with jam – Admiral Fontoon was well into the subject of greed and violence, considering how much of it was technically necessary from a resources perspective.

"How much wealth," he was asking, "can any one person actually use?"

"That's a good point!" said Emily. "After the first few million, how much do you really need to feel like you're all right?"

"Seriously," said Bob. The two of them looked fondly at Doreen. Doreen looked back at them.

"I've got a surprise for you," said Bob when the show was over and he had cleaned up their small plates and bowls from snack time.

"What is it?" said Doreen.

"Tickets," said Bob.

"Tickets to what?" said Doreen. Emily looked at her knowingly and smiled.

"The 'Hey Morning!' show," said Emily, full of excitement. "Admiral Fontoon is going to be on live, with a panel of four gigantic pop stars and a former dictator from South America!"

"We're all going!" said Bob.

"Wahhh!" said Emily. They looked at Doreen and could tell she was very pleased.

The day of the taping of the 'Hey Morning!' show, everybody got up a little extra early, got a little extra clean, had a little extra breakfast, and put on some of their favourite clothes. When they got there, they had to stand in a long queue and go through a security procedure before they were finally ushered to seats and became part of a real studio audience. There were lights and cameras everywhere. The hosts came out early before the proper show just to warm them up and get them laughing. So this was television.

Bob and Emily looked frequently at their daughter during the show, to see if she was having a good time. She was. Doreen would look up to see them looking at her, and she couldn't help but break out into a shy, happy smile. There were pop stars on the stage, bantering with Admiral Fontoon and peppering him with questions.

"So yeah, it's like, total rubbish, isn't it?" one of the pop stars was saying.

"Well," said Admiral Fontoon, "I've always thought there should be way more public transportation, and it should be done nicely. I mean, people shouldn't just tolerate public transport, they should want to wear hats for it."

"Spot on," said another of the pop stars, leading the audience in a warm round of applause.

"This man would make a good dictator!" said the former dictator, to much laughter.

"Benevolent!" said Fontoon. "A benevolent dictator!"

"Hey," said the former dictator, "I *was* benevolent! I was!"

"That's not what I heard," joked one of the pop stars. Everyone laughed even harder.

"All right now," said Smilin' Dave Poppets, the male half of the 'Hey Morning!' hosting duo. "We've got some time for a few questions from the audience. Anybody have any questions? Let's see some hands!"

Hands shot up all throughout the studio audience. There were so many things they wanted to ask.

"Admiral Fontoon, what's the largest object in the universe?"

"What am I, a scientist?" said Admiral Fontoon, to good-natured laughter. "I'd have to look it up. It's probably some kind of gas cloud!"

"Is there a God?"

"Look," said Admiral Fontoon. "There's love, magic, and the Big Bang. Isn't that enough?"

"Who's the best rock guitarist of all time?"

"Buck Dharma," said Admiral Fontoon. "Come on, ask me a tough one!"

"Overall most interesting artist?"

"I'm going to go with the patron saint of broken people, Peretz Bernstein," said Fontoon. "Very poetic kid out of Queens."

"Best general advice you could give anyone?"

"Face yourself strictly with severe eyes," said Admiral Fontoon, "and then cut yourself some slack."

"OK, OK," interrupted Smilin' Dave Poppets, as Cheeky Simpson, the shiny female half of the hosting duo, looked on smiling with her hands pressed together as if in prayer. "Let's not wear the Admiral out here. One last question. Is there one last question? Yes, this young lady right here. Hold on, honey, let me get to you with the microphone."

Doreen Perkins stood up with her mousy brown hair and spoke in front of everyone.

"Mr. Fontoon?" she said in a clear, quiet voice. "Am I" – here she hesitated – "am I pretty?"

Admiral Fontoon looked at her intently, saw her eyes, which shone with youthful vulnerability, imagined her as a newborn baby, and understood how she'd have looked in mirrors and hoped and wondered.

"What is your name?" he asked her.

"Doreen," she said shyly.

"Doreen," said Fontoon, "I've got news for you, sweetheart. You are as beautiful a thing as there is in this world."

Doreen looked up and her face shone with an enormous yet still shy smile, as the audience roared its approval. Bob and Emily hugged each other, and then hugged their daughter.

"Admiral Fontoon, ladies and gentlemen," said Smilin' Dave Poppets, clapping his hands.

"I love this guy!" said Cheeky Simpson.

There was so much fuss over Admiral Fontoon that even Yan Peng couldn't help but be aware of his activities, even after he lost his Firebrand Arm and much of his zest for life during his fight to avenge his master's death.

Chapter Love

Peter Gramlinson had been young once too, and married, and with babies. He and Giacinta had been very much in love.

Giacinta had dark hair and dark eyes. If she hadn't been haughty, Gramlinson could never have married her. Her eyes were capable of flashing, as if they had been plucked from a Russian novel. If she found something funny, for long moments it seemed that time would freeze, her deep dark eyes widening and widening until finally laughter burst out of them, as if from a cage. When she was merry she lifted all hearts within her event horizon. When she was offended, everything that couldn't harden would wither under her cruel half smile.

The Gramlinson of then was not the Gramlinson of now. For example, he could laugh in two startlingly different ways, but in only one way at a time; he could speak in several voices, but not all at once.

The problem was that both Gramlinson and Giacinta embodied irresistible will and immovable stubbornness. Both were hypersensitive to perceived slights. Neither could ever yield, neither could offer the first olive branch, neither had the inclination to consider another point of view. Both laid claim to the moral high ground in all matters. All wounds were eternal. All insults were interpreted in the least generous possible manner. Forgive? Never. Forget? Not on purpose.

Arguments would begin between them slowly, warily, and occasionally could be skilfully defused before reaching critical mass. When diplomacy failed, however, indignation and silent rage would ensue for days, sometimes weeks, occasionally months at a time. And now years.

The final break began on a Monday. On Monday evenings, it was Gramlinson's habit to meet with senior underlings in a local café and manage the process of expanding his shadowy influence. Giacinta would mind the children. Giacinta was an artist, and there were times she reserved for herself too, where it was Gramlinson's turn to watch the children. In short, family responsibilities were shared out according to a certain schedule. However, sometimes special deadlines or unexpected events would force a change; schedules might have to adapt accordingly.

Giacinta worked mostly in papier-mâché and dead media. Her work was in demand in those days, and she found herself at times working more than she wanted. Giacinta believed in work-life balance. She tried not to let her work intrude into the precious hours she reserved for family and pure pleasure. However, sometimes, despite her best efforts, work would spill beyond its boundaries.

The weekend before the Monday in question, Giacinta had informed Gramlinson that her work had piled up. She was tempted to break one of her cardinal rules and spend part of the weekend on a commissioned piece for the lobby of a philanthropic organisation. Knowing how she felt about working on weekends – and being jealous of the implications for his own time – Gramlinson had encouraged her to delay the project, to ignore it, to stand on principle and enjoy the weekend. Time was precious. Work will always try to intrude and a line must be drawn and drawn firmly. Giacinta had agreed.

The deadline, however, had not changed. They both knew that. The work would have to be done sometime, and in the very near future. Their shared agreement to shift it from the weekend was a pact; they were together, bonded by love and respect.

"Well, I better get going," Gramlinson had said that Monday evening, wiping the last bits of his dinner from his lips and chin with the cloth napkin he kept at hand during every meal.

Giacinta pierced him with a wounded look. She didn't have to speak. Gramlinson understood. She had work to do. She was under a lot of stress. She had been hoping that he wouldn't go, that he would stay home and look after Glynnis and Gwen so that she could spend the evening catching up with her project so as to make her deadline. She had been hoping he would not leave her on her own in the cold.

She hadn't actually so much as articulated this expectation. She hadn't thought it necessary, yet Gramlinson felt pricked. Surely a bit of communication would go a long way at these times. Flexibility was good, flexibility was necessary, but communication was the key. He wasn't a mind reader. Not yet.

On the other hand, it was clear that he ought to stay home. There was no other way, not now. Perhaps if he had been more of a gentleman and cared about his beloved more... but why should it all fall on him? He had not agreed to the deadline and he had not failed to manage the necessary work. Now it was impacting on his own time and he was expected to make all the adjustments. So. He would be the selfless one. Again.

He snorted, just slightly, before speaking, but when he spoke it was with cheerfulness. When making a decision to acquiesce, Gramlinson knew very well, it was humiliating to do so begrudgingly. The way to acquiesce is instantly to embrace the new direction wholeheartedly. Anything less would be a half measure. Peter Gramlinson did not deal in half measures.

"Ah!" he said, clearing away some dishes and narrowing his eyes. "Of course, of course. I've been a fool. Naturally there's no question of me going. You must work on your project. You'd have done it at the weekend if I hadn't prevented you. I'll watch the girls. Let me just clear these dishes away."

But it was too late. Giacinta had heard only the small snort. There was nothing in his bag of tricks, no matter how subtle, that she did not know intimately, just as he knew all her manoeuvres. He was treating her like a child now. The snort simultaneously permitted and ruined his so-called generosity.

How dare he, thought Giacinta. So I am free to accept subservience, free to put myself into your debt. Thank you very much indeed, but I decline. You have made it impossible now for me to work. I will not work now under any circumstances. Go. Go to your café.

Gramlinson, too, had been offended. So he had been neither loving enough nor clever enough to have cancelled his Monday plans at once, in advance. But had he not immediately grasped it at the critical moment? Could Giacinta not have matched his effort to create a gracious façade, even if prefaced by a small snort of her own? Two snorts could cancel each other out, could be silently acknowledged and then ignored.

Did she have to be so clumsy, so theatrically wounded? For that matter could she not have simply asked him not to go? It all could have been so straightforward, a question, an answer, an agreement, but no. Giacinta was offended, and her being offended in turn offended Gramlinson. Little Glynnis and Gwen, one a toddler, the other not quite walking, sat blinking in the mute and icy bitterness of that kitchen.

"Go!" cried Giacinta all at once, in multiple layers. All was lost.

"I'm not going," said Gramlinson quietly.

Their evening was a long one. Gramlinson stayed home. To leave in anger would cede the high ground and make it once again clearly his fault that Giacinta could not do her project. By staying, the choice was hers. She could work, or not.

She persisted in her fury. She did not work on her project; she could not. Doing so would be tacit agreement to Gramlinson's emotional blackmail. She would only be doing it at his pleasure, by his grace, in the face of his obvious resentment. No. If he could not see it himself, desire it himself, share of himself freely out of love, then it was nothing. Worse than nothing. She would not accept it.

So it was that neither of them did what they wanted to do. Instead, all evening they competed in the arena of who could care most sensitively for the children.

When, a week later, Gramlinson was observed rolling his eyes at the lengthy and fastidious manner in which Giacinta bathed the children when she knew Gramlinson was in a hurry to leave the house, Giacinta dried, powdered, massaged, oiled, and dressed the girls, and took them out of the house. They never came back.

That was many years ago now.

Chapter Work

Kent liked saying it: 'Yeah, I work for a nonprofit organisation. Goody-two-shoes type of stuff.' 'Yeah, we do environmental stuff, focus on healthy children.' It gave him some high ground. People always responded with respect, sometimes envy. Kent didn't have a stupid job he did just for the money; he had a job that sounded like it actually made a difference.

Sitting in his office, dressed in business casual except for Fridays, which were completely casual, Kent had a computer and a coffee cup that got rinsed every two days or so but never truly washed. Very little was asked of him. He had plenty of time. If he didn't have to go to staff meetings, they might not even know he was there. He hated staff meetings. Everyone gave reports and he was forced to emit a lot of nonsense.

The phone rang. Kent answered it.

"Kent, man, it's me. How the hell are you?"

"Admiral!" he said. "How am I? How about you? You're everywhere. What the hell is going on?"

"I don't know," said Fontoon.

"Seriously, it's amazing. I didn't know you had this kind of mojo. Your career has really taken off! Aren't you coming out with a poetry book too?"

"No. I mean, yes. It's... not quite finished, but..."

"You are so sorted, it's disgusting. When are we going to shoot some pool?"

"That would be great. You have to come up to Buhongo, they have a great table here. I don't know how much you'd like it actually."

"Why not?"

"I don't know."

"Man, you are really living the life. Really living it."

Arlene stuck her head through Kent's doorway. Arlene had hair in a shape from another era and pursed her lips. She wore a lot of blouses.

"Staff meeting, Kent," she said. "Five minutes."

Kent crushed the pencil he had been holding in his hand with such force that the graphite in it turned into a super-hard substance very closely resembling diamond. This he tossed onto his desk, and watched it slowly return to soft powdered graphite at normal atmospheric pressure.

Arlene had the capacity always to seem busy. If she wasn't organising a workshop of project partners, she was preparing reports for funders, and if she wasn't doing that, then she was meeting with big shots, or tippy-tappy typing on her computer, or closing her door importantly and talking on the telephone, or circulating memos.

"Bad time?" said Fontoon.

"Staff meeting," said Kent. "But we should get together. Possible?"

"Definitely. I'll be in touch. In the meantime, man, could you do me a favour?"

"Sure."

"Don't know when I'll get back to the apartment. Would you be able to check my mail for me? Water my plants?"

Kent assured his friend that he would do so. After hanging up, he went to the little kitchenette, ran some water in and out of his coffee mug, and filled it up out of the coin-operated coffee machine.

Kent didn't like being among the first in the room,

twiddling his thumbs waiting for a meeting to start, so he made sure always to be one minute late. The usual procedure was followed in which everyone gave a brief update on their recent activities. Everyone sounded like they really had recent activities that promised to keep the grant monies flowing. Key figures within relevant departments of critical government agencies had been spoken to; responses had been received from workshop invitees; concept papers had been circulated among chummy contacts at major foundations; technical talk about data was bandied about.

Finally, Arlene folded her white, veiny hands together, made a sickly little smile, and said with almost imperceptible scepticism: "Kent?"

Kent had done nothing since the last meeting thirty days ago and had nothing to report so he began to spew imprecise blather about draft proposals and getting key partners on board. Arlene seemed unimpressed until Kent remembered to talk about sustainability. Arlene loved that word.

Arlene nodded happily when she heard it. She unfolded her hands and the blue veins pulsed with pleasure. She proceeded to share a few ideas about how the office could use less paper.

Later on, Kent was having lunch with Burnsley down in the staff lunch room. Both of them were habitual brown-baggers, and when they didn't brown-bag, they went Chinese.

"Man," said Burnsley. "Do I ever hate staff meetings."

"Me too," said Kent. "At least you do cool stuff and have actual work to report."

"Complete bullshit," said Burnsley. "I spend at least seven hours a day downloading music and playing games."

"Seriously?"

"Hell yes."

"But your data re-envisioning..." said Kent.

"Takes me a half hour a day."
"Uh huh. So that leaves half an hour."
"Lunch," said Burnsley, waving a tuna sandwich at Kent Peterson. "A man's gotta eat."

Chapter Tremble

Downstairs in the kitchen, an incredulous Marilyn de Ponze examined a jar that had been handed to her by Dizzie Dezzaro, who stood by with his hands on his hips in sadistic triumph. Marilyn held the jar with the thumb and ring finger of one hand, using the nail of the index finger of the other hand to steady it, her other fingers arching delicately away. In other words she was holding it in such a way as to ensure that the smallest possible number of finger cells came in contact with the jar.

"Well," said Dezzaro. "What do you think?"

"Is it really..." she began.

"I believe so," said Dezzaro.

"But how..."

"What else could it be?"

"I have no idea. How grotesque."

"Yes, a genuine personal atrocity. An unbelievably good find."

"Eh, what's the scuttlebutt?" broke in Northrop Hindlips, just entering the kitchen looking for some bitters to add to his gin. He stopped dead in his tracks when he saw the jar. "Jar of dog's business is all. Probably from the war."

"Well, we were thinking it might be something rather more interesting actually," said Marilyn, handing Hindlips the jar and glad to be rid of it.

"I say," said Hindlips. "I see what you mean, but I don't know what you're getting at."

"Exactly," said Dezzaro.

"Pink Ladies anyone?" Irina had slinked into the room suggestively, one slender leg at a time. She always looked like she had more legs to slink in with should the need arise. She was only showing you the first two.

"Absolutely," said Dezzaro. "Come here, luscious, and have a look at this."

"How perfectly fantastic. Where did you find it?"

"Hidden in the basement, behind some bricks in a hole in the wall."

"Amazing."

"The basement you say?" said Northrop Hindlips. "I say we just get rid of it. I mean it's not a done thing, is it?"

"Well," said Marilyn. "It's a thing. And it's been done."

"By someone," added Irina, idly admiring her own left ankle.

"It wasn't me," shouted Northrop Hindlips. "I swear it!"

The invisible omni-connecting tendrils of the all-feeling universe trembled.

Chapter Busted

"I can explain!" he began, as Irina and the others crowded around. Then he broke down in tears, exposed at last. "No, I can't. It's just weird and disgusting and I don't know why I do it. I've just always found it fascinating. I've been doing it since I was little. I'm sure I'm the only one in the whole entire world. I'm the only one, the weirdest man in the world. Oh the loneliness. Oh god, I've never been so ashamed."

"I never imagined it was you," said Dizzie Dezzaro, amazed. "So you've been jarring your business since you were little?"

"Yes. Ever since I can remember. I've always done it and I've always been ashamed, and now that it's out in the open, it's funny but I feel strangely relieved. Maybe now I can stop. At least there won't be any more hiding."

"No, Northrop," said Irina, her exquisite hands on his shoulders. "No more hiding."

"You must all think I'm so bizarre," continued Hindlips. "It's just, perhaps you've never really studied them, probably not, but once you've got one in a jar and really had a chance to look at it closely, watch it change over time..."

"You begin to fall in love with it?" ventured Marilyn de Ponze.

"No, no, no," he objected. "Don't be insane. Christ. No, it's just strangely fascinating. That's all."

"I see," said Irina. "I'm thinking Whisky Sours."

"Thank god," said Dizzie Dezzaro.

Fontoon

The servants were in motion at once and the thing was done.

"Well," said Hindlips, knocking back his drink in one go. "There can be no question of me staying on now."

"No," said Irina. "I suppose not."

"It might be a bit awkward," agreed Marilyn. "With all of us knowing your horrid secret."

"It's not that we're asking you to leave, of course, Northrop," added Irina. "But we can certainly understand your position."

"The humiliation," specified Dizzie Dezzaro.

"Indeed," said Hindlips, standing up and putting on his hat with as much dignity as he could manage. He shook Dezzaro's hand, kissed Marilyn on both cheeks as she scrunched up her face in a disgusted manner, and gave Irina a long hug. "Please say goodbye to the others for me."

"But where will you go?" asked Irina.

"To the continent," he replied. "I have rooms there."

With that, Hindlips strode out of the room, down the long corridor, through the front door, and into a waiting Hispano-Suiza, which struggled through the mud and along the escarpment before vanishing into the distance.

The others were still in a daze, holding their drinks in silence, when Admiral Fontoon walked in and saw the offending jar on the table in their midst. He actually had to grab onto the back of a chair for support because of all the blood rushing to his face in shock. So. He had been discovered. At last. There was only one thing to do.

"Ah, our dear Admiral," said Irina, and Fontoon read all kinds of insinuations into it.

"If it looks like that's a jar of shit on the table," said Dizzie Dezzaro, "that's because it is."

Fontoon took a deep breath.

"I can explain," he began.

Chapter City

Stickyman was almost home, at last. He was dog tired, figured he'd stop and rest a while. Just perch there on some wall and look around. Take in the sights of the city. Try to forget about the insults of the day. Just do a little breathing.

Man, what a beautiful city. Gorgeous. That skyline at night takes your breath away every time, as long as you remember to notice it. All those buildings, all those lights.

The tops of the tallest buildings poke right into the bellies of the low clouds. There's that zone where the clouds begin where you can still see the lights before they are entirely obscured, you can still see them, but they're all fuzzy, fading upwards into the heavens, the very top invisible. Stickyman loved that. It wasn't so much that humanity had raised its citadels so high that they could touch the sky. No, it was more like the sky had found the futile effort poignant, had condescended to lean down and kiss the world, creating beautiful mystery at the interface.

So many people. So much diversity. So many different people feeling so at home in so many different neighbourhoods, but all within a few blocks of each other. That city mix of music coming out of windows, groups of people laughing, the odd shout, a siren fading in and out, the noise of silverware on plates coming out of restaurants. Stickyman closed his eyes and listened.

So many shadows. So much danger. Frightened people, raised up all twitchy, predatory, hair-trigger personalities, seeking advantage, seeking weakness, bloodsuckers, vampires. Just accidents, crimes, horrors, waiting to happen. Waiting and biding time, hanging out, shooting the breeze, waiting for the shadow, the moment, the hunger, the silent gap, the lashing out, the shriek.

Beautiful, beautiful, all of it beautiful. Beautiful sadness, beautiful tragedy, beautiful pain, beautiful babies gone twisted, gone lonely. At least from up here, on the wall, everything beneath the lights, it's all beautiful, all part of the tapestry. *Maybe I'm just tired.* Sadness is beautiful. One can imagine peace. One can at least imagine the freedom of nothingness, the release. No pain lasts forever. Forever is a beautiful thing. Imagine it: forever.

Maybe I should quit trying to be a hero. It is, let us be honest, stupid. Absurd, in the stupidest possible way. If there is some strange honour in striving, just striving, it is surely overwhelmed by the intense personal madness of persisting in certain futility. We knit our lives around ourselves, make ourselves a little cocoon, become familiar with all its little contours, its little rules, its little rationalisations, its little routines. We make up our own little games, getting everything in our cocoon to be internally consistent, make our excuses when it isn't, never even realising: internal consistency is nothing! What we want is consistency with reality! We go off track, we go following some random trailing branch, spiralling off god knows where, and don't even realise how weird we've become. Nobody tells us. There's nobody to tell us. What are we really attached to? We're attached to nothing. Internal consistency is everything. It's all we have. And if we don't have that, then it's what we don't have. Tangled masses of unresolved ambiguities, each in our own weird little worlds. That's us.

Take it light, take it light. We're only human.

I need some sleep. God, I love this city. Just listen to it. Gorgeous. I want to hug everyone, so tightly I absorb them, become them, inhale them, all of them all at once. I want to tell them it's all right.

I have to quit being Stickyman. It's ridiculous. Who am I kidding?

Stickyman was still pondering the question of whom he was kidding when he heard the crashing smash of breaking glass.

Chapter Crashing Smash
of
Breaking Glass

Kent Peterson wrangled the invitation, but had received it with dread. First, he had agreed to take in Fontoon's mail and water his plants while he was off at Buhongo. He had heard the anguished screams of Pig Stankpool coming out of the apartment across the hall; it had made him feel ill at ease. He had felt like a hypocrite, working for Eco-Child, supposedly caring so much about sustainability and the future of the world's abstract and imagined children, while standing by and doing nothing to help the very real child inhabiting his own world. So he went out of his way to speak with Ed Stankpool one day when he saw him coming down the hall.

"Hi," Kent had said brightly. "I'm Kent Peterson, Fontoon's friend."

"Ed Stankpool," Ed Stankpool had said, holding out his hand.

The two men shook hands. Kent tried to be gentle, but Ed winced. Kent always had that problem. A lot of people's first impression of Kent was that he was one of these try-to-crush-your-hand types of macho jerk-offs. It fed into Kent's sense of personal stupidity.

"I work with kids," Kent had said in what was pretty much a lie. He didn't work with kids. He worked *about* kids. Still, it was a good wedge.

"Oh yeah?" Ed had replied, narrowing his eyes into half-formed suspicions.

Kent wasn't sure where to go now. He wanted to get in there and have a chance to talk to Pig, a chance to see the family in its natural setting, get a sense of the family dynamic, but he couldn't just say 'I'd like to drop by some time to make sure you're not abusing your son.' Then he had an idea. A new lie.

"Yeah, actually, we're kind of doing surveys of families in the neighbourhood, getting opinions, trying to get a handle on people's needs, that sort of thing. Would you be willing to participate by any chance? I could drop by some evening, we could just have a sort of a chat, wouldn't take too long?"

"Nah," Ed had responded. He had left it at that. A lot of people felt the need to come up with excuses when they didn't want to do things. Ed wasn't one of them.

That would have been the end of it except that Marla happened to be snooping behind their front door. Marla liked having guests. It made her feel cosmopolitan.

That is why the door flew open at that moment and Marla's head had come poking out into the corridor.

"Well hah there!" she had said. "Ah thought ah heard voices out here in tha hallway. You must be that friend of that nahce Admiral Fontoon. Ah'm Marla Stankpool. Ah am deelahted to meechoo."

Marla had held out her hand. Kent had reached out and really tried barely to touch it at all, saying "Charmed." He had done well. Marla had not cried out in pain.

"You really must come over for supper one evening," she had said. "Ah think it would be very nahce for our Pig to spend some tahm with a real gennelman."

"Aaaaiiiieeeeegghhhh!" came from within the apartment.

"Tuesday naht?" Marla had said.

Fontoon

And now Tuesday had come, and Kent had the feeling he always had when he made any sort of appointment, namely, he wished he did not have to go. But he generally did go anyway, so now he found himself sitting at the Stankpool dinner table, Ed across from him, Marla to his right, Pig to his left. In the middle of the table was Marla's special meatloaf, made with ketchup.

"Well, let us say grace," began Marla. "It's the civilahzed thing to do. Would you lahk to say the grace for us tonaht, Kent?"

"Umm..."

"Hell with that, let's jest dig in," said Ed, reaching over and getting a big serving spoonful of mashed potatoes into the air before his hand got slapped down by Marla.

"Now, Ed," said Marla testily, "you know we always say grace before supper."

"Yer lyin' Marla," said Ed. "And you know it."

Marla blushed. She had got it into her head that nice people said grace before supper and she had wanted to impress Kent Peterson with their manners.

"Oh that Ed, he's always forgettin' his manners," said Marla as Ed continued helping himself.

"Fat-ass bitch," mumbled Ed.

"What was that, Ed?" said Marla threateningly.

"Nothin'," said Ed.

"Good, cuz ah lahk a little decorum at the supper table," said Marla. "Don't you lahk a little decorum at the supper table, Kent?"

"Well, yes, I suppose I..."

"Fa-hass-bishhh, fa-hass-bisshhhh," mumbled Ed in a sing-songy growl. Marla gave him a stern look. Everyone was digging in now.

"Anyway," continued Marla, keeping a threatening eye on her husband even as she helped herself to a modest little pile of sweetcorn, "it shore is nahce to have a little civilahzed intercourse at the supper table now and again. Ah am so glad you were able to join us tonaht. Ah do lahk that Admiral Fontoon, you know, we have become really good friends over the past few years."

"That is pure bulldinky, Marla," said Ed. "You know that Fontoon cain't standja. He cain't stand any of us."

"Oh, well, I don't know," attempted Kent.

"See?" said Marla. "Kent knows that just ain't true. He lahks Pig, ah know he does. Doesn't he, Pig?"

Pig looked up from under his brow, chewing his meatloaf carefully, and then looked back down.

"Ah'll give him one thing, though," said Ed, surprising everyone. "Ah did lahk that show he did about what a miracle we all are on account of how darn unlahkley it is for us to get borned."

There was an awkward silence here. Ed didn't notice. He had a faraway look in his eye.

"So, Pig," began Kent at last, "how's it going? How's school? What grade are you in now, third, fourth?"

"Twelfth," said Pig. "I passed a bunch of tests. They skipped me."

"That's cool," said Kent.

"Not really," said Pig.

"You don't think so?" asked Kent.

"I'm eight," said Pig. "Everyone else is seventeen and eighteen. Think about it."

"You be nahce, Pig," warned Marla.

"It's pedagogically untenable," continued Pig. "Socially it's a nightmare. However, I try to take the long view. What I mean is my grades are still good. I'm not, like, on the basketball team or anything."

And the home life, Kent wanted to know, the home life?

"And so things on the whole," Kent emphasised, "on the whole they're OK?"

Ed broke out of his faraway look and into the conversation.

"It's not just yer daddy's spermies, that's jest the start of it," he said. "One in a shmillion makes it to the aig and all. Now that's unlahkley enough. We could stop raht there. But then you have to tahms that by yer daddy's one in a shmillion chance and yer ma's one in a shmillion chance, and then tahm's yer grandma and grandpa's, on both sahds mind, all the way back on all sahds until everbody's grandma and grandpa is a chimpanzee, and then you really have to keep going back from there too at least as far back as the beginning of animal lahf six hunnerd and senny million years ago. Now if anybody in any of the branches of the lahn that led to you didn't have the exact one in a shmillion baby they had, you don't get to exist, pure and simple. That's the lesson ah took away."

"Ed for god's sake ah am tahrd of yore nonsense about chimpanzees. Ah am not kidding with you, ah have had it!"

Ed wasn't listening. He was shaking his head dreamily.

"And people take lahf for granted," he said.

"Ed Stankpool, ah have had it with you, absolutely had it. Ah have been up since fahv ay em and ah am tahrd. Ah do and do and do for this family every day and ah cannot take this any more. Ah really cannot."

"You ain't been up but since about noon, Marla, and you know it."

"Don't you start in with me Eddie, ah am in no mood!"

"You sit up reading yer stupid magazines and then you sleep all day and flounce around in yer raggedy-ass nightgown.

That's all you did today, that's all you did yesterday, that's all yer gonna do tomorra."

"Ah have had it! Ah cain't take this any more! Ah am goin' upstairs!"

As Marla stood up dramatically and stomped off. Pig looked at Kent and rolled his eyes.

"Hold on people, hang on here a second," Kent said, desperate, with a pleading outward sweep of both hands.

He saw the look of horror on Ed's face, and initially thought it was because he had dared to intervene in a family argument. Then he heard the crashing smash of breaking glass.

Uh oh, he thought. He turned to look. The window was blasted into a million pieces. The wind was blowing in through the curtains.

Kent had accidentally knocked Pig flying through the window with his outrageously powerful arm.

Chapter Weasby

Things certainly are looking up, thought Weasby, lighting up a cigarette to Shirley's disgust as they lay languidly in bed. Weasby didn't smoke, but he'd always wanted to do that: have sex with a woman and then light up a cigarette. Indoors. That particular dream was now officially checked off the list. Suddenly he saw the look on Shirley's face. Smiling weakly, he put out the cigarette, blew his last smoky exhalation towards the open window, and thought about toothpaste.

Shirley suddenly wondered what she was doing there. True, Weasby had exhibited a very manly sense of command lately, performing his job with ingenuity and confidence. She had never thought of him as attractive, but once she got it into her head that he was cute, well, things had become a bit different. Perhaps going to bed with him was not the wisest thing she had ever done. Getting involved with someone from the office was famously ill-advised. But it was done now. Well, why couldn't a girl have a few wild times? Besides, the office is where you meet people, isn't it? What's she supposed to do, go to a bar and sleep with strangers? Weasby, at least, was a gentleman.

When they had gotten as far as the bedroom and done a bunch of smooching and it was time for the undressing bit, Shirley had let Weasby take the lead. When he put his tongue out a little bit between his teeth as he squinted at the buttons on her blouse and wrestled with them with both hands, she was determined to find it endearing. Certainly he wasn't the first man ever to have trouble with a bra clasp and she didn't mind helping him out there. Weasby had taken off his clothes with a shy little grin on his face, unfortunately leaving his socks for last, so that he stood for a few moments naked except for socks, which is a condition no man should ever allow. Then he sat down and pulled his socks off and immediately got into his pyjamas. Everything else that happened had to happen through his little pyjama hole. Shirley thought about the commendations Weasby had received at work. This was a man with a future.

Was she attracted to her boss, Mr. Bentley, as well? She tried not to admit it even to herself. Above all what she felt for Mr. Bentley was respect. She felt she had earned his respect as well for the efficient manner in which she reliably performed her duties. She didn't want him to think she was, well, a certain kind of girl. Oh, she just didn't know! Life was so complicated!

Getting the respect at work, thought Weasby, *getting Shirley – Shirley! Me! – man, this is more like it. If my mother could see me now.*

Weasby turned and tried to nuzzle Shirley with his nose but she turned away as if by reflex, repelled. She saw that Weasby looked hurt and she gave him a sympathetic smile, along with an affectionate touch on the tip of his nose with her index finger.

"You've been a busy man lately," she said playfully.

"You ain't seen nothing yet," he replied.

"Really?"

"Oh yeah. Think I'm going to rest on my laurels? Not a chance. I've got a few surprises left for old Fontoon. You can count on that."

There was the confident Weasby she had come to admire.

"What are you going to do?" she asked, coyly.

"Oh, you'll see. I'll tell you one thing though. Can you keep a secret?"

"Sure I can."

"When the dust all settles, I've got my eye on the top spot."

"Top spot?"

"Oh yeah."

"You mean..."

"That's right. Seems to me old JB's been gathering a little moss these days. I think it's time for some new blood in the company leadership."

"You're going to try to get Mr. Bentley's job?"

Weasby was really filling his boat up with pride and sailing down the river with it now.

"Sure, why not?" he said. "I've got what it takes, I know I do. After all, he wouldn't be the first old generation guy to be ousted by the up-and-coming youngsters."

Weasby was forty-seven. Mr. Bentley was forty-three.

Shirley now felt extremely uncomfortable. What had she done? It wasn't going to happen again, that much was certain. When Weasby asked her if she thought his pyjamas were silly with the sheep all over them, Shirley wasn't even listening. She felt a kind of certainty returning that she had lost recently. Her loyalties were clear. She knew exactly how she felt about this. Firstly, she would not be spending the night; it was time to call a cab. Secondly, she would be asking Mr. Bentley for a word in private.

How you like me now, Mom, thought Weasby as he turned onto his side to curl up into the foetal position. Then he thought: *Darn it. I still need to brush my teeth.*

Chapter Mom

"Fifty dolliz," said Mr. Burgleman with his hand out.

"All right, all right," said Fontoon, wearily, fishing around in his pocket and producing some crumpled paper money.

"I never known anybody lose his keys as much as you."

"I'm actually really careful."

"I bet. With careful like that you should try reckless. I'm getting rich here."

"No kidding. You could try cutting me a break once."

"I can't do that," Mr. Burgleman laughed as he walked away. "That's bad precedent. How'm I gonna put my kid through college?"

"You're all heart, Burgleman," Fontoon called after him.

"Tell it to the radio, kid," called Burgleman without looking back.

That wasn't going to happen. There wasn't any more radio. No more television. The book deal was off, thank goodness.

There was some kind of ruckus coming out of the Stankpool's apartment. Nothing new about that. Sounds like they smashed a window this time. *None of my business, thank god,* thought Fontoon.

A tupperware container sat outside his door. Fontoon picked it up and examined it as he entered his apartment. Chocolate chip cookies. His mother. He sat down at his kitchen table with the container on his lap and opened it. Freshly baked. *That was actually so nice of her.* Because he was tired, Fontoon felt poignant tears of unutterable beauty come to his eyes, thinking of her baking them, boxing them up, travelling across town, knocking on his door, shrugging her shoulders, leaving the cookies, going all the way back home. He thought he might get a good cry in and feel cleansed by it, but then the tears just kind of dried up in their tracks. *Oh well.* He ate a cookie. Then he seized his telephone and dialled a number.

"Yah?" came the voice on the other end.

"Hi, Ma," said Fontoon. "I just wanted to say, well, thank you. Thanks for the cookies. They're really good."

"I'm glad you like zem," she said. "So how are you?"

"Not great. I kind of... lost my position. It was pretty, well, pretty embarrassing."

"Yah," said his mother.

"Yah," said Fontoon.

"Zat is like life," she said.

"Right."

"Fotta you gonna do."

"Right. It happens. Gotta roll with it."

"Zat's it. You gotta roll."

"It was quite a big disaster actually, though."

"Oh vell."

"Yeah. Well, talk to you soon, Ma. Auf wiedersehen."

"Bye bye."

As Fontoon hung up the phone, a small chunk of his badly repaired ceiling fell down and hit him on the head. With nothing else to do, he thought he might as well go up and knock on old Yan Peng's door. See how his floor looked. See how his studies were going. Maybe learn a little Cantonese.

He ventured back out into the hall. The floors had turned very rubbery. It was like walking on a trampoline.

For this we pay how much a month? thought Fontoon, nearly bumping into one of the walls. The crying and wailing from the Stankpool's apartment was louder than usual. *I need to get out of this place.*

Chapter Mosura

Outside of a cave on Infant Island, the tiny Pichi fairies Emi and Yumi were singing in unison again. There had been a time – after they had been kidnapped, caged, and forced to put on musical shows for Tokyo audiences – when they lost their enthusiasm for singing altogether. For weeks after being rescued by Mosura they'd sat around glumly, still feeling humiliated by the ordeal, and just refused to sing, even after the bongos got going and started stirring up the old feelings. They'd start to speak, only to stop, look at each other, smile wanly, and return to silence. But, by and by, their joyful nature took over and reasserted itself, and within the month they were singing their special songs to Mosura again. Inside the cave, Mosura was glad.

The young woman who often took the same Orange Train as Admiral Fontoon was glad to hear them singing again too. She felt pleased as she showered now under a waterfall, with her shampoo made from the island's indigenous herbs and oils. She too was tiny, and when she sang the world shimmered.

Wrapped in a towel, the young woman floated over to Emi and Yumi and opened her mouth. Emi and Yumi opened their mouths at the same time, and they emitted simultaneous sounds of a high and melodious pitch. It was a conversation. They were complimenting each other. Emi took a comb and started running it through the young woman's hair, gently removing the tangles; the hair fell in wet ringlets to her fragile shoulders. Despite the acne scars, she was pretty. Yumi opened up a mirror out of jungle space so the young woman could tastefully apply some lip gloss and mascara. They all laughed when they saw how beautiful she looked.

The young woman suddenly glanced at her watch and gasped. It was not necessary for her to speak. She was distraught because she was running late now for work. She looked at Emi and Yumi, who offered distraught and sympathetic looks in return. What could be done? She was thousands of miles from the city, and she wasn't even dressed.

Emi and Yumi began to sing in unison once more. This time their song was more urgent. Bongos began to play from near and far and inside everyone's heads. An unseen chorus of many female voices joined in with an insistent refrain. The young woman put on some underwear and a blouse. Then she stepped easily into a pair of trousers that were far too big for her at first; but she began to grow. She grew and grew until they were impossibly tight. Making sure she had her purse, the young woman closed her eyes and let the music build and course through her.

Emi and Yumi lifted her and flew her to the top of the hill, above the cave, where it was rocky. Lightning flashed in the sky and was almost instantly followed by deafening peals of thunder. The singing only grew louder, the bongos more determined.

Finally she came out of the cave, Mosura, enormous and strange. The music grew louder still, the lightning seeming to keep time, the thunder like a giant's timpani. Emi and Yumi lifted the young woman onto Mosura's broad back, between her wings. The great beast took to the skies, slowly at first, and the winds swirled around. Once again the young woman looked at her watch and pursed her lips in concern. Then Mosura was off, beating her great wings, moving ever more swiftly, swallowed now into the clouds, and was gone.

Inside the swirling clouds there was no time, and when they came out the city was there and it was morning.

Climbing down onto the Orange Train platform, the young woman took time to thank Mosura, and was brazen enough to kiss the godlike being on the nose before it rose to return home to Infant Island, leaving the world once again in peace.

The woman surveyed the platform impatiently. Unworthiness everywhere. Would anyone speak to her? Would anyone dare?

Chapter Cantonese

"Come in, come in!" said Yan Peng on seeing his neighbour at his door. "Good to see you! *Neih hou ma?*"

"Gei hou, gei hou," said Fontoon. It meant he was doing OK.

"I'll make tea," said Yan Peng. "Come in! Sit down!"

Fontoon went in and sat down and tried to think up something to say. His eyes fell on the part of Yan Peng's floor that had been repaired. As he feared, the repairs failed to demonstrate the desired level of care and craftsmanship. The wood was poorly matched and surrounded by what appeared to be cheap spackling compound.

"Nice job on the floor, huh?" he said.

"Terrible," said Yan Peng. "I wonder about this building sometimes."

"Me too."

"By the way," said Yan Peng, returning with the tea. "I'm very sorry to hear about the loss of your radio show. It was very good."

"Oh, thanks," said Fontoon, accepting the hot tea and bringing it to his lips. Since the catastrophe was very recent, a question occurred to Fontoon. "How did you hear about that?"

"It's news," said Yan Peng. "Look."

Yan Peng picked up a copy of the *Daily News* from his coffee table and flipped a few pages into it.

"Here," he said, folding the paper and handing it to Fontoon. "Gossip pages."

"You read the *Daily News* gossip pages?" said Fontoon, feigning unconcern despite the dread he felt at looking more closely at the photograph he already saw out of the corner of his eye.

"Always," said Yan Peng.

Fontoon had not been mistaken. Half the page width comprised a lurid colour photograph of a certain familiar jar. Right next to it, comprising the other half of the page, was a photograph of a seated Admiral Fontoon with poor posture, his jaw slack, saliva pooled and spilling over the edges of his mouth. Fontoon recognised the chair; the photograph had been taken at Buhongo at one of the parties, doubtless very late at night.

Across the two photos was the enormous headline: 'HOLY $#&@!'

Admiral Fontoon put the paper back down and pushed it weakly across the coffee table.

"You should read the article!" said Yan Peng.

"Not right now, I think," said Admiral Fontoon.

"Oh," said Yan Peng, only now realising the sensitivity of the issue. "I'm sorry to have brought it up."

"No no," said Fontoon. "It's fine."

The two men sipped their tea.

"Pretty horrendous, eh?" said Fontoon out loud, after starting many sentences in his head, feeling blood rush to his head as the words came out. "I don't mean the floor."

"I know."

"I mean the..."

"The jars, I know. The shit."

"Yeah."

They sat for the next several minutes in silence. Birds outside could be heard making bird noises. The air itself seemed thick and sweet.

"And jesus," began Fontoon.

"The humiliation."

"Yeah."

"The big secret coming out. The embarrassing secret. Very personal, very freakish secret."

"Yep."

"And being asked to leave. Losing everything."

"Right."

Yan Peng paused before continuing with the question that he wanted to ask.

"So," he began. "Why do you like to put it in the jars?"

Fontoon burned with the flushing of his face and his hands trembled. At the same time he was glad of the question and the opportunity to address it out in the open. One must appreciate frankness. He felt a rage, not at Yan Peng, but at his own weirdness and at how the things you most desperately want hidden always come stumbling grotesquely out of some cellar door sooner or later. He waited a few moments before responding, only in the hope that it would give his voice a chance not to quiver.

"It's hard to explain."

"I understand. I don't mean to pry."

"No no."

"There is no need to speak of it."

"No, it's fine, we can speak of anything. It's just..."

"Hard to explain."

"Exactly."

"I understand."

The sound of breathing, and tea being sipped. An airplane noise went by overhead. Fontoon felt ruined. How different things were once a secret was out. How insane it all suddenly seemed. If only it could all be done over and more normally.

From outside, more bird sounds.

"I guess you must think I'm pretty weird," said Fontoon. After he said it he clenched his teeth.

Yan Peng looked at him thoughtfully before responding.

"It is unusual to put it in jars like this," he said. "That is what I think. And unpleasant somehow. I wouldn't want to do it. It seems unusual to me. But also I strangely understand."

"You do?"

"Yes, somehow I do. Somehow. It's a bit like stars you can only see when you don't look at them directly. Have you ever noticed that?"

"I definitely have."

"It's a bit like that. If I don't try too hard to understand it, I can understand it. Like a baby."

"Right. Babies are good at that sort of thing."

"Yes."

"It's just... I tried it once... I don't know why... just to see," continued Fontoon, unprompted. "It occurred to me to do it, so I did. And it was, I don't know, it looked so... and then to look again later, and later again, and then to see them when they're old. It's... I don't know... it's just..."

"You found it interesting."

"Exactly."

"Well," Yan Peng thought hard about how to put it. "There are so many fascinating things, and everybody is going to focus on something, and, well, there are so many possibilities. I don't think it's that strange."

"You don't?"

"No, it's not the strangest thing at all."

"Well, I'm relieved to hear you say it. It is a relief to have it..."

"Of course it would be best if it had stayed private. Hidden."
"Yes. Yes, I agree with that."
"But enough. We let it go. No more speaking of it."
"Yes, OK. We'll never speak of it again."
But we'll never forget it. Neither of us will ever forget it.
Anyway who can control what others think? The important thing is comportment. Fontoon was happy to let the matter fester silently. He couldn't know that even as they sat there and spoke, several dozens of his most non-judgemental followers were putting their own business into jars in a sort of experimental salute to the man they still admired.

It was only then that Admiral Fontoon noticed that Yan Peng was missing one of his arms. Had he always been missing it? No. No, surely this was new. Wasn't it? What if he spoke up and mentioned it and Yan Peng replied that he had never had that arm? How embarrassing it would be. Against his better judgement, Fontoon decided to risk commenting on it.

"Erm," he began, "you used to have two arms, right? Am I insane?"

"No no, you're right," said Yan Peng, looking down at his shoulder, which ended so abruptly. "Yeah. I lost one."

"Christ!" said Fontoon. "When did this happen?"

"Recently," said Yan Peng.

"You're letting me sit here and drone on about myself all this time, and you're sitting there with one arm! I can't believe I didn't even notice, I'm really sorry."

"No, I'm glad. It means I'm not drawing attention to it. It means maybe I'm not feeling too sorry for myself. Anyway it doesn't matter."

"Doesn't matter? Well come on, there has to be a story in there somewhere."

"Yes."

Fontoon

Yan Peng told him the story of how he had fought Peter Gramlinson to try to avenge his master's death, only to lose the fight along with his Firebrand Arm. He wanted to make sure that Fontoon understood that he wasn't by nature the revenge-seeking type, and that he had considered at length several other options. Yan Peng understood that life was about choices. He was aware that he did have the option to consider the matter between his master and Gramlinson closed, and no concern of his. Furthermore, avenging masters' deaths was an anachronistic concept, not merely out of fashion but arguably ridiculous. For starters, it was ridiculous even to have a master. These days they were called teachers. This was the real, modern world we lived in. Yan Peng understood that.

On the other hand, like any young and thoughtful person, Yan Peng wanted his life to have a sense of meaning. Fontoon nodded his head at this part because he shared this desire to have a sense of meaning in his own life. Yan Peng related that what bothered him about the death of his master was that, first of all, it came by trickery and deceit, and secondly that Gramlinson had gotten clean away with no consequences. He doubted very much that Gramlinson even felt guilty about it, or had so much as given it another thought. And if he was very honest with himself, Yan Peng had to admit that as postmodern as he considered himself to be, he retained a respect for tradition that was not entirely ironically detached.

Yan Peng concluded that the situation was intolerable enough to serve as a cause, which would have the additional benefit of conferring upon him a righteous sense of purpose. It seemed to him that a very singular sense of unerring purpose was a fairly rare commodity and that it would be unwise to pass this one up. It would require courage, as well, which made it seem even more worthwhile. It would be dangerous and not the sort of thing that could be fobbed off on somebody else. That was why he made the choices he had made. He would put his life on the line. Total commitment. Unfortunately he had failed miserably and been humiliated and, as already noted, deprived of an arm.

Fontoon searched for the right thing to say.

"That has to be the worst story I've ever heard in my life."

"It also might be the worst one I've heard," agreed Yan Peng.

"You gave it your best shot," said Fontoon.

Yan Peng was silent.

"At least you survived," added Fontoon.

When Yan Peng remained silent, Fontoon felt ashamed and there was more silence.

"Boy oh boy," said Fontoon at last. "What a pair we are, eh?"

Yan Peng smiled.

"Yeah," he said.

"I mean what kind of luck is that?" said Fontoon.

"Bad luck," said Yan Peng.

"Exactly. Bad luck. How do you say that in Cantonese?" asked Fontoon.

"Waaih wahnhei."

"Ngoh tuhng leih, waaih wahnhei," said Fontoon, saying 'Me and you, bad luck' because it was the first thing he could think of in Cantonese that rhymed.

Yan Peng liked the rhyme and repeated it several times.

"You've gotten very good at Cantonese," he said to Fontoon.

"Stop it," said Fontoon. "Nothing compared to your English."

"Well," said Yan Peng, "if you lived in Hong Kong, it

would be easier. You should try writing poems in Cantonese. They're sure to be amazing."

"Ha," said Admiral Fontoon.

Chapter Greatness

There's no point denying it, thought Peter Gramlinson, admiring the beauty of the perfect sphere he held in his hand. *I am great. I have greatness.*

The sphere had been carved from minerals of unknown origin and polished to a nearly luminescent glow. It had heft. It felt good in one's hand: cool to the touch, yet emanating a strange warmth from deep inside at the same time. Its value was beyond money. Gramlinson had stolen it from a secret collection of Chinese national treasures in Beijing, one of many similar stones in his possession; he just loved these things.

There was a natural urge, feeling the sphere in the palm of one's hand, to hurl it, to hurl it as far as one could, if for no other reason than to see just how far that might be. The urge was said to be nearly irresistible if the holder was standing at the edge of the sea. There were legends of the sphere changing hands many times throughout history precisely because of a sudden hurling. Gramlinson took a moment to appreciate the historic nature of this and all his other achievements.

When I think of how I started out! Just another kid from the suburbs hooked on strip malls and half-hour sitcoms. One timely intervention by a ruthless lady mobster with connections to the dark side of the martial world and hey, look at me now! Peter Gramlinson, international badass, mover of men, maker of history. Look out, world! Damn!

Is it so wrong to reflect on one's accomplishments? Let us

call it what it is, thought Gramlinson, let us call it indulging in smug superiority. There is no harm in thinking back on those who have wronged us, and savouring the precise extent to which we have surpassed them and exacted our revenge.

Jackie Zebo. Beat up a hundredth grader? Here Gramlinson laughed bitterly through his nose. The sting of humiliation hurt him even now. I suppose I taught him a lesson in the end, thought Gramlinson. How early it all starts.

Gramlinson didn't run through the entire story in his mind, but what had happened was, the seven-year-old Peter Gramlinson had rashly impugned the fighting skills of his classmate Jackie Zebo after overhearing the two prettiest girls in school say that Zebo could beat up anybody. Jackie Zebo stood about three quarters the height and half the width of an average seven-year-old, but he had a wiry and maniacal strength and most of all he enjoyed total, unquestioning self-belief. He'd race in and beat somebody up and race out before the person even realised he'd been beaten up. They'd just find themselves on the ground and say Christ, I must've been beaten up by Jackie Zebo!

Even then Gramlinson had pride and acted sometimes out of impulse. He stopped in his tracks and confronted the two girls as they sat eating plums under a maple tree during recreation.

"Beat up anybody?" he had said, full of scorn, elbowing his companion, Mark James Ewert, who was always called by his full three names. "Jackie Zebo couldn't beat up a kindergartener."

The girls were duly shocked. With one quick glance at each other, they suddenly and wordlessly stood up and ran, girlish mouths agape. They were heading off to find Jackie Zebo to report this profanation. The young Gramlinson merely laughed, albeit nervously, and continued his way with Mark James Ewert across the field in back of the school.

They had gotten quite far across the grass when suddenly a chill went down their spines. All sound melted together and became low echoes as the sky darkened overhead. Children's laughter managed to pierce through the veil of dissolved sound, as if emanating from a photograph held years away in a grandfather's trembling hand. A time-lapse thunderclap could be distinguished amid the general rumble. The world shifted into slow motion, except for the clouds, which shifted into fast motion.

From as far away as the eye could see, a tiny figure raced out of the flat scene into three dimensions. The figure raced at terrifying speed, but seemed to take forever to arrive. Peter Gramlinson and Mark James Ewert both realised at once that it was Jackie Zebo, and that he was coming straight for them. They were going to be beaten up. There was nothing they could do but wait.

For an eternity Zebo remained far away, a tiny little character with pumping legs and steam coming out of his ears, and then in an instant he was upon them. Gramlinson braced himself, not even really afraid, feeling as if he were in a dream. But the Zebo went right past him and leapt upon Mark James Ewert, who obligingly tumbled to the ground and laid in a submissive posture. Jackie Zebo mounted him and took a few slappy pokes at his face.

"Can't beat up a kindergartener, huh? HUH?!"

"You can! You can!" yelled Mark James Ewert as Gramlinson looked on in horror and relief.

"Yeah I know I can!"

"You could beat up a fourth grader!" added Gramlinson obsequiously.

"Uh huh, uh huh! You jerks!"

"You could beat up a sixth grader!" cried Mark James Ewert, raising the stakes.

"You could beat up a hundredth grader!" shouted Gramlinson, completing the debasement.

It was a seminal event in the life of Peter Gramlinson and he soon got his revenge. It was only weeks later that Jackie Zebo openly mocked Gramlinson at school over the length of his trousers. Gramlinson, still burning with hatred, responded with provocative words. Jackie Zebo ran at him to beat him up, but Gramlinson somehow grabbed hold of Zebo's arm and began simply turning round and round. He found he had rendered Zebo helpless through the use of centripetal force. Soon Zebo was crying for mercy and the two prettiest girls in school were laughing. Gramlinson bided his time, and eight years later, when they were fifteen, he dated one of the girls, only to cheat on her with the other one. The girls are no longer friends.

Am I evil? Gramlinson pondered the question and looked at his perfect mineral sphere. I guess most people would say so. If you look at all the sadism and the screwing other people over. The killing. Yeah, it starts to look bad. But I don't feel evil. I think I'm a good person. Was I bad to my family? Was I really so bad? I never raised a hand to anyone, I tried to accommodate everybody's needs. I'm not the one who left. Who's selfish? I miss my little girls. If I were evil would I miss my little girls?

Isn't it about survival? Win and survive, lose and, well, goodbye. OK: I'm not that nice. Guilty! Is it sensible to be nice all the time? All this niceness is just a bunch of idiots with a false sense of security. That's all it is. I've earned what I've got. A little power. I guess that gives me some rights. This is the real world we're living in here. Most people just don't have what it takes to face up to it and deal with it head on, in the only way that works: aggressively.

Oh man, he breathed, shaking his hand out, looking at the sphere, feeling the urge to hurl it, enjoying the knowledge that he wouldn't, enjoying his sense of self-control in that regard.

God, it would be so great just to hurl this thing! I'm dying just to hurl it! Can you imagine? Just to stand up and wing this thing away? I feel like I could hurl it a mile!

Chapter Catch

The smashing crash of breaking glass makes Stickyman look up, instinctively covering his eyes to protect against falling shards. Yep, a window got smashed up there all right. A window got smashed and something – or someone – is plummeting straight down at him. Stickyman squints upwards to try to get a better view.

A smallish figure... in fact it looks like... yes... yes it's a child! *Holy chicken sticks,* thinks Stickyman, *kid's actually going to hit...*

They say you can live your whole life in an instant. The fact is most worst nightmares don't happen, just as most dreams don't come true. But when they do, all the mundane nonsense that takes up so much time is pushed aside all at once and in that instant a man learns who he is, learns whether what he's made of is worth a damn or if he's just been living some kind of sad delusion. Moments like these, defining moments, don't come too often in a life. Maybe just once. Maybe just as the lights go out for good. Maybe every moment of our lives, every moment we push defining moments aside and defer, and ignore, and pretend, is a defining moment just the same.

Anyhow, sooner or later one of them is going to land on you like ninety-four pounds of Pig. If you're lucky, your hands will be sticky enough to catch it.

"Whoa!" shouted Stickyman on impact.

"Whoa!" shouted Pig, and they looked at each other, trying to make sense of what had just happened.

"It's OK, son," said Stickyman. "I've got you. I've got you, and you're going to be all right."

That's when he noticed a second, much larger, desperately grasping figure plummeting downward right behind young Pig. After a moment of cringing embarrassment in the Stankpool's apartment, Kent Peterson had realised over the course of perhaps two long seconds that his most earnest apologies were not going to be nearly enough this time. Kent knew what he had to do. He got up, did the short run across the apartment, and dived out of the window right after Pig.

He hoped he might catch him, shield him somehow, maybe catch onto a flagpole or some other unlikely thing, or failing that, die in the attempt. It would be better than standing there in the apartment shrugging at Ed and Marla with the wrong expression on his face. But in his adrenaline rush, he had jumped too far out of the window, and it was too late anyway.

Stickyman watched upwards as Kent Peterson sailed down towards him, well outside of sticky grabby range, watched as Kent passed him, experienced a brief moment of surreal eye contact, and then watched him go down, down, down, and... wham. Into the concrete surface of the back alley far below.

A nauseating sound.

Chapter Tea

"Eeee, Arthur," said Auntie Minnie in a small voice, "I'm dry." She had reached the end of a row and her hands had plopped into her lap.

"I'm parched, me," rejoined Uncle Arthur, groaning as he put down his newspaper and lifted himself out of his armchair to go and put the kettle on. Auntie Minnie smiled and carried on knitting. There was nothing more comforting than rituals preserved from the old country.

Soon Arthur had assembled all the bits and pieces: the teapot, with two spoonfuls of Co-op 99 in it; the cosy, ready to put on top; two teacups on two saucers; a creamer full of milk; a tea strainer, the kind that tips and has a small flat pan attached to catch the drips; a small plate with four digestives on it, two plain and two with chocolate. Shortly after arranging all this paraphernalia, the electric kettle was puffing steam, its little orange light went out, and the on-off switch automatically flipped back up to the off position. Without wasting a moment, Uncle Arthur grasped the kettle firmly, poured just the right amount of boiling water into the teapot, placed the cover on, and slipped the tea cosy over the whole business. When he brought all these things on a tray and set the tray down on the table in the living room, it was official: teatime.

"Eeee, that's a lovely cup of tea," said Aunt Minnie after her first sip, observing the unwritten rule about mentioning how lovely the tea was.

"I'm a new man," said Uncle Arthur, reaching for a plain

digestive, saving the chocolate one for last.

WHUMP!

The hideous whump sound came from just outside the window.

"Eeeeee," said Aunt Minnie, and the cup in her hand rattled so much that considerable tea was spilled over onto the saucer. Saucers are such a good idea.

Uncle Arthur set his cup and saucer down carefully. He had not spilled any, but then he was fairly hard of hearing. He went over to the window, moved the curtains aside, and lifted the lower sash. A rush of fresh, cool air came in. Why hadn't they opened the windows earlier? A lovely evening. Invigorating. Groaning could be heard.

"Ouch," said Kent Peterson from his position on the ground.

"Are you all right?" shouted Uncle Arthur, perhaps slightly louder than necessary.

Kent was slowly sitting up. He looked skywards, peering, trying to pinpoint the window he had fallen from, just to amaze himself with the distance involved. He could see Stickyman up there, looking down, holding Pig. Thank god for that, thought Kent. It had been a pretty good drop. Was anything broken? Probably not. He moved his shoulders around, clenched and unclenched his fists, bent his knees and unbent them. Yeah. Everything was fine. He was all right.

"Ask him in for a cup of tea," said Aunt Minnie.

"Would you like a cup of tea?" shouted Uncle Arthur. "I think you'll need one."

"I could murder a cup of tea," said Kent Peterson.

Chapter Meteorite

Between the last rocky planet and the first giant one made out of gas is a messy region jam-packed with asteroids. The four biggest asteroids make up about half the mass of the entire belt, and most of that is Ceres, which is thought of as both an asteroid and a dwarf planet. It is quite a bit smaller than the moon, but among the asteroids it would be known as the Big Fella.

Ceres is also, by far, the most spherical of all the asteroids. Things don't generally get to be spherical in space unless they've passed the size test: if you're big enough, your own gravity crushes you into roundness. Big enough, for a rocky object, means about six hundred kilometres in diameter. Ceres is nine fifty. No other asteroid makes the grade.

The rest of the asteroid belt comprises a ragtag bag-load of solar systemic hoi polloi, unwashed rocks of various little unimpressive sizes and irregular shapes. If you squished them all together into one unified ball, including Ceres, they'd still be smaller than the moon. They'd hardly be worth squishing.

With so many rocks floating around out there, it's not too surprising to find that they bash into each other now and then, breaking into even smaller pieces. Around and around they go, jostling in a busy orbit that would be just perfect for another little rocky planet instead of a bunch of rugged individualist mineral composites that have difficulty getting along with each other. Of course, they're not all the same and it's only natural that they divided up into rough camps. At around two hundred and fifty million miles from the sun, there's a neighbourhood dividing line. On the sunward side, the metallic asteroids spin, while their rocky cousins stick to the outer path. Even when they've been melted and mixed, they don't really integrate; you just end up with a metallic core surrounded by a rocky mantle.

However, some great beauty occurs at the interface of core and mantle when these bad boys are shattered by impacts. Pallasites, for example, consist of olivine crystals in an iron-nickel matrix. In other words, they are greenish and shiny and practically glow sometimes with reflected light. They make some of the rarest and most gorgeous of meteorites.

Meteorites are usually bits of smashed asteroid that whizz around in space after being ejected by impact from their proper orbit, and manage to hit Earth and survive intact all the way through the atmosphere to the surface. They can also be smashed bits of moon or, believe it or not, Mars. It seems tremendously unlikely, but the facts speak for themselves. Having made their escape, these little Martian ejectoids with the universe at their disposal go hither and yon, and some of them head in the general direction of Earth by virtue of Earth being in-between Mars and the sun and the sun having the most gravity of anything in the system. We are forced to accept that some of these bits run flat into Earth because Earth was in the right place at the wrong time.

In any case, there must be a lot of smashing going on out there and a lot of little whizzers, because if there weren't, then Earth wouldn't have been hit by a minimum of thirty-nine thousand, seven hundred and forty-six meteorites, and that's just the documented cases so far.

People have been hit by them.

Chapter Bacon

Admiral Fontoon's pockets certainly felt a lot lighter after he dared to give Enchanting Vendor Girl twenty-five saved-up pennies with his payment. In order to help her with this quantity of small coins, he had helpfully organised them into five stacks of five, which he placed one by one onto her small countertop. He couldn't help but notice her broad smile when he looked up.

"What would you do without me keeping you in pennies?" he said, casting the transaction in a certain light.

"I have no idea," she said, her eyes revealing only a fraction of the laughter she was feeling inside.

She likes me, Fontoon mused as he sat down on a nearby bench to enjoy his coffee and his bacon, egg, and cheese sandwich on a fresh roll. What he loved second-best was the unwrapping: peeling back the shiny foil to observe the sandwich, wrapped in an under-layer of wax paper and sliced, then separating the two halves to have that first look at how much bacon there was in there. Then the first bite. Right in the middle. Plenty of everything.

Fontoon actually closed his eyes, the better to focus his senses on the experience of chewing cheesy egg bacon in the brisk morning air. When he opened them again, he discovered that he had been joined on his bench by none other than Chase Krugley.

"I'm a vegetarian," said Krugley, affably. "Been one for many years. But I'll tell you something."

Here he paused.

"Go on," said Fontoon.

"Bacon is my weakness. I love bacon. God, is that the single best smell in the world or what?"

"I think it might be," Fontoon agreed.

"May I have a bite?"

"A bite of my sandwich?"

"If you don't mind."

Fontoon was taken aback. Of course he minded. Who likes sharing sandwiches? Krugley could see his hesitation.

"Just a small one," said Krugley, reassuringly. "It's just it looks so good. I don't want a whole one, so..."

There had to be ways of refusing gracefully but Fontoon couldn't think of one.

"Sure," he said. "No problem."

He reluctantly handed the sandwich over to a very greedy-looking Krugley. Hopefully he would just take a small respectful bite; no. Krugley opened his mouth wide and took a premium bite out of the choicest section of the sandwich.

"Oh, my god," said Krugley with his mouth full, eyes closed in almost obscene pleasure. "That is so good. Oh, that's good."

Fontoon accepted the sandwich back, frowning at it with transparent unhappiness.

"Don't you just hate it," began Krugley, wiping his mouth with the back of his silken sleeve, "when people take a bite out of your sandwich? Isn't it awful?"

"Well, I..."

"Heads up!" cried Krugley suddenly, lunging at Fontoon and knocking him clean off the bench on which they had both been sitting.

Not two seconds later, a screaming red hot downward projectile shattered the bench and buried itself inches into the sidewalk with a sound like a thunderclap, leaving a small crater. Little shards of broken concrete and dust particles were kicked out, many of them pinging against Admiral Fontoon and Chase Krugley, who lay entangled in a heap next to a nearby fire hydrant. Krugley was the first to stand up and brush himself off.

"Meteorite," he said calmly. "Fortunately, I heard it coming."

"Meteorite?!" said Fontoon, slowly rising. "How do you know it's a meteorite?"

"Look," said Krugley, pointing at the crater, wisps of smoke coming out of it, a black and green object the size of an elongated, twisted baseball steaming at its centre. "What else could it be?"

"That's insane," said Fontoon.

"It happens," said Krugley. "We were very fortunate."

Fontoon bent over and sniffed warily at the crater.

"Think it's too hot to touch?" asked Fontoon.

"It was a screaming ball of fire a few moments ago," said Krugley.

"I think it's cooled off," said Fontoon. "I'm touching it."

Fontoon quickly poked it with his finger tip, then again a bit more slowly. It was warm, but no longer searing.

"Pick it up," encouraged Krugley.

"Should I?" said Fontoon. Very cautiously, he did. It fitted nicely into his pocket.

"Do you know what I would do if I were you?" said Krugley.

"Give it to a museum?"

"I'd keep it. It's fantastic. In any event – let's stroll, shall we? – I just wanted to say to you that I'm sorry about what happened at Buhongo. I really am. I have no idea why you do the things you do with jars, but personally, I don't judge it. If anything, in my opinion, it bespeaks a poetic disposition. I just wanted you to know that."

Krugley put his arm around Fontoon's shoulders as he spoke. Fontoon was ready for everyone to stop talking about what had happened at Buhongo, but he appreciated a nice gesture when he heard one, and he thanked Chase Krugley for saying it.

"I mean it," said Krugley. "For my money, hey, it's a jar of shit. Several jars, if I understand it. Could be hundreds of jars full of hundreds of pieces of your own shit. Big deal." He took his arm from around Fontoon's shoulders and gave him a comradely punch on the shoulder. "That's all it is. A bunch of shit."

"I appreciate that," said Fontoon.

"Naturally the media stuff is out of the question now, the jars have become a distraction, there's nothing we can do about that. You're finished as far as that's concerned. You've become a, for lack of a better term, a comical figure now. God, people are stupid, aren't they Admiral?"

"Sometimes."

"Sometimes, well said. Sometimes. I like that. You have the forbearance of a saint, you know that Admiral? A saint. And of course there is a funny side to it, right? Perhaps you don't see it that way. But people have gotten laughs out of it and that's not a bad thing. Laughter, Admiral, I don't know if you can see this right now, but laughter is not a bad thing."

"Laughter is good."

"Exactly. Exactly. Listen to me."

Krugley stepped in front of Admiral Fontoon and stopped him walking by putting his hands on his shoulders right in front of a cross-town M23 stop. He looked imploringly into

Fontoon's eyes.

"I still believe in you," said Krugley, pausing to elongate his meaningful stare. "And do you know what? Because of you and your radio show, I now get around the city on buses. You know why? Community. Take care, Admiral. There will be opportunities. I've got my eye on you."

Just then an M23 pulled up to the curb and opened its doors. Krugley got on the bus. Leaning out just before dipping his metro card, he called to Admiral Fontoon.

"You have looked into the cosmos," he shouted. "And it has thrown a rock at you – not everyone can say that!"

He dipped his card; the bus pulled away and was gone. Fontoon still had the meteorite in his hand. He looked at it, gave it a little sniff, and put it into his pocket.

When a space rock enters the earth's atmosphere and becomes by definition a meteor, it is known among the fan base as a Fireball Event. A community of interested people has developed ways of sharing information on these events, tracking them, and classifying them into various categories. They are mapped and shared via social media virtually in real time with surprising precision. In one particular household, an alarm system alerts its owner to events likely to result in a meteorite; when the event is nearby, there is a special alarm, and a rapid response sequence is initiated immediately.

Admiral Fontoon still had the other half of his bacon, egg, and cheese sandwich, although it was well past the optimal temperature now. He clutched it in its little paper bag and sat down on a new bench. When he had finished eating it, he used the napkins in the bag to wipe the oil from his fingers. Then there was the dual sadness: the end of the sandwich, and the rest of the day to face.

A bicycle messenger rode up, hopped off his wheels, and

squinted around the general vicinity. He took out his phone and used his fingers to poke and swipe at it, then looked up and squinted again. He was handsome, Fontoon noticed, and suited the combination of his multi-coloured, skin-tight bike shorts and dark grey Gotham Girls Roller Derby hoodie. Fontoon also noticed that the man was squinting directly at him.

"You the guy with the meteorite?" he said.

"Um, yes," confessed Fontoon, presuming he had been caught by some kind of roving scientific policeman.

"Awesome," said the messenger, handing Fontoon an envelope, before leaping on his bike and wheeling away in one fluid motion.

Fontoon opened the envelope. There was a piece of paper in there, heavy with high rag content. He took it out and unfolded it.

Some kind of invitation. Mr. Peter Gramlinson wanted to see him.

Chapter Switch

They had all gathered at Minnie and Arthur's: Kent, Stickyman, and the Stankpools. Marla Stankpool was sobbing the beautiful, total tears of a mother reunited miraculously with her beloved child after believing that all was irrevocably lost. She held Pig in her arms tightly and shook. Ed stood by them, resting one hand on Marla's shoulder, the other on Pig's head, afraid to speak lest he, too, would start blubbering. Everyone felt it, the beauty of the moment. Nobody spoke. The only sound, apart from the odd audible sob, was the sound of tea being sipped.

Kent Peterson hung his head, too ashamed to speak, too enervated to leave. He sat as close to the corner of the room as he could, staring at his shoes. He would have turned his chair around and actually faced the corner, except he sensed that it would have been absurd, and there would have been no place to put his teacup. Stickyman saw and understood and made his way toward the other man one sticky step at a time.

"Eeee, well," said Aunt Minnie. "Top-up?"

Marla scrunched her teary eyes and nodded, and everyone else followed suit. Top-ups all around.

"Eeee," said Uncle Arthur. "That's quite a wallop you've got there, Kent, eh?"

Kent stared downwards and shrugged.

"Pig," he began. "I don't know how to tell you how sorry, how totally..."

"I know you didn't mean it." Pig was nothing if not philosophical, but his parents eyed Kent with a wariness verging on hostility.

"How ya feeling, kid?" asked Kent. "Are you hurt bad?"

Pig wriggled his way free of his parents and checked his limbs. He stretched them all out, stretched out his fingers and toes. He rolled his head around his neck and shrugged his shoulders a few times, moved his jaw around.

"I'm good," he said.

"Well thank the Lowered for that," said Marla, casting a dirty look in Kent's direction.

"Now Marla," said Ed.

"Don't you now Marla me, Ed Stankpool!"

"All right, Marla,"

"Because ah am tahrd."

"Ah know you are Marla."

"Just tahrd!" Marla began to cry again. Auntie Minnie poured her another top-up and pushed a chocolate-covered digestive towards her.

Uncle Arthur had been peeling an orange in his pocket, and he now loosened a section of it with his thumb and surreptitiously popped it into his mouth. He only had the one orange, the one plus two others, which he was saving. It was just as he swallowed that he spoke.

"So," he began. "You just sort of swiped him clean out of the window did you? Just like..." He made a sweeping swipey gesture and Kent hung his head. "I only mention it because of the strength."

Stickyman had managed two steps and was near enough to sit down and talk to Kent Peterson.

"It's true enough, what Arthur says," said Stickyman. "It would appear that your strength is quite staggering."

Kent grimaced and stayed looking down. Stickyman understood.

"Listen," said Stickyman, "you can't blame yourself. With strength like that, accidents are going to happen, they're just bound to. Thank goodness I was in the right place at the right time, so let's just count our lucky stars here and not get too down on ourselves, don't you think?"

Kent didn't feel that he had the right to cut himself any slack. He felt that the only honourable way to be, the only way he had a right to be, was completely ashamed and crestfallen. But still, secretly, down at the bottom of his well, he did appreciate the encouragement. Despite himself, his grimace slackened. Stickyman perceived it and continued.

"All any of us can do is make the best of what we naturally have," he said. "We're going to make mistakes. You have to forgive yourself. None of us can get by without forgiveness. We have to forgive each other, you know why? Because otherwise how can we keep going? And if we have to forgive each other, then you know what? We're allowed to forgive ourselves also. I feel like I'm not being clear."

"But..." started Kent.

"I know. I'm not saying we go too easy on ourselves either. That's the other side of it, the other side of the coin. You see? We take it seriously. We're human. We mess up. What I'm saying is forgiveness is totally essential. What I'm saying is, buck up, soldier."

"Eeee," said Uncle Arthur, popping an orange segment quickly into his mouth. "What a palaver."

"Well it sure is an honour to meet a real live superhero, Mister Stickyman, that's all Ah've got to say," said Marla.

"What a load of horseshit, Marla," said Ed. "Jest yesterday you was saying Stickyman was a sad, bad joke who shouldn't even ought to bother. No offence, Mr. Stickyman."

"None taken."

"You shut up, Ed, Ah did not."

"You did so. Just as you was making the dinner. Ah remember distinctly, you said..."

"Ed Stankpool you shut your mouth raht now or Ah'll..."

"Please," interjected Stickyman, making as if to move towards them, but of course his feet stayed stuck where they were since it really wasn't worth the effort. "Marla, I don't know whether you said it or not, but you're right. I am a sad, bad joke. I really shouldn't ought to bother."

There were a lot of noises along the lines of awwww and nonsense and you shouldn't say such a thing and you just saved a boy's life and that's not a sad joke by anybody's standards. But Stickyman persisted.

"Nope," he said. "I'm grateful for what's happened here today. It's a moment I've been waiting for, hoping for, for a long time, believe me. But let's be honest. I've fought against this realisation for many years, but it's come time to admit it: Sticking around and hoping is no way for a superhero to be. I've got to face it and I am facing it: I'm not strong enough for this game. I'm not strong enough to wear the Sticky suit."

"Hey," said Kent, feeling that he ought to say something. "Shouldn't this be time for you to buck up? Soldier?" He hung his head again, just a bit. *Stupid thing to say.*

"Why don't you let Kent wear it?" said Uncle Arthur, and when all eyes were on Kent, he popped another orange wedge into his mouth and chewed. After he swallowed and there was still silence, he added, "He's strong as a goddamned freak."

"It makes sense," said Pig, to a supportive generalised murmur. Aunt Minnie thought about getting the kettle back on.

Stickyman wrestled with his feelings. It did make sense. He had struggled so long against the Sticky suit, just trying to lift one stupid foot or clumsy hand at a time and flip and flop his stupid way around. But this Kent fellow, he'd have no trouble with that, no trouble at all. How strong was this guy anyway?

In the Sticky suit, Kent would be able to leap and bounce around the city like a velcro ping-pong ball on rocket juice. He could climb and spring his way up the side of the Empire State Building quick as spiders and launch himself effortlessly like a human pogo stick and land on the roof of the Public Library eight blocks up. He could crisscross his way up a street by leaping back and forth from one side to the other against buildings, hopping on top of buses for a ride whenever his fatness made him tired. If he saw a crane swinging out of control or a construction worker falling off some scaffolding on a high-rise, he could jettison himself with his powerful legs and be on the scene in split seconds, and moreover, when he got there, he'd be strong enough to set things right. In fact, it would be good exercise for him, and maybe he wouldn't be so out of shape all the time. It would get his blood flowing and that would show in his daily attitude. Probably be the best thing ever to happen to him.

Stickyman sensed that all this was true and knew that it would be good for the city. Yet he had only just stopped being Stickyman himself, and he wasn't even sure he completely meant it. Really he was just being a bit dramatic and trying out the words to see how they sounded. Certainly it was still his right to continue as Stickyman if he chose to, let's not have a rush to grab his suit off him the moment he lapses into reflection.

But aren't I just being jealous and petty, thought Stickyman, afraid that Kent will make a better Stickyman than I did? Well so be it. Let's finally have a really super Stickyman. The kid is right, it makes perfect sense. This city needs a hero, goddammit, and I'm not going to be the one to deny them.

This Kent Peterson will make a great Stickyman, and I'm honoured to pass the torch along to him.

"Pig's right, Kent," said Stickyman aloud at last. "You were born for this. You're a natural. Here," he said, taking off his sticky gloves and offering them to Kent. "Take them. Take them and do good!"

"Nah," said Kent. "I appreciate it and all, but I'm not the superhero type. I'd feel, I don't know, stupid. No offence."

"Eeeee," said Auntie Minnie.

Good, thought Stickyman.

Chapter Dark

Alyosha Ilyvich Razumikhin was drunk when the dark mood came, and when it came he smiled, because he saw the way forward. He had to face himself strictly, with severe eyes. No wiffle-waffling this time. Straight through to the other side. It was the obvious only thing to do. He'd sit in the tub and do it with a razor. He deserved nothing. Enough is enough.

Chapter Chance

Ding dong!

Admiral Fontoon had decided to accept the invitation for two reasons. Firstly, he could take the opportunity to stand up for his friend Yan Peng, who had lost his Firebrand Arm to this terrible man. Secondly, it sounded like his meteorite might be worth something.

Fontoon had decided not to consult with Yan Peng before making his way to the big house across the river. He was afraid that Yan Peng would try to talk him out of going, would tell him not to get involved, that it wasn't any of his business. Yan Peng wouldn't have wanted anybody interceding on his behalf under any circumstances, especially not with a man as dangerous as Peter Gramlinson. But Fontoon was envious of Yan Peng's sense of purpose, and this was a way to borrow some of it. Fontoon was going to face this fellow strictly and have some severe words.

Gramlinson answered his own door. He was handsome, dressed impeccably, and had very expensive-looking silver hair. He had a surprisingly open smile as he extended his hand towards Admiral Fontoon.

"Come in, thank you so much for coming," said Gramlinson. "Admiral Fontoon himself! I confess I'm nervous. I feel I'm in the presence of a legend. I can't believe it's you. Let me congratulate you on your good work with Buhongo. I am an avid listener of your weekly broadcast."

"That's all finished now," said Fontoon, entering Gramlinson's enormous house.

"Is it? Was it the jars? People are so narrow-minded when it comes to other people's perversities. What a shame. It was an excellent show. I particularly enjoyed your piece where we all had to imagine how very tiny we are. I got a real sense of it. It gave me a lot of perspective."

"Thank you," said Fontoon, who was already very uncomfortable with how friendly this all seemed to be. He stood uncertainly in the foyer.

"Now then," continued Gramlinson. "If I know anything at all about Buhongo, I'd say it was the custom at this time of day to have a Gin Fizz? Or would it be Pink Ladies? Or is it bad form of me to bring up that ungrateful place? Shall we have sherry? Or tea? You're not a whisky man. Or are you?"

"Maybe just a bit of fizzy water for now."

"Fizzy water, I like that. Do you know what my youngest daughter used to call that?"

"Tell me."

"Busy water."

"Cute," said Fontoon reluctantly.

"And somehow apt."

"Those bubbles do seem pretty busy."

"Exactly! Let's have some. I'll have white wine in mine. A spritzer. Girlish, I know. Please don't mock me! Come in! Sit down!"

Fontoon entered a kind of drawing room with ceilings that were easily twenty feet high as Gramlinson arranged the drinks. When he sat on the sofa the cushions were so firm and so silken that he felt like he was going to slide forwards off it and onto the floor.

"Big house," said Fontoon as Gramlinson returned.

"Guilty. I designed it myself, you know. And it did occur

to me, dammit I said, this house is goddamned big. So do you know what I did?"

"What?"

"Follow me. You have to see this."

Fontoon followed Gramlinson to a door on the other side of the room. Gramlinson opened the door and went in. Fontoon tried to follow him but could not; there was no room. He bumped right into Gramlinson and had to take a step backwards.

"This is what I call my Small Room," called out Gramlinson from inside. "It is minuscule. There's barely room for one person in here. You couldn't possibly even sit down in it. I come here when I need to feel cramped. I'll go out the other side so you can come in."

Gramlinson opened the door on the other side of the room, which he could do without moving an inch. He proceeded to go through it, then called across the twenty-four inches or so of the room to Fontoon.

"I'm through!" said Gramlinson, shouting as if he were much further away. "Your turn!"

Fontoon wedged his way into the Small Room, pausing momentarily to experience how uncomfortable it was.

"This is probably the smallest room I've ever been in," he said.

"If there's a smaller one I wouldn't want to go in it," replied Gramlinson. "Stay in as long as you like!"

Admiral Fontoon thought it polite to stay for about fifteen seconds to get an appreciation for it, and then he nodded and said 'OK' and came out. He had to duck to get through the door and into the next room. He hadn't noticed Gramlinson ducking, although Gramlinson was several inches taller. It was as if the door had shrunk, but of course that was impossible.

The new room on the other side was entirely white, so white that one could distinguish no features. It was very difficult to tell even where the walls were, or the ceiling. It was like being in heaven, thought Fontoon.

"Let me ask you a question," said Gramlinson, the two of them simply standing in the whiteness. "When's the last time you were with a woman?"

Fontoon looked at him quizzically, trying to make sense of the question.

"Sexually," Gramlinson clarified.

"Well, I..."

"I'm sorry. Is that too personal? I was just curious. But go on, answer, why not? It's obviously none of my business, which makes it safe to answer."

"Well, it's been a while, frankly."

"Years."

"A couple of years, yes."

"Two years?"

"I don't know, two, three years, something like that."

"Six? Seven years?"

"I'm sure it hasn't been that long."

"But it might be that long."

"It's possible. I actually try not to do the math on that one."

"Yet you must know. I won't press you. Do you know what we could do?" said Gramlinson. "If you like, we could have a party here, as licentious as you please. With a single phone call, it could be you, me, and any number of exquisite women."

Fontoon's face made it clear he had no idea what to say.

"Not common tramps, of course," continued Gramlinson. "These would be beautiful women of culture, and, I assure you, very open-minded and relaxed. I could even leave. It could be just you and the women if you prefer. Just say the word, Admiral. I would be honoured to arrange it."

"No, thank you," said Fontoon, who could not imagine any way he would feel comfortable accepting this offer.

"It's a shocking offer," said Gramlinson, "I realise that. It's enormously presumptuous, please forgive me. Let me simply add that, if you prefer, I can arrange for them to show up spontaneously at your own home at some future time, with my assurances that nobody would ever know I was involved. Even you might forget. I'll say no more about it. Just wink at me if the idea appeals."

Now Fontoon had to endeavour not to make any motion with his eyelids that could be construed as a wink. This effort lent an air of tension to his entire face.

"No," said Gramlinson, "you're a romantic. I can see that very clearly. We're alike, you and I, in that regard, if you don't mind my saying so. Love. Love is the answer. There's really no substitute. I'll tell you a secret. I was in love once myself. Oh yes, it's true. Very much in love, very much indeed. I think I told you about my youngest daughter. I have another as well. Two girls. They'll be all grown up by now. Oh yes, I know all about love. Shall we move on?"

"I think it's probably a good idea."

"Excellent," said Gramlinson. "Let's have a serious talk, you and I. I didn't invite you here for nothing, you know, not even to talk about love. Let's go have a proper sit down in a proper chair, shall we?"

"All right," said Fontoon, and the two men went through another door to the sitting room. The room also featured a fireplace with a mantelpiece, above which was mounted an iridescent human arm with wisps of smoke still wafting from the end where it was separated from the rest of the body.

"Yan Peng's arm," said Fontoon, with some anger.

"Yes it is," said Gramlinson, who had gone to the drinks cupboard. "You're friends, the two of you, of course. I'm well aware of it. Astounding. I'm having a Bronx. I make them after the fashion of Luis Buñuel. Ice cold gin, held closely next to a bottle of fine vermouth; let sunlight pass through. Then a tiny splash of freshly squeezed orange juice. Would you like one?"

"I want the arm," said Fontoon.

Gramlinson smiled as he walked back and settled into his favourite chair with his drink, fixing a warm stare on Admiral Fontoon.

"That is admirable," said Gramlinson, gesturing with his glass. "I like Yan Peng very much. I took no pleasure in his defeat, I'd like to emphasise that. You wouldn't like being me. Business, business, business! The things I have to take into account. Reputation. Matters of unyielding principle. A dreary bore. It's an extraordinary arm."

"So you'll give it to me."

"No."

"Why not?"

"It's not done."

"The meteorite for the arm."

"No. But I like your style. Would you write a poem?"

"What do you mean, write a poem?"

"You're a poet, I'm asking you to write me a poem. On commission. I'll give you a thousand dollars for it, but I'd like it to be done in ten minutes. I'm going out on the balcony. I would like to smoke a cigarette. Unfashionable, I know. I do it only very rarely. Special occasions. Like today."

"I'm not writing you a poem."

"Five thousand."

"And the arm."

Fontoon

"I can't give you the arm."

"I don't write on demand."

"You can certainly do this and it will be good for you. Quite apart from the money. I'm doing you a favour."

Fontoon frowned and it was clear he was trying to articulate an objection.

"Ten thousand dollars," said Gramlinson. "In addition to what I'm prepared to offer you for that meteorite."

"I'll write something," said Fontoon, trying to project disgust. "It might be very bad."

"That's not humility, I know," said Gramlinson. "Humility is badly over-rated. People ought to have an unapologetic comfort with their own powers. People may hate you for it. Fine. Hate them back. Contempt is a great defender of love. You simply stated a fact: your poem might be bad. I respect you for that. I'll pay anyway. Oh, and Admiral. I want it in Cantonese."

Gramlinson strode over to one of his many bookshelves and pulled out a slim green Cantonese-English dictionary, which he tossed carelessly on an end table near Admiral Fontoon.

"I don't expect you to be strictly grammatical," Gramlinson continued. "I do expect it to rhyme."

He took his wallet out of his pocket, peeled off a single Salmon P. Chase in good condition, easily worth five times the face value, and stuck it under a corner of the dictionary. Then he left the room and smoked. Ten minutes later he walked back in as Fontoon was scribbling down the last line. Fontoon looked up and saw him, and pointedly put down his pencil while looking Gramlinson straight in the eyes.

"Read it," said Gramlinson.

Fontoon read it. It went like this:

Fontoon

Daihyatjeung yi taai daaih
Daihyijeung yi taai sai
Daihsaamjeung ngoh hou jungyi dahnhaih
Gojeung yi taai gwai.[2]

Gramlinson didn't say anything at first, but merely strode back over to his armchair and sat down thoughtfully.

"I knew it," he said finally. "It's wonderful. Writing in a language you don't understand is the way forward for you."

"What is the point of all this?" asked Fontoon.

"Your radio show was really something, you know. You have no idea how influential it was. There was some very rash talk in some very high places. You stirred some new feelings. There's been talk of ditching greed and violence for loving cooperation. In high places, mind. And then, alas, the jars. It's thrown everything into the air. As if you weren't fascinating enough, there is now also the meteorite. May I see it?"

Fontoon took it out of his pocket and handed it over. Gramlinson inhaled sharply and closed his eyes as he held it.

"It's a pallasite," said Gramlinson, speaking the word in such a way as to indicate that pallasite meant special. "Not only rare but the most beautiful of all meteorites."

"It almost hit me."

"Extraordinary. Do you know how many meteorites in all have been found and documented, all together?"

"Nope."

"Nearly forty thousand. Of those, only sixty-one are pallasites. This makes sixty-two. Would you like to know how many of the pallasites are in my personal collection?"

"Yes."

---

2 The first chair is too big; the second chair is too small; the third one I like very much, but that one is too expensive.

"Forty-seven. Obtained by various means."
"You really like them."
"I really do."
"Let me have the arm."
"The arm for the pallasite?"
"Yes."
"No."
Fontoon sighed.

"Don't be an idiot," said Gramlinson. "Now, ordinarily a pallasite transaction is about money. But seeing as it's you, which is astonishing, that wouldn't do at all. But Yan Peng's arm has no exchange value. Think about it. What happened between Yan Peng and his master and me is a private affair. Yan Peng risked everything to challenge me, and the grievous loss he suffered was one he earned. Now you would come in here, with frankly nothing remotely comparable in the way of training or commitment, and get him his arm back with a commercial trade. Have you thought for one second about how that would make him feel?"

Fontoon's sudden uncertainty showed.

"It is a ridiculous idea," said Gramlinson. "It is asinine. I hope you don't mind my saying so. Think bigger. What is Yan Peng's arm to you? Be honest. You have been on the verge of changing the world, Admiral. That dream is not quite gone, you know, it's tottering. I could perhaps help make or break it. I do have some small influence in these matters. A word from me to the right people can sometimes make all the difference."

"I don't understand," said Fontoon. It felt good to admit it.

"We'll have a game of pool to decide the fate of the world. If you win, going forward it's all tiny people on a little blue ball in space happily helping each other."

"If I lose?"

"Mayhem. And I get the pallasite."

"The truth is, I'm not very good at pool. I won't win."

"I see. Let's make it simpler. Break up a rack."

"What do you mean?"

"Hit the cue ball into a neat arrangement of closely packed billiard balls, thereby dispersing them according to the standard minimum criteria."

"Yes, yes, but which rack?"

"Which do you prefer?"

"I'll say nine-ball."

"Nine-ball then. Are we agreed that a legal break requires you to hit the one-ball and drive at least four balls to a rail?"

"Yes."

"Well there's our challenge!"

"That's all I have to do? Make a legal nine-ball break?"

"You can manage it? Reliably?"

"Yes, I can do it."

"Not too much pressure? You can do this?"

"I can do this."

"Well then," said Gramlinson.

"OK," said Fontoon.

"Shall I rack?" said Peter Gramlinson.

They rose from their chairs. Gramlinson led the way through a side door into the billiards room, where an eight-foot table stood with leather pockets, green baize, and thick, ornate legs of carved oak. As Gramlinson arranged pool balls one through nine into the requisite diamond shape, with the one-ball at the head and the nine in the centre, Admiral Fontoon selected a cue from the rack on the wall.

On his way to the head of the table, Fontoon paused to inspect Gramlinson's handiwork. Each ball was flush against all of its neighbours and aligned from front to back like an arrow: a perfect rack. Fontoon looked at Gramlinson and nodded. Gramlinson bowed slightly and nodded back.

I can do this.

Fontoon shook his shoulders out to loosen them up and took a deep breath. He tried to breathe low down in his abdomen, and keep his hips nice and flexible. He wiggled his fingers around the butt of the cue as he gripped it. Everything focused, relaxed, in tune.

Fontoon put the cue ball right on the head spot and went into his stance. He looked down the table at the one-ball and back to the cue ball, all the while taking warm-up strokes. He took another deep breath and focused his gaze completely on the cue ball. With each warm-up stroke, the tip of his cue aimed straight for the centre of the cue ball. Three more strokes and then he'd follow through. He didn't have to murder the ball. Just a nice clean forward motion all the way through, shoulders relaxed, hips pushing forward at the same time. Easy does it. Three. Two. One.

Tick.

Chapter War

"Hello?" said Strongman Simms. It was how he always answered the phone. "Oh, hello, Mr. Gramlinson sir! Thank you for calling sir! Yes I'm very well indeed, I've rarely been better, thank you for asking, sir! I trust you're well, you're always well; are you well, sir? Super. Super news. If you're well, we're all well, that's what I say. What can I do for you?"

The Strongman looked around his office and admired it. He sat in one of the most comfortable office chairs money could buy. Bookshelves? Bingo. Desk? Solid. He thought about how good it was to be the president as he listened to the words of Peter Gramlinson.

"Oh, you mean about disbanding the military!" he continued, after listening for a few moments. "Yes, a very beautiful idea, I agree with you there. No, not yet; we're just about to get started. No, of course not, not without your buy-in. Yes, we did get a little excited. Thank you, sir. I'm glad you can see how exciting it might have been.

"Yes, that's it, that's it exactly. Yes, we'd all been listening to him. Right. Yes, we all found ourselves feeling that way. Frankly, I was moved by the general spirit of what the fellow was saying, you know, about, well, about a lot of things, about the question of why should there be anything? You know what I mean? How did he put it? Why should there be anything, I think he said it just like that and somehow it hit me. It is a damned good question. In my opinion."

The Strongman paused to listen again for a few moments.

"Yes, nothingness, that's right," he continued. "When you think about nothingness for a while, really think about it – nothingness – no space, no time, absolute nothingness, then the question arises: hey yeah why *should* there be anything? Everything bursting forth like that. Why should it have *bothered*? Exactly, it's... exactly, exactly... yes, reverence, I would use that word. Awe, there's another word. Perfectly good word. I don't know, makes you feel a bit one with everything, if you see what I mean. Kind of makes the old bloodlust go a bit flaccid. Heh heh."

The Strongman's secretary came in with her own special shape and put some papers on his desk as he idly reflected that it wasn't as easy to get dirty sex as people probably figured it would be for a sitting president, on account of being watched so closely all the time. That was a down side.

Dirty sex. When was the last time he had truly dirty sex? It had been years. Jesus. It was that lady from Russia. He was working behind her and just innocently putting his thumb in there when suddenly she reached back and guided his whatsis right into it and he had not to act shocked and just go with it. And then she didn't even make him wash it before she...

"What's that now?" The Strongman was still on the phone. "Well, had heard something, didn't know what to make of it. In jars, right? So you're saying... well, OK, if you say so. No sir, I don't have any objections exactly. I had just been spending so much time lately thinking we were past all that, thinking of all the fragile people on the little ball in space, joining hands and all that sort of thing... No no, I'm sure you're right... Look, if that's what you definitely want, we'll do it. So, just go ahead then? Right. Any particular country? OK. No, no questions. Thanks a lot for the call, Mr. Gramlinson. As always, anything

I can do, just give a shout. Bye bye."

Welp, he thought as he sat back in his chair: *More war.*

Chapter Next

"Nice break," said Yan Peng.

"Yeah," said Admiral Fontoon. "Now that I don't need it. How many was that?"

"Nine in a row."

"One more, then we'll play a game."

"OK."

Yan Peng was racking them up for Fontoon so he could practise his break, over and over again. The goal was ten legal breaks in a row. They had come down to The Reward at an off time, and nobody was waiting for the table. Plastic cups in the holes saved them a lot of coins. Fontoon waited until Yan Peng had made a perfect diamond. He watched as Yan Peng examined all the points where the balls were required to be in contact, using his hand to block the overhead lights so the glare could hide no defects. When Yan Peng gave the OK, Fontoon took his stance. He had given up thinking much about his preparations. It had gotten him nowhere. Now he was just taking his stance, doing a few warm-up strokes, and letting fly.

The balls made a very satisfying cracking sound; Fontoon had completed a better than merely legal break for the tenth time in a row. He allowed himself a small smile and a sip of his beer.

"Shall we play a game?" asked Fontoon, setting down his glass.

"Let's," said Yan Peng.

"You break," said Fontoon. "I'm sick of it!"

This time Fontoon made the rack, and Yan Peng took the cups out of the holes so they could play properly. With no warm-up strokes whatsoever, Yan Peng proceeded to make a spectacular break, sinking five balls, including the nine.

"I never should have given you that arm back," said Fontoon. "It's patently unfair."

Yan Peng smiled.

"Still can't quite believe Gramlinson let you leave with it," said Yan Peng. "Wait. Tell me that part again. I'll never get tired of hearing it. You line up your shot, and you miss, right?"

"Abject failure," said Fontoon, gathering the balls to rack them again. "Cue ball scratch."

"So, the terms are, you lost the bet."

"Lost the bet," said Fontoon, completing a full rack of all fifteen balls. "Eight-ball?"

"Fine. Tell me again how you got the arm."

Fontoon described again how, immediately after his foul on the cue ball, he was sure the skies actually darkened and low peals of thunder rolled across the world. He looked up, and in the flashes of lightning Peter Gramlinson appeared for that fraction of a second to be floating, with long white hair and a long white beard, and wearing colourful robes. He appeared to be laughing, only it was as if there were two people laughing at once, one at a very high pitch and the other normal. But it was a trick of the light because as soon as the lightning flash ended, Fontoon could see that Gramlinson remained a well-groomed man from western civilisation in an expensive suit. And he wasn't laughing. He had a sympathetic expression on his face.

"I handed him the meteorite," continued Fontoon. "Neither of us said a word. I walked back into the sitting room, went over to the fireplace, reached up, and took your arm down.

And he just walked me to the front door and opened it. Not a word. And I just left."

Yan Peng shook his head in amazement.

"He lets you take the arm. Doesn't try to stop you."

"Yep," said Fontoon.

"And just lets you go," he said.

"Yep," said Fontoon.

"You don't know Gramlinson," said Yan Peng. "You don't know how strange that is."

Fontoon shrugged.

"You know what I think?" continued Yan Peng.

"What," said Fontoon.

"I think he likes you."

"Yeah, OK. Your break, sunshine," said Fontoon.

At that moment there was a commotion at the front door. There was a lot of shouting going on and a few people looked as if they had been knocked to the ground. The door looked like it had been ripped right off its hinges and part of the adjoining wall had been decimated. The bouncers were shouting at somebody who was trying his best to apologise. It almost looked as if the door had been crumpled up into a ball in frustration.

"Sorry I'm late," said Kent Peterson as he approached the table.

He reached out to shake Yan Peng's hand. They had met in passing, but had not really known each other. He couldn't remember Yan Peng's name, but didn't ask, because he felt that he was supposed to know it already. Hot sparks flew out as super-strong hand met Firebrand hand. Everyone shrugged it off.

"How was the funeral?" asked Kent, pleased that he had remembered to ask and trying to use the correct tone of voice for such a question.

Fontoon nodded and felt sad all over again.

"Nice," he said.

"As these things go," added Kent, understanding.

"Right," said Fontoon.

"Did you go as well?" asked Kent of Yan Peng.

"I did," said Yan Peng. "For moral support. I didn't know Alyosha. But the Admiral says I would have liked him very much."

"Was it weird seeing the people from Bawanga again?" asked Kent.

"Buhongo," corrected Fontoon. "It wasn't that weird. I mean, it was always weird there, so it was just kind of normal. It was strangely nice. Irina, she's kind of the leader. We hugged. It was nice."

Yan Peng shrugged and broke up the rack impressively.

"I got next," said Kent, gingerly placing a coin on the table.

"I heard you had dinner at the Stankpools," said Fontoon.

"Who'd you talk to?"

"Marla."

"Oh," said Kent, blushing. "Yeah. I don't think I'll be invited back."

"Doesn't sound like it," said Fontoon.

Yan Peng proved to be unbeatable over the course of the next two hours. By the time Admiral Fontoon was in his pyjamas and brushing his teeth that evening, he was exhausted. Poor Alyosha. If only they could have been better friends, but then what can one do with people like that? There wouldn't have ever been anything to say. All you get is an overstuffed feeling full of inexpressible wishes. Fontoon thought it would feel great to cry, but sometimes it just doesn't happen.

Fontoon climbed into bed. He thought about not setting the

alarm, because surely after all he had recently been through, he deserved to sleep as long as his body wanted. But no, he thought resolutely. Up and at 'em. Besides, he wanted to drop in on old Mr. Pappy. Not that he wanted his job back – no sense moving backwards. Whatever would be next, it would have to be something that felt forward-ish. He simply wanted to visit the man. Maybe thank him. It's a good idea to thank people who have cut you some slack in this world. Yeah. Better set the old alarm.

With a sigh, Admiral Fontoon reached down and slipped the noose around his ankle, and drifted off to sleep.

Chapter Now

Admiral Fontoon had no way of knowing it at the time, but in less than five years' time, he would have a cult following throughout Asia. Dr. Li, very young, very hip, a freshly minted PhD in his back pocket, would take advantage of his knowledge of what was *au courant* on the savvy Hong Kong streets to help mainstream the underground sensation of Fontoon's Cantonese poetry. Li had made his name with his tremendously beautiful dissertation on the oeuvre of Leslie Cheung. Now he taught – that is to say, in less than five years he would teach – anything of sudden cultural significance.

Dr. Li would stride into his classroom excitedly one day, unable to restrain the smile that was breaking out all over his face. He would be holding a few sheets of paper, which he would be tapping importantly with the back of his hand, as if to indicate, this, my friends, this here is something, this here will amaze you. He would stand up in his black jeans and artistically tattered jumper, peer at them mischievously over the top of the papers, and proceed to read aloud to his class of some one hundred and forty eager young minds:

> *Tingjiujou geido chin a?*
> *Ngoibihn haih bingo ga?*
> *Daaihyidi pahngyauh mouh dihnyauh.*
> *Keuideih yiu tong ngaam ma?*[3]

---

[3] Tomorrow morning costs how much? Outside belongs to whom? Other friends have no gasoline. They want soup, isn't that so?

Some one hundred and forty heads would nod earnestly, many with mouths that would display knowing smiles. Edgy stuff. Very very now.

Dr. Li would walk across the front of the room and sit quite casually right on top of his desk. "Anyone?" he'd say, setting off waves of conjecture and insight among the trendy young intellectuals arrayed before him.

Chapter Heaven

"Are you all right, master?" inquired Alyosha, his brown eyes wide with caring about the answer to the question. "Let me put some more cool water on your forehead."

"Please," said Miguel, putting a fond hand on Alyosha's shoulder. "Don't call me that."

"As you like," said Alyosha, dipping the wash cloth into the silvery bowl. Having squeezed out the excess water, he patted Miguel's brow and scanned his face for any sign of discomfort.

Miguel sat and surveyed the landscape of fluffy clouds that spread out infinitely before him. When he looked down and squinted, Alyosha knew what he was trying to do, and he sprang into action.

"Let me help," he exclaimed, and got down on his hands and knees to clear away a patch of cloud so Miguel could look down and see his family clearly.

Miguel looked down and squinted for several moments, Alyosha next to him doing the same.

"There!" said Alyosha, pointing.

Miguel looked and saw his mother and his brother, working as usual. He watched, smiling, for a long time, Alyosha silently massaging his feet and crying tears of joy.

Chapter Spoon

"But it's not fair!" said Weasby, on the verge of tears, as Jenkins and the rest of them looked down decently. Only Shirley and Mr. Bentley looked directly at him.

"You're a cancer, Weasby," said Mr. Bentley, coolly. "There's no place for you in this organisation any more."

"You won't get my spoon," said Weasby.

Hesitant looks were exchanged. Finally, as if on some unspoken signal, Jenkins voiced the question:

"What spoon?"

"A special one," said Weasby with wild insolence. "You're washing the dishes, you put it in the sink? It lands concave side up, right underneath the tap. Water splashes everywhere."

"All spoons do that," ventured Edgars, his tongue a cowardly knife.

"Not every single time," said Weasby.

Everyone grumbled.

Weasby gathered up his belongings and pouted.

"It was my idea to send him all those graduate school pamphlets," said Weasby with grave dignity.

"No it wasn't, JB," said Jenkins. "That was one of mine."

"Shirley?" said Mr. Bentley.

Mr. Bentley knew that Shirley didn't just have a razor-sharp memory; she kept impeccable records. Her word was pure gold.

"It was Mr. Jenkins, Mr. Bentley," said Shirley.

Mr. Bentley narrowed his eyes and nodded. His hands were

on his hips.

"Take your things," he said to Weasby, "and get out of my office."

Weasby gave Shirley one last wounded look, but his efforts were wasted. She viewed him only coldly now. He took his things, and he got out of the office.

In the offices of the Weasby Wrecking Company, loud whoops of celebration could be heard reverberating through the corridors.

Chapter Bongos

He did hit the snooze button once, but on the second alarm, Admiral Fontoon propped himself up on his elbows, took a deep breath, and decided he was awake enough. He sat up properly and removed the noose from around his ankle, then made his way down into the kitchen.

If he was going to make his connections out to Wossafocken Point, he was going to have to keep things moving. There would be no bacon, egg, and cheese along the way today. It would have to be a quick bowl of cereal and out. However, since he was feeling unusually resolute, there was one thing he would remember to do: take with him the application form for graduate school in poetry. He'd been bombarded by these things for months and done precisely nothing about it. Today that would change. He could fill out the application form on the train and get it into the mail before coming home at the end of the day. This would be a day for moving and shaking. Tonight, he would go to bed feeling good about himself.

Fontoon smiled when he saw the Boingy Boingy Man. The commute was a whole different animal when you were doing it not because you had to, but because you wanted to. He felt like he was visiting a previous life, inhabiting some old eight-millimetre film footage of himself as a child. Fontoon looked forward to seeing the Boingy Boingy Man do his boingy boingy tricks, bouncing up the stairs, taking his favourite spots. He wasn't disappointed. Same old Boingy Boingy Man.

Unbeknownst to himself, Fontoon managed to annoy

several people simply by appearing to be too relaxed during the commuting rush. He wasn't any slower than anyone else, after all, he still had to make his connections. No, it was just something about the look on his face. He had on a bewildering half-smile, even as everyone crushed at the doors and fought the people trying to edge in, even as they poured down the various stairways, even as he got caught behind an elderly woman with far-away music in her head. By the time he got to the Orange Train platform, Fontoon was feeling positively jaunty. To think, he might see Andy at the bus stop – Fontoon was inordinately excited.

Suddenly there was a great blast of wind and a sound like a beating of enormous wings. Admiral Fontoon whirled around to confront the startling sound, but when he turned all he saw was that girl, the young woman, the one with the impossibly tight trousers and the curly wet hair and the proud acne scars. How regal she was! And before he knew it or thought about it or could stop it, Fontoon had begun to speak.

"Look at you walking around among us like you're not an angel just dropped right down here out of heaven!" he said. "Who do you think you're fooling, girl?"

As he spoke these words, he had time to become alarmed that he was speaking to her, first of all, and also that he seemed to have adopted some sort of persona. When he finished speaking he put his hands on his hips and winked at her.

"I mean seriously!" he added.

He had no idea where to take things from there. It was in her hands now. Everything depended on her reaction.

The young woman looked at him, and her expression turned from one of guarded suspicion to one of wry amusement. She opened her mouth to the quickening of his heart, and the sound of distant bongos began to play, and play, and play.

Chapter Bloat

It was a Tuesday in the distant future five billion some odd years from now and the human species had long since ceased to exist. Nobody called it Tuesday at this point; nobody thought about people, certainly not the mutated extremophile sulphur-dependent microbes that were all that remained of life on earth. They had better things to think about, such as the sun, which was well into its late-stage process of becoming a bloated red giant star by virtue of having turned so much of its hydrogen fuel supply into helium. It had already swallowed Mercury and Venus and it was breathing down Earth's neck with little regard for the consequences. The temperature on the surface of the planet was six hundred and fourteen degrees Fahrenheit in the shade and rising.

Down in the ruins of the city, inside a small, long-abandoned apartment, underneath an old refrigerator, a tossed and lonely pencil could not take it any more. Its last contact with a human hand was five billion years ago, and that last touch was angry, frustrated. Poor little pencil. Mass produced, yet somehow so exacting and meticulous.

Any number of moulds and parasites might have gotten to that pencil first, far far earlier, but no. Didn't happen. However, things had been getting steadily worse. By now, a sloppy, extravagant heat belched in constant red waves from a bloated star mindlessly destroying its closest children. Now the pencil had no chance. Finally in the end it reached its combustion point and burst into flame, as more and more things were doing these days. It burned for a little while until it was completely consumed, at which point the fire petered out. There was just a little pile of ashes and a fading wisp of smoke. End of pencil. Finito.